M000020458

DEADLY

AFTERMATH

NANCY CHURCHILL

Copyright © 2015 Raging River Press, Yorba Linda, California.

ISBN: 0990903001

ISBN 13: 9780990903000

Library of Congress Control Number: 2014953709

Raging River Press, Yorba Linda, CA

Things either are what they appear to be;
Or they neither are, nor appear to be;
Or they are not, and do not appear to be;
Or they are not, and yet appear to be.

Rightly to aim in all these cases is the wise man's task.

—Epictetus (ca. AD 55–135)

This book is dedicated to my wonderful daughters,
Suzie, Cindie, Karen, and Becquie,
who continue to share my enthusiasm for life.

DEADLY
AFTERMATH

People Waiting to Meet You

The Penningtons
    Grace, the mom
    Amanda, the oldest daughter, FBI agent
    Rachael, the middle daughter, Bullhead City Police Department detective
    Meg, the youngest daughter

The Spencers and the Turners
    Elliott Spencer (a.k.a. Turner)—How do you describe evil?
    Derek Turner, his brother
    Marisa Turner, his sister

Josh Meyers, Catalina Police Department detective

The Davises
    Greg, Josh's partner at the Catalina Police Department
    Stella, his redheaded sister

Luke Wilson, CIA, old friend of Grace

The Kraemers
    Payden, the older brother
    Jessie and Jordan, Payden's twin sisters

Rosie, Meg's friend from the Conservancy

Plus a selection of various and sundry characters who pop in and out

I

"For God's sake, get an IV started. He's bleeding out."

Josh Meyers's blood spread eastward as the Oasis Casino's dock rocked from boat chop. The pooling design resembled Van Gogh's *The Starry Night*, only in red.

The bullet, meant for Rachael, had found its way to Josh.

A paramedic pushed Rachael aside. "Move. I've got this." He grabbed a loaded syringe and inserted the sixteen-gauge needle deep into a vein as his partner applied pressure on the gunshot wound. "Too damn close to the carotid. We're losing him."

Josh was in and out of consciousness, and his mind drifted: he pushed through the casino crowd, felt the explosion from the detonated bomb, watched the gamblers scramble for the flying chips, ran in slow motion toward Meg, and saw Rachael take aim at some man fleeing in a boat. He knew he was a cop, but he didn't know where he was. Black converged and smothered the images.

2

Rachael Pennington ran to the end of the boat dock, untied a casino WaveRunner, and took off into the night.

"Come on, come on, you piece of junk." She revved the throttle on the watercraft as she closed in on the jet boat careening down the river. Not this time, you bastard. Not this time. She urged the PWC forward. I'm coming, Meg. Hold on. I'm coming. Lights reflecting off the water from the casinos lining the river now guided her toward the fleeing craft. She was seconds behind the boat. Her WaveRunner hit the boat's swim step, sending her flying over the engine cover. Protecting her head, she turned shoulder down as she catapulted through the air and landed between the seats of the lead boat.

"Damn you," Elliott Spencer screamed. He jammed a life preserver against the throttle, holding it at full throttle, and grabbed for her.

"Kill him, Rachael. Kill him," Meg Pennington yelled. The effects of the drugs were waning. She wanted to help her sister, but her hands were cuffed. The boat's erratic speed tossed her back onto the seat.

Rachael struggled to her feet and tried to knee him in the groin as the vessel plowed down the treacherous Colorado River. Elliott rolled left to avoid the blow and grabbed the fire extinguisher. He reared back to hit her, but Rachael dodged the swing and rammed the heel of her palm into his thyroid notch.

Elliott's eyes rolled up. He fell backward and teetered on the edge of the low freeboard. Freezing water from the boat's side wake spewed across his face. Rachael reached for him, but the momentum of her blow had knocked him off balance. He grabbed for the steering wheel but managed only to spin it as he was ejected from the boat. The jet was now heading toward the shoreline, open throttle.

"Grab the wheel," Meg shrieked as she struggled against her handcuffs.

Rachael snatched the wheel, looked around to set her position on the river, and whirled the jet starboard. "Hold on."

Meg flew across the boat to the port side, cracking her shoulder against the fiberglass.

"We just passed Harrah's," Rachael murmured, her eyes searching the black Arizona shoreline for another landmark. The boat's bow dipped into the river and then slowed. "It's a straight shot downriver. I'm turning it off for a minute." She turned off the boat, her hands trembling from exertion, her emotions raw.

Rachael knew this part of the Colorado, but not like Meg, whom the locals knew as "queen of the river." She squeezed between the seats, pulled Meg to an upright position, and removed the cuffs.

Meg, still queasy from the ipecac and Rohypnol cocktail Elliott had given her in the casino, was alert enough to turn and look for him in the water. "I don't see him." Her voice turned tense. "We're close to shore. He could swim that far and get away. Start the boat. Turn around."

"It's too dark. We'll never find him." Rachael sat down beside Meg and sucked in a deep breath. "I need to get it together. Just wait, damn it."

The boat glided downstream, propelled by the fast current. It was peaceful, in stark contrast to its occupants.

"I'll be able to see the white water if he kicks. He can't get away again. Come on. Hurry up." Meg stood and peered through the moonlit night, antsy to get her sister's cooperation.

Before Rachael had a chance to reason with Meg, a helicopter light moved along the shoreline. "Wait. That could be Amanda." She grabbed her two-way radio. "Mandy, that you? Signal me if you see us. I'll turn on the lights." She moved to the dash and pulled on the boat's running lights. A moment passed.

The pounding sound of the helicopter's rotors scrambled the signal, but Amanda responded. "It's me, sis. Meg okay?" The chopper soared back and forth across the dark shoreline.

"Yeah, but Elliott got away. I knocked him out of the boat. About five hundred feet back. East side of the river. Somewhere between the Edgewater and the island."

"I'm on it." The helicopter banked left, returned to the shoreline, and directed its light over a spot by the River Lodge Campground. "Oh, happy day. Spotted the son of a bitch. We're landing."

"Is he on shore?" Meg scrambled to take the receiver away from Rachael.

"Just crawling out. Gotta go."

"There, you see? It's over." Rachael pushed Meg away. "Settle down."

Meg leaned against the engine cover and stared into the dark, watching the helicopter disappear as it landed. "Amanda has him? For sure? Can't get away?" Doubt coursed through her words. She had intimate knowledge of Elliott's cunning and resourcefulness in evading the police.

"For sure."

The boat slid into a sandbar and jarred to a stop. "Guess I'd better pay attention to where I'm going," Rachael said as she picked up an oar, leaned over the port side, and pushed off. She engaged the blower switch and started the engine. "Time for us to head back and get you some medical attention." She turned the boat against the swift-moving water, using the casino lights to guide her.

Meg wouldn't give up the search. "There's a car driving down in the area where Amanda landed." Worry seeped into her words. "What's with that?"

"Probably backup." Rachael, intent on not running into another sandbar, didn't divert her attention.

With instincts running red hot, Meg blurted out, "Shit, listen to me. I don't think so. There's something going on."

Ignoring Meg's comment, Rachael glanced over at the shoreline as they passed Harrah's Casino. She reached for her cell phone and quickly dialed dispatch. "Rachael here. I've got Meg. Send a car to meet us at the Oasis boat ramp. Need to get her to the hospital. Any word on Josh?" She hit the speaker button so Meg could hear.

"Will do. Nothing new on Josh. He went by ambulance to the hospital."

"Alive?" She had to know. She clutched the phone, trying to wring out the right answer.

"Yeah, but he didn't look good." Lillian, working the dispatch desk, was a close friend and wanted to relay more positive news. She tried to maintain a professional attitude, but her voice broke. "I'll try to keep you updated. Sorry."

"Thanks." Rachael steered the boat past the Colorado Belle Casino and throttled down. She could see the outline of the Oasis boat dock and closed in on it. It took her three tries to maneuver the boat into the slip, as the current fought her all the way.

Meg's shoulder was painful, so she didn't argue over the hospital idea. That bastard. He was so close to getting me again. Her previous encounter—the torture, the cigarette burns, chew marks on her body, the rape—swam through her brain. She shuddered as the pain and despair reappeared. A year had passed, but moments like this made the memory resurface and tear at her soul.

Rachael saw Meg shudder and knew what she was thinking. "Meg, relax. It's over. You're safe. Okay?" There was no doubt in Rachael's mind that Meg would get past this. Sturdy stock defined the family. Meg was resilient, tough on the exterior; but still a sense of innocence prevailed…an innocence everyone wanted to protect.

"Yeah, just had a chill." Meg turned and peered across the river through the black night, finally locating the car lights. "Rachael, I don't think that's a cop car. It's not driving down the road, and it kinda looks like an SUV sneaking through the bushes." She narrowed her eyes, trying to focus better, and then the lights seemed to disappear.

"Probably undercover wheels, but I'll call it in as soon as we hit shore."

"Hmm." Meg knew better.

By the time Elliott realized his overconfidence had placed him in jeopardy, it was too late. Rachael, a Bullhead City Police Department detective, had outmaneuvered him. The three explosive devices he'd hid in the Oasis Casino had detonated as planned, and the ensuing chaos had left an opening for him to slip through and kidnap Rachael's sister, Meg. But then nothing had gone as planned. Now, as he pulled himself out of the frigid Colorado River, he heard the helicopter closing in and saw the floodlight. He was forced to realize his mistakes. Ejecting from a speeding boat wasn't in his plan. But fate had intervened, and here he was.

The bullet Rachael had fired during their struggle on the casino's boat dock had caught him in the shoulder, a through-and-through shot. Bitch. How did you catch up with me so fast? His whole year of planning for a second meeting with Meg had gone woefully wrong.

Elliott used his good arm to crawl forward, looking for a place to hide from the helicopter circling overhead. Crunched up in a small ball, he held his shoulder and whimpered, a reaction foreign to him. His icy clothes chilled his skin. The night was a typical one hundred degrees, and the hot sand should have helped but didn't. He fought the fatigue that accompanied shock and the loss of blood, but his shivering, confusion, and drowsiness were signs of hypothermia. He knew it wouldn't be long before he passed out. Meg, that beautiful, sensual girl. Was she really worth all this? Sounds were getting closer. Footsteps? Someone was coming. The helicopter had landed, he was sure. He tried to turn, but the pain from the gunshot wound was too intense. One eye cracked open, and he peered through the dark toward the approaching figure. "Is that you, D—"

Amanda Pennington's FBI standard-issue Glock pushed into his painful shoulder. "Expecting someone else, Elliott? The cavalry? Sorry to disappoint you. FBI. You have the right to remain silent." She was winded. Sprinting from the helicopter through the heat had drained her energy, but finally catching Elliott gave her the strength to wrestle his arms behind him and cuff the serial killer. He was too spent to resist.

"Amanda. You. Damn." His speech was slurred. "I should have known there was something going on with you. Too smart for a cocktail waitress. But FBI?" He tried to search back through his mind for any clues giving away her true identity, but he was too weak to care. He knew he'd been played.

Amanda could hardly contain herself. She jerked his arm and snapped on the cuffs. "You ass. Why don't you struggle so I can shoot you? Payback for what you did to my sister."

"Your sister? Meg's your sister?" How could I have missed that? He fell forward. The sand smothered his face, and he didn't have the energy to move. Hot grains filled his nostrils and scratched his eyes.

"Yeah, my sister." She grabbed his hair and jerked him up. "Do you know how much I hate you for what you did to her?" She callously brushed the grit from his scraped face and glared into his vacant eyes. "You sick bastard." His wet, greasy hair started to slip through her fingers, and she twisted it harder and pushed his face in the sand again.

He gasped for air. "You can't kill me. You're FBI," he muttered, spitting sand through his teeth.

She grabbed her two-way. "Chris," she said to the helicopter pilot, "I've got Elliott. We'll be there in five. Keep the chopper going. We'll head to the hospital. He's been shot." She straddled Elliott and reached down for the cuffs. "Stand up, asshole."

"Roger. Need any help?" Chris could hear Amanda's heavy breathing.

"No, I'm good. Call—"

Cold steel slammed against her temple and disrupted the sentence.

Derek Turner, Meg's weekend friend from Yorba Linda, was Elliott's younger brother, a well-guarded secret to all parties. His job over the last year had been to befriend Meg so when the time arrived to abduct her, Elliott would know how to finalize his plans.

Derek had been successful in hoodwinking Meg, who had accepted his quasi advances. He knew she was curious about why he'd stopped short of going all the way. The occasional kiss was all he'd given her, and he'd been relieved when she finally gave up on him as boyfriend material and added him to her brat pack list of close friends. He'd continued to drive from Orange County to Bullhead once a month to party with Meg and his other new friends, and then he'd reported back to his brother, Elliott.

Derek remembered the fun days he'd shared with her last summer.

"Come on, let me drive your boat," Meg had yelled, tugging at Derek's arm.

He liked her aggressive style, and her innocent beauty overwhelmed him. "You're too girlie. Probably wouldn't know how to handle it."

"Ha." Meg moved forward, plopped down on Derek's lap, and took over the steering wheel. "I'll show you girlie. Maybe you'll get lucky, and I'll show you how I can handle more than a boat."

"Big talk, little action," he responded. Her lithe body seemed to float in air as she moved toward him. Tan from the summer sun, she flashed an impish smile that radiated confidence and happiness. Meg was the whole package.

Her long, wavy blond hair had tickled his nose as she squeezed into the small opening between the steering wheel and his attentive groin. Those were the fun, flirty days with Meg. By instinct, he knew any further advances on his part would be reciprocated, but he also knew Elliott would punish him if he touched her.

Elliott, now known as an infamous serial killer and one of the FBI's Ten Most Wanted, had focused on Meg two years ago. As the only Bullhead TV news reporter, he had deceived everyone about his real identify. He had the run of the town and was invited to all social gatherings. Although he wasn't a handsome man, he always managed to snag a date for the weekends. Keeping the town abreast of the latest gossip, he gleefully roused the city's ire when the serial killer appeared for three consecutive years without apprehension by the police. Now stunned by the revelation of his identity, the city wanted justice for the rape of Bullhead's favorite daughter, Meg. The citizens wanted revenge, but they'd had to wait a year until he resurfaced.

In general Derek knew the plans Elliott had for Meg last year. He would grab her, take her to his desert compound, and try to mold her into his lifetime mate. What Derek didn't understand, or elected to deny, was that the initial seduction, which would last only eight hours on a train, would entail torture, rape, and sodomy. Meg's verve for life, along with her beauty, grace, intelligence, fun-loving nature, and caring persona, had all impressed Derek. Once he'd grasped the extent of his brother's maniacal actions, the first stone of a crumbling wall of devotion to Elliott broke away from the familial mortar.

**

Elliott's current plan for Meg's abduction had also included Derek's cooperation. Though only three hours had passed, it seemed like a lifetime. "Hang out with Meg. Ignore me in the casino when you see me. I'll be in FBI attire. There'll be explosions. I'll grab Meg, take her to the boat, and get away. Cover my ass, just in case."

Derek hadn't argued. He'd been on the wrong side of Elliott's wrath before, and experience told him how easily one of Elliott's problems could be eliminated. Murder was Elliott's specialty. So out of fear, Derek acquiesced. As the C-4 exploded in the casino, he watched Elliott push a drugged Meg toward the exit.

"Where the hell are you going?" yelled Mike, a member of the brat pack, as he watched Derek run for the exit. "You fuckin' coward."

Smoke and debris filled the room as Derek broke through the terrified crowd and headed for the parking lot. Sounds of sirens filled the hot air as he jumped into his SUV and started the engine.

"What the hell?" Amanda? He mentally questioned why the casino cocktail waitress was climbing into a private helicopter waiting on the helipad. He decided to follow her. Driving over the Laughlin Bridge, he turned south on Highway 95. Minutes later, as he watched the helicopter hover over a trailer park across the river from the Edgewater Casino, he steered the van over the curb and drove down a dirt road, reaching a remote, shrub-covered area. The helicopter dropped out of sight. Only the moon directed his way now. He hated guns, but he grabbed his .38 from the glove compartment and hastened through the underbrush. Shit, I'm an attorney. What the hell am I doing running around like James Bond? Damn you, Elliott, for putting me in this position.

When Derek slammed the butt end of his .38 into Amanda's skull, her knees buckled, and she sank into the hot sand. He checked for a pulse and was relieved to find one.

Confused and dazed, Elliott grabbed for his brother. "Where the hell've you been?" He coughed up some blood and shook his head, trying to focus. "She almost had me." Elliott's knees refused to hold him up, and he collapsed beside Amanda.

"Keeping up pretenses. I saw you pushing Meg out the door. Thought you might need some help." He dug through Amanda's pockets for the handcuff keys, removed the cuffs, and helped his brother to his feet. "How's Amanda involved in this?"

"Apparently she had us all fooled." Elliott lost his footing again and fell against Derek.

"Hurry up." Derek slipped an arm under Elliott's shoulder and pulled him along. "The pilot will be getting suspicious. Let's get the hell out of here."

Elliott's last bit of energy gave out, and he sagged into his brother's arms.

"Hospital," he gasped. His wound had opened again, and blood was flowing from the hole.

"Hospital? Hell, no. They'll recognize you. And you've got FBI clothes on."

"Wrap my face. Hurry. Go get the car. There should be gauze in your first aid kit. Cuff the girl. Throw her in the trunk." He grimaced with each word, and his breath came in quick spurts.

"She's FBI, a federal agent. Are you nuts? No." He managed to drag Elliott next to a large boulder and struggled to prop him up. Blood transferred to the front of his shirt.

"We may need her." His knees were giving away again. "Don't argue."

"What about the gunshot wound? For God's sake, Elliott. Bad choice. I can't explain that." He knew the decision was wrong.

With a last burst of energy, Elliott lurched forward. Derek reached for him, watched his brother's eyes lose focus, and caught Elliott seconds before he passed out. He struggled with Elliott's weight but finally lowered him to the ground, turning his attention to Amanada.

Derek cuffed Amanda's hands, duct-taped her mouth, and rolled her over. As he stared down at her lovely, unconscious body, her strong frame and well-toned figure, he mentally adjusted to her FBI status. It surprised him. He had missed that when she was an undercover cocktail waitress. Just a sexy broad then. What else had he missed?

He raced through the underbrush, located the car, and drove back to the shore. Struggling with her dead weight, he snagged Amanda's hair on the license plate before rolling her into the trunk. When he started to slam the lid, her two-way blared out. "Damn." He reached into her pocket, retrieved the radio, and turned it off. The chopper pilot was trying to find her. Meg's sister? FBI? Everyone in Bullhead thought Amanda was a cocktail waitress and dancer at the Oasis, but no one had suspected this. He did recall that Amanda had been invited to Yorba Linda for Christmas with Meg's family last year, but the event had been explained away.

Elliott stirred again, and Derek managed to help him into the front seat. "Take off your jacket. Put on my shirt." Derek stripped off his shirt and helped Elliott change, a slow process. Once they were changed, he fastened his seat belt, maneuvered the car through the brush, and drove away from the helicopter. Highway 95 was hectic with police cars and ambulances still responding to the casino bombing, but he found an opening and turned left into the middle of the chaos, his heart beating like crazy.

"Pull over here. Get off Ninety-Five. Wrap my face before we get to the hospital."

Horns honked at him as Derek crossed two lanes of traffic and ducked into a dead-end street shy of Silver Creek Road. He left the air on as he rummaged around for the first aid kit and finally completed a bad job of wrapping Elliott's face.

Six ambulances were lined up in front of the ER, and they could hear sirens approaching from across the river as they slowed down in front of the hospital. Derek pulled to a sharp stop at the curb adjacent to the Silver Creek ER. A nurse rushed to the car and helped lift Elliott onto a gurney. She quickly assessed his condition.

"Gunshot wound?" She looked at Derek. "We weren't expecting this. Just explosion victims."

An ER doctor joined her. "What's going on? You a relative?"

"No. Look, a cop commandeered me and my car at the casino. Said this guy got shot by a stray bullet, and there weren't any more ambulances. Shit. That's all I know." Derek slid a cell phone under Elliott's back and stepped away, trying to make a quick exit to avoid further questions. "I gotta go. My girlfriend's waiting for me at the casino." He threw his arms up in the air in a dismissive action and started for the car.

The doctor looked at the long line of ambulances, and to Derek's relief, he nodded to the attendant. "Bypass ER. Get him to surgery. Put pressure on the wound now." Slinging his stethoscope around his neck, he moved toward the next waiting ambulance.

Derek couldn't believe his good luck. He headed down 95 for Orange County with Amanda in the trunk.

***

Rachael and Meg arrived at the hospital minutes before Derek, and Meg was ushered to a room on the second floor. Worried about Josh, she inquired about his injuries. She was devastated to learn of his surgery, and she insisted on seeing him.

"Absolutely not, young lady. I just got you hooked up," replied the attendant. The woman continued checking Meg's vitals as she squirmed around in the bed.

***

Rachael waited for the doors to close as Elliott's gurney was shoved into her elevator. She hadn't seen Meg since the ambulance had dropped her off, and she was deep in thought about Josh and Amanda. She glanced at the gurney and sympathized with the patient's burned face, which was covered in gauze. As the door opened, she rushed down the hall to Meg's room.

Elliott, who had been sliding in and out of consciousness, recognized her through the slits in the gauze and turned away, hoping his bandaged face—his impromptu disguise—would hold up. Elliott's gurney was pushed into room 204, which was across from Meg's room.

"Wait, this patient is scheduled for surgery," said the attendant.

"Change of plan. The PA looked at him, and they aren't doing surgery. We'll clean him up. The ER is packed."

As they started his IV and monitors, Elliott recognized Meg's voice drifting across the hall and was thrilled. His recall was instant, remembering the first time he'd gazed on her young, naked body and the exquisite torture that had followed. *Oh, I loved ravaging your tender body, especially when the blood would spill over your sweet breasts. If your fuckin' sister, Rachael, hadn't intervened, well...* He pushed the thought around. *Rachael, you'll pay, and my payback is a bitch.*

If anyone had looked past the facial bandages, he or she would have seen Elliott smile at his good fortune. *Oh, darling, look what we have here. Maybe I'll slip between your sheets tonight. Your stallion awaits.* The sheet rustled a little from the beginning of a pathetic erection just before he passed out.

5

"I don't want to stay in the hospital. I'm fine." Meg struggled against the tightly tucked sheets. She fought to untie her gown. "Where the hell are my clothes?" The nurse came over, put on the blood pressure cuff, and attempted to insert a needle in a forearm vein. "What's that for?"

"Just an IV. The doctor ordered it. Your shoulder was dislocated, and we're waiting on the results of the tox screen to see what kind of drugs are in your system. You'll be our guest overnight—so he says."

"Bullshit." Meg snapped her head around to face the nurse. "My shoulder is fine."

"That's because they set it for you when you were out. Now settle down."

Meg, resisting her usual hotheaded, pushy way, decided to compromise. "Tell you what: if you find out how my friend Josh is doing, I'll stay the night. Find out if he's in surgery." She fell back onto the bed, exhausted by the slight exchange of words. She hated hospitals. They reminded her of Elliott and pain, so she decided to cooperate, to play nice and get out of there.

The nurse grumbled something profane and left the room.

***

Meg's semiprivate room was separated by a curtain. On the other side, lying apathetically in the sterile bed, was a young woman whose dark hair, matted with foreign matter, was tangled around her face. Singed eyelashes and a

14

multitude of lacerations marred her face. Jordan Kraemer moaned slightly, and Payden drew immediately to her side, gently touching her shoulder with his calloused hand.

I'm sure your bloody face will heal up fine, honey, but what about the rest of you? "Jessie, Jessie. How ya doin', baby sister?"

She tried to open her eyes, but they were heavy with pain and medication. Through the tiny slits, a worried smile came into focus. Why are you calling me Jessie? She mouthed a word, but again only a moan emitted through her blood-caked lips.

Payden recoiled when a loud, angry voice of the female persuasion rang out from down the hospital hallway. "Where did you take her? She needs a private room with twenty-four-hour security."

As Rachael shoved her way into the room, Payden glanced around the curtain and watched as the head nurse intervened, blocking her way.

"Hold up. Look, lady," the staunch RN began. "I know the situation. I know this is your sister, and we'll make sure she's safe. Bring on the security as long as they don't interfere with her care. The hospital is under siege with the bombing at the casino."

"Tell me something I don't know. Out of my way." She pushed past the nurse.

The nurse pushed back. "More ambulances are on their way. They have to go back for even more injured. We've got ten people in the morgue, and we aren't staffed for all of this." Undeniable frustration and fatigue registered on the nurse's formidable face, but she stood her ground.

Rachael continued yelling, which annoyed Payden. "Why can't Meg be in the same room as Josh? Where did you put him? The last time I saw him he was spurting blood from his neck. Where the hell is he?" She pushed the bedside table away from Meg's bed.

"Mr. Meyers is in surgery. He'll go across the hall when he's out of ICU. The best we can do." The nurse clipped off the last sentence and abruptly left, leaving Rachael stunned by the quick dismissal.

"Shut the hell up, lady. Your sister's not the only one that's hurt," roared Payden before any more of Rachael's yelling could penetrate the room. He pushed the privacy curtain out of the way and charged toward her. "Did you say *Meg*? I've been watching the TV about this Meg Pennington. She's the bitch responsible for all this. Too bad that sicko didn't get her this time."

Rachael turned, took four bounding steps, and was in his face. "You asshole. Who do you think you are? Go to hell." She raised her hand to punch him.

Payden grabbed her arms and forced her against the wall. Looking at her face, he could see the pain and anger that filled her. He relaxed his grip and stepped back. "Sorry. I had no right to say that. It's not easy for any of us." He turned and started for Jordan's bed. "But my sister, Jessie, is lying right here, and her twin sister's lying in the morgue."

Why do you keep calling me Jessie?

6

Payden Kraemer pulled the straight-backed chair next to the hospital bed and sat down. His typically strong physique failed him as his shoulders slumped forward and his chin dropped. The sudden outburst with the woman behind the curtain confused him. God, what's wrong with me? Jordan moved slightly. He reached for the bed and pulled himself to a standing position. His rumpled clothes, tousled hair, and two-day beard growth was in direct contrast to his normal manicured style. A president of his own computer company during the day and a cowboy at night—that was his life, not this heavy drama. One hand pushed a wisp of brown hair from his sister's cheek.

She moaned.

"Jessie? Talk to me, baby sister." Nothing. He settled back into the chair and closed his eyes, recounting the last few days before the accident. Everything had been perfect. The twins had entered the barrel-racing competition at the Rodeo National Finals in Las Vegas with winning odds. The Thomas and Mack Arena had been filled to capacity as the girls raced to victory. Jessie's horse had started strong at the beginning and cleared all barrels, while Jordan's horse had sideswiped a barrel, losing two precious seconds. Trophies, money, accolades. The identical twins had it all, but they didn't always accept it in the same way. Payden had noticed Jordan's typical jealous attitude emerge at the photo op after the event, but he knew it would disappear in time—at least, he hoped it would.

As a reward for a job well done, Payden insisted they drive to the Oasis Casino in Laughlin for a well-deserved minivacation. While the city didn't support all the nightlife Vegas did, he knew the girls would relax more, swim in the river, gamble a little, and breathe.

He pulled up to valet parking, got out, and talked to the attendant. Both Jessie and Jordan got out. Then instant recall got a little blurry. Jessie or Jordan? They were dressed alike with their tight jeans and plaid shirts—one blue, one red. He remembered grabbing the luggage and going inside the casino. Was it Jessie or Jordan who forgot her purse and cell phone and went back to the car? Jessie or Jordan? Red shirt?

The blast from the C-4 killed one sister instantly. The blue shirt. The surviving sister had cleared the rotating entrance doors when the bomb exploded; she was knocked out, but the injuries were minor—scrapes, bruises, and cuts from flying glass. The red shirt.

Final identification was difficult, but both Payden and the police relied on the evidence. The purse and cell phone that had cleared the revolving door and the red shirt buttoned on the girl belonged to Jessie. So Jessie it was. Jessie had survived. Jordan had not.

Jordan moaned again. Payden, you idiot. Why do you call me Jessie? Then the answer appeared through her migraine headache, and she mentally grinned. It's a fuckin' mistake. A mistake. She allowed her mind to wrap around the thought. Intriguing. Why not go with it for a while? The trophy would be mine. I wouldn't have to live in her shadow anymore. It's a win-win.

When Payden leaned over and kissed her forehead, she strained to open her eyes and moaned. "Payden?"

"Oh, Jess. Thank God. I've been so worried."

"Where's Jordan?"

7

Derek slammed the car door and took off down Highway 95, leaving the hospital in the dust. So far, so good. Damn, that was close. He cranked up the air-conditioning, noting the 110-degree heat penetrating his windshield.

Amanda squirmed around in the trunk of the car. Knocked unconscious? She didn't know how long she'd been out, but a gnawing headache was working its way to her frontal lobe. She managed to roll onto her back and started kicking the lid.

Derek ignored the noise until he reached Walmart. Cursing under his breath, he parked at the edge of the parking lot, away from the store, where no one else would hear her—or care enough to check on the noise. Too hot. After purchasing a throwaway phone, he started for home, clicked on the cruise control, and settled back for the four-hour trip, using the time to reflect on the past year and contemplate the next. Things had to change.

From the beginning he'd known Elliott was a criminal, but both he and his sister, Marisa, had steered away from his exploits. Once Derek had graduated from Western University of Law, Elliott had reminded him that someday it would be payback time for the college debt, a day when he would enter the "family business," which consisted of drug smuggling and money laundering. Initially Elliott had lived in San Jose by himself and excluded his siblings from his illicit business, but one day he'd called.

"Derek, I'm moving my business to Bullhead City, Arizona, which will also encompass Laughlin, Nevada. Be ready. I will be calling in your marker."

Elliott had failed to tell Derek that his move from San Jose was necessary since the police were getting too close and his unmentioned crime of killing was getting too much publicity. The subject was never to be discussed again. It would be as Elliott wished. Derek understood that his job would be mainly logistics, seaplane arrivals, contacts in Tijuana, and overseeing Marisa's bookkeeping. No hands-on drug connection—his participation was only as a facilitator, which was handled by phone. Derek felt the off-site managing was okay, but after six months, Elliott called with a strange request.

"There's a girl named Meg Pennington in Bullhead. Works at the dam. Hangs out at the Oasis Casino. Befriend her. Report back to me."

"Report what?" Derek wondered whether Elliott was ready to give up the call girls he loved to use, misuse, and eventually knock around. Maybe settle down?

"Everything. Where she goes, address, work hours, friends. Everything."

I remember the first time I saw Meg; she was hanging out with her friends at the river bar. She sparkled. Bright, beautiful, spontaneous, flirtatious. A rare jewel. What was Elliott thinking? She would never, ever be interested in the likes of him.

He made friends with Meg and her brat pack, backed off from an open invitation from Meg to become romantic, and reported all of her movements to Elliott.

Egotistical, self-centered, and brash described Elliott's reputation in town. He was smart enough not to make an outward move on Meg, but he took time to develop a perfect plan for his desires. For two years the city lived in fear of the serial killer, and up to the minute when Elliott kidnapped Meg, Derek had had no inkling that his brother was the monster. The aha moment came when the FBI identified him, much to Derek's chagrin. And now, he would be considered an accomplice.

Cruising down Interstate 40, he checked the temperature and wondered how long Amanda could last in the trunk. His mind quickly reverted again to the very present problem of Elliott. He merged onto I-15, pulled off the freeway at Barstow, and ordered a burrito, three large Cokes, and a jumbo cup of ice water at the Del Taco drive-through window. After driving five minutes, all signs of civilization were left behind, so he took the exit and drove down a dirt road. As he opened the trunk, he instantly realized Amanda was suffering from acute dehydration. "Amanda, wake up. Drink." He yanked the duct tape from her mouth, helped her up to a sitting position, and shoved the cup of water to her raw lips. It spilled.

The sun was directly behind the man, and while Amanda recognized his voice, her eyes failed to make the connection. She had no way of holding the cup, so he quickly removed the cuffs. She squinted and with shaking hands grabbed the cup and drank. She could feel the cold water trickle down through her body. "Thanks" was all she could muster. Her incoherent mind tried to sort out how Derek had found her in the back of this strange car. With her free hand she picked at the duct-tape residue on her mouth and rubbed her raw wrist. Her head was throbbing with pain, and the glaring sun added to her discomfort. "Derek? How did you find me?"

"Find you?" Then he realized the situation. "Oh. No wonder you're confused. I didn't find you; I knocked you out. You were going to arrest my brother."

The truth shook her. "Elliott? Your brother?" And then every unsolved question from the last year was answered. "Oh."

"Yeah. Big surprise. You don't know how many times I thought Rachael was going to catch us, but I never dreamed that you were FBI." The thought of having the feds messing around with his life was staggering. "Not all that smart, are you, huh? Look. If you behave, I'll let you lie down on the backseat and soak up the AC."

"Please."

Amanda cooperated and was relieved to rest, lying on the backseat as the cool air drifted by. Her mind, somewhat refreshed, started analyzing the last few hours and the startling realization that Derek and Elliott were brothers. How had she missed that? When the bottom line finally materialized, she was left with the undeniable fact that she was in a world of hurt.

Thirty minutes of silence passed, and as traffic got heavy, coasting down the Cajon Pass, Amanda decided to engage Derek in conversation.

"You know, Derek, I was never convinced that you weren't involved with Meg's missing key to the dam, but I couldn't piece together a motive."

"Hmm." He concentrated on the road.

"Well, now. Elliott's brother? Didn't have you pegged as the right hand to a serial killer."

Derek remained silent at first. Then, realizing Elliott would probably kill her, he decided to participate in the conversation. "Circumstances were beyond my control. I never wished any harm to come to Meg."

"Do you know what Elliott plans for me?"

"No. I did hear him say he was going to annihilate your whole family, though." He waited and then said, "Probably shouldn't be making any big plans."

Derek noticed Amanda was trying to make contact with a passing motorist. Cuffing her hands in front hadn't prevented her from pushing her face against the window and showing her constraints to anyone driving down the pass. He pulled off I-15 and drove through Victorville into the desolate desert.

Reaching into the glove compartment, he pulled out a syringe, loaded it with two ccs of ketamine and opened the back door. Amanda was ready for him and kicked him in the face as the door opened. She hurried to a sitting position and scooted forward, making a quick exit from the car, as Derek flew across the sand.

Within ten feet of the car, Derek caught up with her, knocking her down with a fully loaded shoulder thrust. Once down he put a knee in her back. "You bitch. Had to make things worse." Cuffs in place behind her back, he shoved her toward the car, and she fell headfirst into the backseat. "Duct tape it is," he said as he tore off a piece of the silver tape and applied it to her already-bleeding lips. He thrust the needle into her arm, and she relaxed into a deep sleep.

Once she was out, he continued down the freeway in silence, turning onto Highway 91and later taking the off-ramp to Yorba Linda. Rolling hills, trees, and grass awaited him, in sharp contrast to the sand and brush of the barren desert. He passed Savi Ranch and continued on to East Lake Village, where his sister was waiting.

When the garage door opened, Marisa dashed through the man door to see her brother. The image of a prone body caught her attention as she passed the car, and she abruptly stopped. "Who's she?"

Derek pressed the remote and closed the garage door. "FBI."

"What the hell is Elliott thinking? Bringing an FBI agent here? He's lost it." Marisa stared at the crumpled shape in the backseat. "Is she dead?"

"No, just out. I gave her a shot of Elliott's ketamine. Help me pull her out of the car."

"What happened to your face?" Marisa opened the back door and grabbed Amanda's ankles.

"The bitch kicked me. Hurts like hell. She won't do that again. I taped her eyes and ankles." Frustration flowed through his words.

Derek and Marisa, struggling with the limp figure, finally dropped her onto the garage floor. Dragging Amanda across the concrete and through the laundry room door, Derek winced when her head bounced on the threshold. "We'll leave the cuffs on. Guest room will be best." Panting from the exertion, he tried to pull her through the bedroom door, but her inert body got stuck, and he cursed. "Damn it. Come on, Marisa. Get your ass over here and help."

With Marisa's help, they wrestled Amanda onto the bed. "No use suffocating her." Marisa tugged on Amanda's hips and finally rolled her, standing back to look at the beautiful woman. "Guess we don't need the blindfold now. You know how Elliott feels about witnesses." She yanked off the duct tape, tearing out more of Amanda's hair and eyelashes in the process. "Sorry 'bout that," she said, then paused to smile. "Might as well get used to the pain, missy. Welcome to hell." She pulled the remaining duct tape from Amanda's mouth and stood back as the split lips oozed blood.

Blinking away the dry eyes, Amanda focused on Derek. The ketamine was still impairing her thoughts, and she fought her way through the mental haze. Pain ripped through her head, but she struggled against the impulse to cry.

"Awake, are you? Wondering what's next?" He recognized the hatred spilling from her eyes. "What? Still reeling from the truth about my relationship to Elliott?"

She didn't reply.

"Well, since my brother never leaves witnesses, here are a couple of items you probably didn't realize, you great FBI person. I stole the dam key from Meg and gave it to Elliott. He threw that cocktail waitress over the dam during the monsoon. Remember? That happened on my first date with Meg."

Amanda watched him and categorized the information.

"What else? Oh, not enough time to tell it all." He smiled his handsome, crooked smile, which most women found irresistible.

"Why?" Amanda's voice was raspy.

"Why?" Derek thought about that. "No choice, if you must know. I like my limbs, my face, and my life, for that matter. Elliott gives the orders. We are his expediters. No questions asked."

"Strange. Meg usually isn't fooled by the likes of you. Maybe a little ditsy but a lot of common sense too."

"Ah, yes. That was her downfall. Too trusting, too caring. I've never met anyone so in love with life."

"Seems like some of that should have worn off on you. Her innocence, maybe."

Derek faltered. He knew Meg had made a difference in his life. "Good try, Amanda. I've read the FBI manual about an agent being in your situation. Make friends with the enemy. No deal." He leaned over the bed and put duct tape back on her mouth. "Enough for now."

"What's Elliott got in mind for her?" asked Marisa. "There's no way he'll let her live, and I don't want to be any part of killing an FBI agent. God, he's lost it. He's taking us down with him." Marisa crossed the room, glanced out the window to see whether everything looked normal, and then closed the plantation shutters. Worry and concern walked with her.

Derek turned back to look at Amanda, not knowing how to answer his sister. "Help her into the bathroom. I'll wait outside. Amanda's clever, so be careful. We shouldn't talk around her. You know Elliott has people to take care of the gory stuff. He won't make us do it," Derek said, but he wasn't convincing enough to make Marisa believe it.

"We'll have another guest tomorrow," he whispered to Marisa.

Locating scissors in the dresser drawer, Marisa cut the tape around Amanda's ankles and pulled her to a sitting position. "Stand up. Time to pee and then off to bed." She shoved her toward the bathroom, and once inside, she unzipped her jeans and pushed her down on the toilet seat. "Pee."

The bathroom door was left ajar, and Amanda tried to capture the gist of the conversation floating in from the hall. When she heard the word *mother* followed later by *Grace*, she panicked. Mom? What's going on? Mom doesn't stand a chance against Derek.

8

Rachael stepped into the hospital hallway so Payden wouldn't accost her again and tried for the umpteenth time to reach her mother. Twelve voice mails had been left on both the Yorba Linda landline and her cell phone. The sisters had decided to keep Grace out of the loop regarding Elliott's most recent attempt to kidnap Meg. Lying to her was tough, but they'd known she would be right in the middle of the action if she knew what was planned, and that would have meant another person to guard. Rachael regretted the decision now.

"What the hell's going on? Where's Meg?" were the first words out of Grace Pennington's mouth when she finally returned the calls.

"Calm down, Mom. Meg's fine. In the hospital but only for a checkup." Rachael tried to change the subject. "Where have you been? I've been calling for hours."

"New York, business. Had to meet with my agent. I'm at John Wayne now, waiting for a ride home. Give me the details." When danger and her girls were involved, no syrupy conversation passed over Grace's lips. Her focus became like molten steel.

Rachael, taking time to explain the FBI sting operation in detail—how it went down, who was involved, and details of how it ended—carefully selected her final words to calm Grace and hopefully dull her sharp tongue. "Meg is fine. Josh has been shot, and Elliott is supposedly caught."

"What do you mean, *supposedly*? What the hell kind of word is that? And what about Amanda? You haven't mentioned her part."

Rachael tried again for the perfect words, in contrast to Grace, who never spared any words when something went awry. "Last we heard, she had a gun pointed at Elliott and was going to take him to jail via the helicopter, but—"

"But what? She's missing? No, no. This is not happening again." A huge sigh poured through the receiver. "I'll be there tomorrow." The phone went dead.

Rachael slowly returned to the room. This was typical Grace. Always abrupt so you wouldn't see her emotions. I feel like I've disappointed her again.

***

Grace immediately dialed an old number, one she hadn't used for years. "Luke, I need a favor."

"Is Meg okay?"

"Amanda's missing."

"I can be there in six hours."

"No. No time."

"What do you need?"

"A tracking device, of sorts. For me. Can you help?" Grace waited.

After a few moments, Luke said, "Here's the address. Be there by four o'clock today. Are you in danger?"

"I, ah, just want to be prepared for any circumstance. You know me." She chose to ignore his real question because she was acting only on her intuition. Grace wasn't surprised when a tear escaped her eye. She could always count on him, and she called him only when the matter was urgent.

Luke said, "Of course. You know—"

"I know." She could feel his passion through the phone. Grace disconnected the call.

9

The male attendant and scrub nurse wheeled Josh down the hall from ICU into room 207 following his surgery. He hadn't regained consciousness from the repair of his carotid artery, but that wasn't unusual, according to the physician in charge.

Rachael wasn't happy with that conclusion, but she didn't make a fuss. She took his inert hand and massaged it, the hand that had touched her body and brought love to her life. "Hi, honey. It's Rachael." His pallor disturbed her. "You're going to be okay. Meg's okay, too." She waited for him to move, to respond, but there was nothing. Doctors always say unconscious people can still hear. Rachael's normal tough-cop exterior eluded her. Her almost-auburn hair crept over one eye as she leaned over to kiss Josh's mouth. She didn't cope well with the waiting game, and yet here she was. Shit. I was supposed to have your engagement ring on my finger by now, Meg was supposed to be in college, and Amanda was…Well, who the hell knows about her?

Always reluctant to cry, she fought the tears. She was the strong one, but the year had taken its toll. She watched Josh for some sign but saw nothing, so she settled in the chair as the nurse changed his IVs. Probably time to check in with the department. She dialed the number.

"Cap, I'm in the dark here. Have you heard anything about Amanda? She's off my radar now, and that's not like her."

"Nothing new. Glad you called in." He closed the door to his office and slid into his swivel chair. "We've got a car going over to the trailer park to check it out." The PD was crowded with FBI personnel, and the reporters were vying for an interview. "Guess someone from the trailer park spotted an SUV in the area at the time of the shooting."

"What shooting?" Rachael straightened in her chair, then stood and paced around the room.

"Back off, Rach. I don't know yet. You know I'll call you."

"Oh, shit. Meg saw a car earlier, right after the helicopter landed. I ignored her. Maybe an SUV?"

"Wasn't ours. Chopper pilot just called in a 'no response' from Amanda. Sorry."

"What? The pilot lost contact too?"

"Looks like it. Don't know for sure, but I'll call when I hear. It's a mess, Rach. A lot of folks were injured at the casino. Some are taking advantage of the flying chips. The casino's still in chaos, so most of the guys are there."

"Okay. Keep me in the loop." After ending the call, Rachael sighed, kissed Josh's forehead, and returned to Meg's room. She found Meg doing her "Meg thing," trying to cheer up her new roommate, Jessie.

"Well, I can ride horses, too. Last summer I spent some time in Catalina, and I rode every day. It's absolutely beautiful there when the sun sets and you're plowing through the surf's edge. Romantic as hell. You need to try it." She chattered on, unaware that Jordan's twin sister was lying dead in the morgue.

"That's nice." Jordan turned her back on Meg, wishing tears would come but feeling nothing. What had happened? The mix-up? Does anyone know? Oh. She mentally walked through the scene when the explosion had knocked everyone around. I was carrying Jessie's purse. Her credit card for check-in. That's how it happened. I was waiting in line to register while Jessie was outside getting the luggage from the parking attendant. She was killed at the same time some guy was decapitated. The vision of her sister's torn body was caught in her mind's eye. She turned to Meg. "Sorry to be so short with you. I'm—well—I don't know what I am. Half of me is gone." She gave Meg an almost tearful version of how her sister had died.

Meg was horrified. "I didn't know about your sister. All of that's my fault. The monster wanted me. Can't tell you how sorry I am." Meg teared up from the personal burden of guilt that strangled her heart.

Payden entered the room, overheard the conversation, and realized there was an opportunity for the girls to help each other in their grief. "Wow, two broken fillies. Why don't you girls get past it? Maybe start planning your future?" He knew that sounded insensitive but felt it might change their focus from pitiful to pissed. It worked.

"You jerk. Back off. Your sister's in pain." Sitting straight up in bed, Meg yelled at him and then winced from her injured shoulder. "Men—no sense of timing." She shook her head, shot him a well-practiced disgusted look, and rolled over on her side.

Thoughtful, kindhearted, protective, spontaneous, and spunky. Payden liked those attributes and knew they would be beneficial in his sister's recovery. "Okay, Meg. Don't get your panties in a twist. Jessie says you can ride. How about a visit to our ranch in Norco when you get better?"

Jordan bristled. She wasn't sure she even liked Meg. "Say no, Meg. Norco is, well, Norco. Nobody visits Norco unless they are escaping from Orange County into horse land. Our native bird is the fly."

Payden interrupted, "Hey, baby sister. Since when do you put Norco down? That was Jordan's job." He shot a double take Jordan's way.

"Sorry." Jordan bunched up the sheets and turned toward Meg, realizing her mistake in personality.

Meg decided to drop the attitude and join in the conversation. "Seems to me like just a wide spot in the road when I pass it on Interstate Fifteen. Too far from the water for me. If it's not the river, then it has to be the Pacific. I'm an original water bug."

"Do you have any plans?" Payden pushed, impatient to keep the conversation going.

"Can't see going back to work for the dam people again. Really don't know what I want to do." She pondered. School, maybe? What else is there? Bullhead or Yorba Linda? Maybe Catalina? She knew Grace would be pushing her toward college.

"Well, if you're any good with horses and people, we have an opening for a ranch hand. Pay isn't much, but you could flop in the bunkhouse for free." Payden rolled a smile toward Meg along with the invitation.

Meg took a deep look at Payden. She felt he was really trying to help. A real cowboy. He was tall with a slender build, but he looked strong; wavy, unruly brown hair stuck out from under the cowboy hat. He wore jeans, boots, and some kind of brass belt buckle. Her quick assessment was positive, but how many times had she been wrong about the men in her life?

"What? Mucking stalls? Wow, Mom would be so proud of me." Her eyes drifted up and down his tall frame, and he knew it. "What's with that oversized belt buckle?"

"Oh, just picked it up at a garage sale."

"Don't let him kid you. He's the number-two bareback rider in the country. Won that at the rodeo finals last year," commented Jordan. She was proud of his accomplishments, and the thought flew through her mind that now he was the only one to brag about. Jessie always beat me at barrel racing. Pissed me off. She was lucky. I should have Jessie's good luck. Jordan questioned the thoughts of hatred and jealousy that raced through her mind. When had they started?

It was refreshing for Meg to meet someone who didn't flaunt all his talents. A little bashful? Interesting. "Big deal. What, you bought a box of Cracker Jacks at the rodeo, and the buckle was the prize?"

"Hmm, you really are a piece of work, aren't you?" He liked her quirky style, and even while wearing no makeup and lying in a sterile white bed, he recognized her formidable beauty. Payden had been too busy with life to hook up with many women, but he realized this girl was certainly one to be reckoned with. "You're probably too wimpy to work a ranch anyway," he said, ready to banter with her. "Cracker Jacks?"

"Wimpy? Never been accused of that before."

"First time for everything," he said, though he was thinking, Sassy little chick.

Meg read a lot into his words. Flirting? "Doesn't sound like a lot of fun, so instead, Jessie, how about spending a day or two at my house in Bullhead? You can rest and soak in the river while I take care of some business. Then, rather than going to Norco, we'll swing by Yorba Linda for a day or so and then head to Catalina Island. I think my sister's going there too, and we can rent a house. They used to have stables there, and maybe we could find a place for you to practice barrel racing. The Pacific Ocean is all around, and I know a ton of island peeps. How about that?" Her enthusiasm was growing.

"Thought I'd be going home with my sister." Jordan rolled over on her side, fighting the sound from her belly she knew was going to erupt into involuntary moaning. She had never known grief, the heartrending pain of losing a loved one. It took her breath away for a minute, and then the grief transformed again. She wanted to correct Meg and scream out, "I'm Jordan!" but something inside stopped her. Something sinister.

Meg didn't know how to respond to that, so she rolled onto her right side, pushed back the sheet, and swung her legs over the side of the bed. Pulling the wheelchair over, she plopped into it, untangling the IV lines along the way. Snatching a sideways look, she watched as Payden gathered Jessie in his huge arms, thinking how lucky Jessie was to have someone love her that much. The guilt about her participation in the grief gnawed at her insides.

Jordan silently reacted to Payden's embrace. Has Payden always loved Jessie more? Is he happy that his precious Jessie survived? He's never hugged me this way.

Payden watched Meg as she wheeled through the doorway, with one hand guiding the IV stand, gave her a half smile, and questioned his strong interest in this young girl.

10

Amanda was definitely missing. The entire FBI staff assigned to capture the serial killer incorporated their focus on finding her.

"Okay, Chris. Take it from the top one more time. Your chopper spotlight tracked Elliott as he crawled out of the river. You landed in the trailer park lot off Ninety-Five, and Amanda ran through the trailer area, headed to the water." Ron Wendt, FBI special agent and Amanda's boss, continued questioning the pilot.

"Yeah. She yelled at me to call for backup and to stay with the helicopter, which I did. I wasn't armed. When backup arrived, I directed them down the path that Amanda had taken."

"They didn't find her." This is why we don't use civilians, he thought. "They didn't find Elliott. The only thing they found was some blood, signs of a struggle, and tire track. Did you hear a shot or a car—anything?"

"No. I shut the engine down when backup arrived, but honest to God, no gunshots, no car noises. And no one passed me going out through the trailer park entrance. I would have stopped them." Guilt crept into his voice as he spoke. He glanced around the room and felt other people recognized his remorse. Amanda was his friend; he should have done more.

"Forensics is down there now. They're taking blood samples. Water patrol is out with some volunteers from the dam on WaveRunners, checking the shoreline." He glanced out the window, stood, and walked around the desk.

"Sun will be up soon. Make the search a little easier," he mumbled, then turned to Chris. "Anything else to add?"

"Not really. If Elliott had been shot, that was probably his blood. Doesn't mean Amanda was shot or hurt. He must've had an accomplice. Damn it. Amanda's strong; she would've nailed his ass if he was alone."

"True. It seems quite a coincidence that you were standing by, and I don't like coincidences. Why didn't she use the FBI chopper? It was stationed right across the river from the casino." Wendt began to doubt Chris's story. "Did she contact you earlier?"

"Look, Amanda and I go way back. She asked me yesterday if I would keep an eye on the Oasis tonight. Guess I was closer than your chopper, and she went for it. You'll have to ask her." Chris was tired of answering the same questions. "If you're through with me, I'd like to take the bird up and check the shoreline."

"Your call," Wendt answered, "but don't interfere with our chopper. Keep in touch. If you spot anything, don't go charging in. I realize you know the river better than we do, but you're not FBI. I'm not enlisting your help. Got it?"

As he left, Chris yelled over his shoulder, "Yeah." Under his breath, he sent a parting remark. "Thanks a lot, asshole."

Agent Wendt turned to the rest of his unit. "Double-check the hospitals...all newly admitted patients. They might have missed the gunshot wound with all the emergencies coming in, so look for any white male, age forty to fifty, signs of hypothermia. Someone check all the ER rooms, private practice MDs, urgent care facilities—hell, even the veterinarians. Let's get this guy."

Chris belonged to neither the FBI nor the Bullhead Police. He was an independent pilot who'd grown up with Amanda and her family on the river, and he'd had a secret crush on Meg since he was nine. His knowledge of the river, the people, and their habits was always helpful to Amanda when she needed special assistance. He felt he'd let her down this time. *I should have left the chopper and helped her.* His guilt was staggering. *I'll catch up with Rachael and lend her a hand. Don't worry, Amanda. I'll find you.* He checked his instruments and gas level, and with a determined look, he pulled back on the stick and lifted off.

II

Grace Pennington carefully considered her last-minute packing. The SuperShuttle was scheduled to arrive within minutes to take her to the Ontario Airport, and then the hour flight to Bullhead City would follow. Grace had hurriedly purchased airline and SuperShuttle tickets online, and she sent a text to Rachael confirming her arrival time so someone could meet her at the Bullhead airport. Twenty-four hours had passed, and Grace was anxious to start her hands-on healing of Meg again. Medication? Check. Cell phone charger? Check. Cash? Check. Visa? Check.

Grabbing her overnight kit from the closet, she tossed moisturizer, blush, and eyeliner into the bag and stopped to look in the mirror. "So, old lady, just turned fifty-two, did you? When was the last time you danced on a table?" She leaned toward the mirror and in the revealing florescent light examined her face. There were a few more lines, a few more gray hairs that needed to be colored blond, a few more brown age spots trying to work their way to the surface. She shrugged at the reality of it all, looked around, and decided all other items were replaceable on this short trip.

Returning to the kitchen, Grace rested against the black granite and stared out the bay window. "Damn squirrels are back. I'll ask the girls to buy me a shotgun for Christmas. Tired of them eating my macadamia nuts." Grace lived alone but talked out loud a lot. When asked why, her answer was short and terse: "I want my voice to be ready when the president calls." Today she had more than squirrels on her mind. The "Creator," a nickname her daughters had given her, focused on the immediate problem of Amanda's disappearance. She touched the newly implanted device behind her ear. The incision and implant had been virtually painless, with only two small sutures needed to close the incision. She watched for the van, and while her eyes glanced up and down the long driveway, her mind was focused to the point of tunnel vision. Did Elliott have anything to do with Meg's hospitalization? She had prayed he would never show up again, but she knew better. His insatiable lust for Meg would never be curbed. He needed to die.

Rachael called again, hoping Grace had cooled down from their last conversation. "No, Mom, listen. Elliott was never alone with Meg. She's okay. Dislocated a shoulder. We're running a tox screen, but everything else is fine."

"Mentally?" Grace waited. "The truth."

Rachael paused, formulating the truth or a semblance of it. "You know Meg, Mom. She's an expert at hiding her feelings. Tough exterior, but I think… okay. She'll need some time to settle down."

Grace felt relieved that Elliott hadn't hurt Meg, that he hadn't had time to draw her back into the dark abyss of sexual mayhem. It had taken over six months for Meg to finally face the reality of her torture last year and to return to a quasi state of normalcy. Grace wondered how much of that had been real and how much had been an act put on for the family's benefit.

Pulled back from her daydreaming, Grace realized the SuperShuttle had arrived and was turning around, backing onto the garage approach. The driver opened the back of the van and placed the small carry-on bag inside. Grace grabbed her purse, and after setting the alarm, she went outside.

An attractive brunette approached. "Morning, ma'am. You have a beautiful yard. Nice day to travel. Any other bags?"

"No, that's it. You're early."

"Yes, ma'am. Traffic was light on Ninety-One for a change."

"Are you scheduled for another pickup in Yorba Linda? Derek Turner on Via Marwah?"

The driver started the engine and checked the printout located on the dashboard. "Yes, ma'am. We're on our way there right now. No other pickups, and then off to the airport we go. Plenty of time."

Grace climbed into the passenger seat and relaxed as the driver quickly covered the three miles to Derek's house. She ran her fingertips across the new implant behind her ear again. Still a little swollen. She mentally practiced how to activate the device as she brushed her shoulder-length hair back into place. Yes, she thought, the CIA has some nice new toys since my operative days. It looks like this might be the year to give my girls a little CIA history lesson. As they pulled into his driveway, Grace wondered whether Meg had really been interested in this attorney Derek. I probably should have run a background check on him, but he seemed so benign. He'd been gambling with Meg at the casino when she was kidnapped the first time, but then he disappeared. She wondered if that was the same situation this time. Probably afraid of violence. Too wussy for my Meg. At least he cares enough about her to visit today. Guess I'll have to play nice.

No bags were in the driveway when they arrived at Derek's house. Grace sat alone in the van as the driver walked across the manicured lawn to the front door and rang the bell. Derek quickly opened the door and approached the van with the driver. She watched his masculine stride, his usual good looks amplified by his summer tan. Six foot four; an admirable six-pack; and brown, wavy hair. The type Meg always falls for.

"Good morning, Grace. You're looking lovely, as usual."

"Well, thank you, Derek. No bags?"

"Oh, still inside. I bought a gift for Meg, and I wanted to show it to you before we left. Do we have a minute, driver?"

The driver nodded. "No problem."

"Great. Meg loves surprises." Grace's radar needle twitched. Hmm. Don't like the looks of this. She switched to full alert as her old CIA training took over. Inside the house, Grace was surprised to see moving boxes littered throughout the living room. "You moving, Derek?"

"Let me see. Am I moving? What do you say, sis? We moving?"

"Sis?" Grace turned to meet his sister, but only the driver stood in the room.

"Oh, yeah. Your cute, little driver is actually my sister, Marisa. Also sister to one of your favorite people." He struck a haughty pose in the doorway, pushed his hands into his pants pockets, and waited.

A sinking feeling overtook her. Grace knew without asking who that was. How stupid to walk right into this situation. She had been trained better.

"You must mean Elliott. I never had the privilege of meeting the monster." She maintained her poise, but gut-wrenching hatred swirled in her stomach. She returned his look, straightened, and waited for the next mental blow.

"Well, we have a little reunion set up for you here. Not Elliott, I'm afraid. Come on into the bedroom. I think you'll be happy with our choice of partners in hostage." He gloated.

When Grace saw Amanda lying on the bed—hands, feet, and mouth taped—she sucked in a deep breath and held it. Grace never got hysterical; rather her reaction was the opposite. All through life, when calamity came calling, she would become transfixed, melt into molten steel, and attack the problem. Emotions were for later. This was far worse than any nagging nightmare. Her nerves hardened, and she became gravely quiet. "Have you hurt her?" She watched as Amanda wrestled against the tape, trying to send messages with her eyes.

"Not yet, but Elliott is working on a huge farewell party for you."

Hmm...Think...Think...

12

Since there was no slug to analyze, the police who questioned Elliott accepted his explanation of waiting for the ferry on the boat dock when the gunfire had erupted. Rachael, being the detective on the force, would usually have done the questioning. But at the time, she was on the other side of the hospital curtain, attending to Josh, who had regained consciousness. Elliott's wound was through and through, so the PA irrigated the area, sutured the ruptured veins with dissolvable thread, and used Dermabond glue to close the hole. To prevent infection, one side was left open. In addition, he received a transfusion for blood loss, he was treated for hypothermia and exhaustion, and the staff, who were still overwhelmed with the onslaught of trauma victims, left him to heal. When the facial bandage was removed, he insisted on a dark room, feigning eye irritation. He rolled to his left side, staring at the privacy curtain that separated him from his future.

Straining to hear the conversation in the next bed, he recognized a familiar voice, one that belonged to an enemy who needed to be annihilated. Rachael.

"Come on, Josh. Please. Open your eyes." Pleading seemed to fade into despair.

When silence followed, Elliott smiled. I hope you're dead.

Minutes passed, and finally Rachael started again. "Hi, sailor. Welcome back. We've been worried."

Elliott heard the chair scrape on the floor and the rustling of the sheet.

"Rachael? What happened?" Josh's voice sounded thick, and a bewildered tone emerged.

"You were shot, Josh. You're in the Bullhead City Hospital. Any of this sound familiar?"

"Rachael?" he asked again.

Their conversation diminished in volume, so Elliott reached for his phone. Eavesdropping on dribble didn't interest him.

"Yes, sweetheart, it's me." Rachael choked back a tear. "Thank God."

"What's going on? Why are you here?"

Rachael leaned back and wilted. "Don't you remember?" She panicked. Amnesia? Their history gone? A year of Meg's torture, a year when she and Josh had finally connected on Catalina Island, a year when he had waited for Rachael to say yes to his proposal. All gone? She needed to be close to him, so she leaned forward. "Josh, it'll take a bit for me to bring you up to date. Just rest now. You'll remember with time." She gave his hand a quick squeeze, a squeeze that wasn't returned.

Josh blinked, and then his weary eyes closed. "Tired," he mumbled before he drifted off.

Rachael began her lonely vigil again, whispering, "You're the reason I take a breath. I love you. Please find your way back." She relaxed in the chair, looked around the sterile room, and pushed her thoughts into the reality of the moment. It was almost time for her mother's flight to arrive, and no one had news of Amanda. She uttered out loud, "What a friggin' mess."

Friggin' mess? Elliott smiled at hearing her emotional pain and checked himself from laughing out loud. You'll think "mess" when you hear what happened to your mother and sister. Ah, sweet revenge.

He whispered in the phone to Derek, "There's a stretch of desert on Highway Forty between the two rest stops with only one off-ramp. Take that turnoff, drive at least ten miles on the dirt road, and then dump Grace and Amanda. Shoot 'em and leave 'em there for the vultures. Naked would be good, with hands and feet tied."

"What? Speak up." Derek pushed the phone tighter to his ear. "I can't hear you."

Elliott slowed down and covered the phone but didn't add any volume. "Listen, stupid," he said and repeated the plan.

"Are you sure you want to kill an FBI agent? That's a whole other mess. And what for? They'll be no threat to us after we leave Bullhead." Derek hesitated to voice his overwhelming dread of the plan, fearing Elliott would make him suffer for any further challenge.

"The only remaining Pennington will be Meg when I'm finished."

"What about Rachael? She's relentless. She'll stop you."

"Don't argue. I'll take care of her. Have you emptied the house?"

"Yeah, of everything that involves our business. The rest, like prints and stuff, won't matter. They'll ID me within minutes after they realize what happened to Grace."

"Don't get sloppy. After you drop off Grace and Amanda, come to the hospital. Call from the car. I'm going to check myself out before someone recognizes me."

Damn. That's another four-hour trip. "Done."

When Rachael stood and started to leave, she opened her phone and dialed the FBI for an update on Amanda. Elliott could hear her footsteps stop at the door when he murmured, "Grace and Amanda." He froze, then quietly closed the phone, tucked it away, and pretended to be asleep. He heard her footsteps as they rounded the privacy curtain, and he listened to her shallow breathing as she stared down at him.

Rachael studied his face, trying to adjust to the changes, but every feature had been altered. Different hair. Different facial contour. Plastic surgery? It had been too dark in the boat to notice.

Questions still lingered regarding what she thought she'd heard, and once in the hall, she tried to open the patient's chart on the computer. A password was needed, and she had no time to screw with it, so she left in search of assistance. Elliott listened as the screech of her rubber-soled shoes carried her down the hallway.

He called Derek again. "Put a rush on it. The bitch is getting nosy."

13

When Payden left the hospital room, Meg moved close to Jordan. Her shoulder had been reset, and while there was some lingering pain, she managed without pain medication. "Wow, your brother is so overprotective. We haven't had a chance to really talk. He hovers." She moved Jordan's leg and plopped on the bed.

"He gets that way." Jordan really wasn't too interested in talking yet and tried to dismiss Meg. If I'm the new Jessie, I can't afford to talk around Payden too much. He'll catch me in a blink.

"No one tells me anything around here. I can't find out about Josh, and now my sister seems to be missing."

"Is she the FBI one?"

"Yeah. And to make matters worse, my mom is on her way to town. Speaking of being overprotective, Mom's like a pit bull. Your mom the same?" She swung her other leg on top of the bed and crossed them, at ease with her immediate surroundings.

"Lost her when I was ten. It's just been my sister and Payden." Saying the words out loud hardened Jordan. Raised for twelve years by her brother and always second place.

Meg regretted her question. "Sorry. Do you want to talk about your sister? You guys were twins, right?" She leaned against the footrest, hoping to keep the conversation light.

Jordan resented the intrusion, but on some level she did appreciate that Meg was making an effort to help. "We were best friends. Did everything together. We'd just finished the barrel-racing competition at the rodeo when she was killed. She got first place, and I placed second. Oh, no. It was the other way around." *Good thing Payden isn't here.*

"Your whole family competes in the rodeo? Must be fun, and fun's my middle name." She started to braid her long blond hair, and, realizing her hospital gown was untied in the back, she laughed and tied it. "Almost flashed the attendant."

"It is…well, was. Rodeo people are great. Like family." Her mind drifted off as she recalled the Las Vegas finals. The cute clown had sidled up to her after her ride and asked her out. She had had big plans for him. *Make it worthwhile. Maybe go all the way. Something Jessie wouldn't have thought of doing, pure little bitch she was.* Jordan shook her head, trying to throw those negative thoughts out into space.

"Can you make a living chasing the rodeos?" questioned Meg, trying to keep Jordan engaged.

"No, unless you're number one and work the circuit. I'm a stunt woman with the film industry, too. That helps keep bread on the table."

"Now you're talking. What movies have you been in?"

"Mostly westerns, like the old *Dances with Wolves*, you know. Although I do a lot of swimming, car stunts, and rappelling. Payden has a fit if it involves car crashes, but they're the most fun."

"Well, I can see his point. So, you're on a first-name basis with Kevin Costner?"

"You are so dumb." That finally got a laugh out of Jordan.

"Sounds like you girls are having fun," said Payden as he entered the room. "Look who I found in the lobby."

Moving through the door were Jordan's rodeo friends—two clowns, three girls who competed against her, and four strapping cowboys, all colors and sizes. They swarmed around Jordan's bed, and Meg had to move or get trampled. No one questioned Jordan's identity. As they vied for her attention, Payden took Meg into the hall.

She fussed around with her gown, wishing she had her river clothes on, her cutoff jeans and T-shirt or at least one of her push-up bras, and laughed internally at her obvious interest in Payden.

"Is there any way you could stay with Jessie for a while?" He helped her in the wheelchair and didn't remove his hands from the armrests. Leaning forward, he lowered his voice and continued. "When she gets home, there's going to be so much to remind her of her sister, and, well, I don't know how she'll make it."

"Payden, she's got a room full of friends in there. I'm a stranger." Meg's hand came up and pushed him away. The closeness disrupted her thinking.

"They'll be a constant reminder of what's happened. I'm thinking a fresh start would be better for now."

"Look, I'm kind of a wounded pigeon myself. Jeez. Don't know that I'll be much help."

Payden could see he was making progress and pushed. "Could you at least give it a try? I could use the help, please."

Meg sensed his concern and love. Shit, there go the heartstrings. "It'll cost you big-time," she said with a smile. Hmm, here I go again, Mom, dragging another stray dog home.

14

"I understand you need permission from the head nurse for me to look at a patient's file." Rachael was getting nowhere with the floor attendant. Her agitation oozed. "Here's my badge number. Please. This is very important. Will you try?" The attendant scooted down the hall. Rachael took a seat across from the nurses' station and dialed another number.

"What do you mean, she wasn't on the flight?" Rachael listened to the airline representative's explanation, thanked her for the information, and ended the call. Taking a deep breath in an attempt to combat her frustration, she scrolled down on the phone list, finally locating the SuperShuttle number. "I'm calling about a pickup scheduled for this morning." She gave the address to the dispatcher, tapped her fingers on the granite desk, and waited for the attendant's measured answer.

"Yes, we were scheduled for that address," came the reply, "but no one was there when we arrived. We waited for ten minutes, called the phone number, and rang the doorbell. Still no one, so we proceeded to our next stop. Sorry."

Rachael's mind was whirling. First Amanda. Now Mom? "Wait. Your next stop. Where was it? Was it local?" Rachael waited again for the reply.

"Yes, it was local."

Rachael's mind went directly to Derek. She had never trusted the bastard, and he hadn't been seen since the explosion. Meg had mentioned that he lived in town. Coincidence? No. "Was that on Via Marwah in Yorba Linda? Did you go there?"

"That information is confidential. I'm sorry."

"Hold it. I'm a police officer and need to know. The woman you didn't pick up is now a missing person, and you will be implicated in the crime if you don't cooperate. And I mean now. Were you scheduled to pick up Derek Turner in Yorba Linda?" She waited.

"Supervisor Sloan. What's the problem?"

Impatiently, Rachael reiterated her question and waited again.

"Yes, we were scheduled for a pickup there. The driver called in and said there was a note on the door. A cancellation. Two cancellations in one morning. Not good for business."

Rachael disconnected without saying "thank you" and stared into empty space. Calm, stay calm. What the hell is going on? Don't panic. She sorted through the facts. Okay, first Amanda disappears while arresting Elliott. Now Mom disappears while meeting up with Derek. Think. Think. What's the connection?

She called the FBI and asked them to increase their search parameters to include Grace, then called the Yorba Linda Sheriff's Department. After explaining the situation, she stayed on the line while a squad car made the quick trip from the satellite office to the house on Via Marwah.

"Hey, Rachael. We're here at the house. Hold on."

Rachael listened as they banged on the door and announced themselves.

"Shit, Jim. Door's ajar. Pull your gun."

Sounds filtered through Rachael's phone, and finally communication continued.

"Sorry, Rachael. Whoever was here has gone. It's a mess."

"What do you mean? Blood?"

"No, just tossed. Papers, clothes, dirty dishes. Whoever lived here left in a hurry. Took their clothes, bathroom stuff, and that's about it. Found some hair snagged on the door fame from the garage."

"What color? Long or short?"

"Brunette," came the answer. "Long."

"Bag and tag it, would you? No, wait. Leave the scene alone. The FBI will handle it."

"FBI? What's going on, Rachael? This is a local situation. We'll handle it."

"No time to explain right now. Just put the crime tape around the house, and the FBI will take over the case within the hour."

"What case?"

"Missing persons. Will fill you in later. FBI will handle the BOLO for Derek Turner and my mom. Thanks ever so much for your help." So I'm alone. Josh is wounded, Meg's a mess, and Mom and Amanda are missing. What next? And then her mind raced back to the other patient in Josh's room.

"Nurse."

15

Derek drove to the Hertz car rental, picked out an Escalade, and returned home. He and Marisa quickly hustled the women into the car and got away twenty minutes before the sheriff's department arrived. Marisa headed to San Clemente in Derek's car to set up a new business office. Access to the ocean for seaplane landings was essential, and this small city would provide a good cover for their drug and money laundering operation. It would be necessary to establish another stronghold on Catalina Island, but that would be Elliott's job.

Halfway between the two rest stops on Interstate 40, as Elliott had calculated, was a side road leading to the depths of the desert. After driving two miles, Derek found the perfect spot, way off the road, isolated, and desolate. Dust enveloped his car as he pulled to a stop behind a small rise in the dirt road. The temperature reading on his rearview mirror indicated 114 degrees.

"End of the line, ladies. You don't look so intimidating now, Amanda, with no gun or badge. And poor old Gracie. Always interfering and micro-managing your daughters' lives. Do you realize how much Meg resents that?" Sweat poured off his face as he began to wrestle his victims from the car. "I'm probably doing Rachael and Meg a favor, dumping you out here."

Derek yanked Amanda out of the SUV first and shoved her across the hot desert sand.

"It's 114 degrees out here, ladies. Hope you like it hot."

Amanda managed to shift her weight and land on her side, avoiding the blistering sand in her face. Grit and rocks tore into her bare arms.

Grace was next, and for some reason, maybe even a small inkling of compassion, Derek sat her down beside her daughter rather than shoving her. "Elliott said to shoot you and then leave you, but I don't like the sight of blood, so you'll just have to bake to death. And you can keep your clothes on. I have no desire to see you two naked." He looked around at the nothingness that surrounded them; there were only a few scrub bushes too ornery to die in the desert.

Grace tried to mutter a sentence from behind her duct-taped mouth. She persisted by flashing her eyes violently around and trying to form "eye-words." Finally, Derek tore the tape from her mouth. "What the hell do you want? Quit screwing around."

"I know that leaving us water is beyond your orders, but since this is the last time I'll be able to talk to Amanda, please remove the tape on her mouth too. If we decide to yell, well, who would hear us? Coyotes? In reality, that would only exacerbate your plan."

Her calm countenance bothered Derek. She should be pleading. "*Please*? You said *please*? Meg said you were a freaky person when threatened." Derek thought through the request. He was already crossing Elliott by not killing them, and yet somewhere inside, his willingness to obey Elliott was waning. The perverse side of his brother was increasing, and Derek's desire to be involved in his brother's plans had diminished. "Dying wish? Well, I guess I can grant that." He slowly pulled the tape from Amanda's mouth, knowing it caused more pain. "The fire ants, coyotes, and vultures will enjoy your screaming, so go ahead."

Amanda caught a glimmer of humanity in Derek and pushed. "Do I get a dying wish too?"

"Why not?" He grabbed his water and gulped down a swallow, then poured the rest out onto the blistering sand. "More where that came from," he said with a smile.

"I know Elliott is a psychopath, but it seems like you have some humanity left in you. Did you ever really care for Meg, or was your friendship a part of Elliott's plans to kidnap her? How involved were you in her abduction and torture?" FBI training. Involve the perp.

"That's your dying wish? Information? I was thinking maybe you'd ask for some shade. First of all, I'm gay, which played into Elliott's plans. I had no interest in Meg."

Amanda could see he had difficulty saying that. His attitude changed, and he couldn't look at her. "Really? Meg said you swam naked in Willow Cove with her. Great kisser, as I recall," she said as she urged him on.

"I had to use mouthwash every time. My sister can attest to that. Elliott hates that I'm gay, but at least he didn't have to worry that I would defrock his girlfriend. And, for the rest of your question,…I had no involvement in Meg's abduction. Hard to believe, but I didn't know my brother was the serial killer. Learned that at the same time the rest of the city found out."

"I don't believe that you're gay. I've seen your interactions with Meg. It's a ploy to satisfy your brother. Maybe just afraid of Elliott?"

Derek was intrigued with Amanda's profound and accurate analysis but elected to ignore it and didn't respond. Doesn't matter now, he thought.

"Did he ever tell you how he tortured her?" Amanda pressed. "Meg was supposed to be your friend." Sweat that had been accumulating on her forehead finally dripped into her eyes. Amanda pinched them shut and tried to ignore the sting.

"Look, I don't approve of much that my brother does, but like the rest of the world, I'm afraid of him. You got that part right. Meg was just too delicious for him to pass up. Easy to fool." Derek began walking around the women, picking up sharp rocks and tossing them away.

"Oh, Meg's not easy. Her only shortcoming is her willingness to trust everyone. When Rachael finds Elliott, he'll pay. Shoot first, ask questions later, as they say. That will be his day to die."

"Well, if she's as smart as you say, she should check out her current environment."

Amanda twisted around. He had dropped a bombshell. "What are you talking about?" Amanda was doing her best to pump him for information, even with the unlikely chance that they might escape their imminent death.

"He's in the same hospital as Meg. Same room as your old friend, Josh. How's that for great detective work?" Derek finished his search and walked over to the car.

"You lie." Amanda began to squirm in the sand. She needed to see his face. She needed to negotiate with him.

"Nope. I dropped him off after grabbing you. You slept through the whole thing."

"Well, Rachael is there with Meg. Hell will freeze over before he can touch Meg again. I know my sister. She's nobody's fool."

"Plan is for me to pick them both up in about three hours. Too bad you'll never hear the end of the love story. He has great plans for their honeymoon." He opened the door, and the heat poured out as he sat behind the wheel.

"He's a dead man. If Rachael doesn't kill him, Meg will."

"No, don't count on it. He has a way of making even the most aggressive woman succumb to his ways. Not a fun thing to watch." He put the keys in the ignition and started the car.

"You animal. I'm going to hunt both of you down and kill you!" she yelled. She looked at Grace, who remained passive. "Nothing from you, Mom?"

"No, not to worry." Grace sat in the hot sand and watched as if viewing a new TV drama.

Such a poised, short answer. Amanda gave her a quizzical look.

"Sorry to have to end this, but the air only works with the door closed. Good luck with the coyotes. Are you sure you don't have something to add, Grace? Last chance." He mocked her.

"Whatever scrap of meat is left over after Rachael catches you will be mine to smash. Don't underestimate the Pennington women."

"Ain't gonna happen." He slammed the door shut, spun the car around three times, creating a thick dust bowl, and drove off down the dirt road, heading toward Bullhead.

Amanda coughed her way through the dust and scooted around Grace's back until she reached her tied wrists. "I hope he used duct tape 'cause zip ties are a bitch. Hold still, Mom. Let me check on it."

"Oh, honey, don't work too hard. I figure in an hour from now we'll be out of here."

"What are you talking about, Mom? We're in the middle of nowhere, and there isn't a chance in hell that anyone will start looking here. We have twenty-four hours at best." She glanced up at the searing sun. "It has to be a hundred ten degrees. We'll be lucky to make it through the day." She finally reached Grace's hands and then started looking for rocks. "Good, it's duct tape, but Derek threw away all of the sharp rocks close by. Bastard."

"First of all, Amanda, we need to reposition ourselves in the sand. Scoot over here again and turn around a hundred eighty degrees so that your butt is about where my knees are going to be." With that, Grace toppled over onto her side.

"What the hell are you doing, Mom?"

"Don't argue. Just do it. I need your hands next to my right ear." She remained motionless.

Amanda decided the heat was already getting to her mom, so she cooperated. After a few repositioning moves, Grace was satisfied with the setup.

"Okay, push my earlobe against my head. Two short times."

"Oh, good grief, Mom." Exasperated, Amanda twisted her hand around until she could feel her mother's ear. "Two times, huh?"

"Short bursts. Do it now."

Amanda was surprised to feel a raised area of skin on her mother's ear. She complied. "So what now? Does this turn on the TV in Bullhead or something?" She couldn't take any part of this seriously.

Grace, always in control, answered, "Look, smart-ass, there's a surgically placed GPS implanted there, but it needs to be activated. You have to locate the new sutures by touch and push on them. If you do it right, I'll receive a quick pulse. Now try it again, without the sarcasm."

Somewhere between disbelief and hope, Amanda felt around Grace's ear until she located the sutures and pressed two times. Her second try hit pay dirt.

"Okay. Now we're cooking." Grace laughed. "Funny pun, huh? Let's figure out how to get in a sitting position, and we can talk."

"You think? What's with this GPS thing? The FBI doesn't have anything like that."

Grace scooted around and smiled at Amanda. "Oh, Mandy. There are so many things you don't know about your mother. I guess now is as good a time as any to bring you up to speed."

"Mom, what are you talking about? Like what? You cheated on a geometry test in the ninth grade? You danced on a table in San Antonio?" Amanda was too concerned about their present situation to be interested in small talk. She wiggled around again, facing her mother. The fierce sun was turning her legs red. She needed a plan.

"Snippy little scruff, aren't you? No, I'm not talking about an eight on the Richter scale; I'm talking about off the scale entirely."

Amanda laughed, a snorting kind of laugh, close to a scoffing sound. She raised her right shoulder and managed to dry some sweat that was dribbling down her cheek. "Mom, I know that these are grim circumstances, but there's no need for the dramatics. We need to figure a way out of this."

16

"There you go," the pudgy nurse said to Elliott as she removed his IV. "You're making marvelous progress. You'll be ready for discharge in no time." She tried to puff up his pillow, but he stopped her hand in midair.

He grumbled an acknowledgment to the condescending nurse and tried to raise his other arm. Moderate pain restricted his range of motion. *This is enough recovery; I need to get out of here.* It seemed the room was closing in on him.

When the round nurse shuffled out of the room, Elliott turned onto his side and struggled to sit up. A wave of nausea swept over him. He waited, then stood, inching his way to the bathroom. The hospital gown flopped open in the back, but that was no concern to him. His mind, once again alert, contrived a plan for the next few hours. Derek would play an integral part in his escape from the hospital, along with setting up their next move. By eavesdropping, he had gotten excellent intel on the Pennington family. He flushed the toilet and started back to bed. Each step felt easier, and a determined, focused Elliott settled between the sheets.

***

Rachael rushed into the room, slightly out of breath. The captain had called her in, and she had spent most of the morning helping the FBI gather evidence and information at the casinos. She had returned to the hospital as soon as she could get away. "Josh, how are you doing? Any new memories floating around?" she asked. She tried to remove the tension from her voice as she hesitantly took his hand.

"Rachael…Well, no. I've been thinking. Is there a chance that you could call Stella? She's a nurse. Works at the hospital on Catalina. She'll know what's wrong with my memory."

Rachael didn't like the sound of that; she had never heard of Stella. "The best doctor in the area has looked at you. I can get another specialist if you want."

"Yeah. But Stella knows my history." He rubbed his forehead and grimaced. "She'll know what to do," he insisted.

Rachael dropped his hand and stood back. "Who's this Stella? Did you have a thing going with her?" Rachael straightened her blouse and moved her Glock to the right, feeling a little rumpled by her appearance and their conversation. "Sorry. I shouldn't act so possessive." She knew Josh disliked that personality flaw.

"No problem." He tried to smile his famous crooked smile, but it only half appeared on his face.

Deciding to switch the topic, hopefully to a more neutral ground, she said, "Your captain called this morning, anxious for you to get back to work. They can hold your spot for another week, but then they'll have to get another cop assigned from LA if you're not ready." She turned her back on him, grabbed the chair, pulled it next to his bed, and held her breath. This tidbit of information would upset him, but he needed a shot of reality.

"God, Rach. A week? I don't think that's possible." He cautiously turned in the bed, searching for something. "Where's my phone? I'll text him."

"Josh, no clue. Sometime between when you got shot and ended up here, it got lost. I'll check into it."

He raised an eyebrow. "Are you keeping it from me?"

The question stunned Rachael. "Why would you ask that? What's going on? Why so suspicious?"

"You're acting protective. I can take care of myself." His voice went a pitch higher, and a darkness crossed his face. Hostility was mounting. "I'm asking the doctor to discharge me to the Catalina Hospital tomorrow. I'll have a better chance of recovering there."

Tired of pussyfooting around, Rachael fumed. "Damn, you sure are one stubborn jerk. Fine. Have it your way." She saw Meg rolling through the door in her wheelchair and decided it was a good time to exit. "Why don't you share your shitty attitude with her?"

Meg was quick to recognize the firestorm erupting. "Not to worry. I'm here to take care of that." She wheeled into the room and gave Rachael a nod to leave.

Rachael didn't react at first, refusing to be dismissed by her sister's high sign.

"Meg? Little Meggie, the brat? Wow. You've changed. I don't know that I'd recognize you on the street. What is this? Old home week? All the Pennington women converging in one spot?" He rolled onto his back and sighed. The confrontation with Rachael had exhausted him.

Meg bumped her wheelchair into his hospital bed, backed it up a little, and then stood. Leaning over, she gave him a chaste kiss on the mouth.

Rachael bristled and started for the door. She had work to do and elected to leave rather than watch Meg flirt with her boyfriend.

"That should have triggered some memory waves." She threw her sexy, yet impish, smile at him. "It's only been nine months since our Catalina tryst."

"What the hell are you talking about?" Josh almost panicked. "What's with the kiss?"

A questioning look passed over her face. "Okay, if you must play dense, I'm here to set your memory straight." She piled on his bed.

From behind the privacy curtain, Elliott strained to hear every word. Just hearing Meg's voice caused an immediate response, and he grabbed his growing erection.

Meg started her intimate story, identifying Elliott as the Bullhead serial killer and recounting her kidnap, rape, torture, and the final blow of being tossed from a seaplane into the Pacific Ocean last year. She dwelled on her rehab on Catalina and on how Rachael and he had reconnected to the point of his proposal.

"I proposed?" He glanced down at his ring finger. "Apparently she said no?"

"Didn't say anything—just ran. Typical Rachael. With an open field, I made a pass at you."

"You're kidding. You're just a teenaged brat." He smiled. She had matured into a dazzling young woman, so he soaked in the compliment.

"Wrong again. I'm twenty-three. You rejected my proposition and threw me off the dock and laughed. I should have punched you as soon as I got back out of the water." Now it was her turn to smile.

Josh stared at the lovely Meg, trying to absorb all the information. "I told you no? What the hell was wrong with me? Wanna try it again?"

Her smile morphed into laughter. "Well, well. Is this the first glimpse of the old Josh's humor?" Meg finished the long story with an up-to-date timeline. "Elliott attempted a second abduction in the Oasis Casino last night. Set off bombs, drugged me, and threw me in a ski boat. Shot Rachael in the chest—but she had on her vest. He nicked your carotid; hence, you're here. And then he got away again. Now Amanda's missing, Mom's missing, and we think Derek, my supposed friend, might be involved in all of this."

"Whoa, that's a lot of shit to take in. Tell me about Amanda and Grace. What a fuckin' mess."

"You got that right." After throwing more facts at Josh, Meg returned to the problem with Rachael. "Josh, give Rach a chance. You two were ready to set the date."

"I'm in love with her? I remember our puppy-love relationships every summer on the island, but other than it being nice to see her now, nothing else is coming through. I should remember proposing. That's serious."

"Give yourself some time, Josh. It'll come back. She is so ready for the ring. Don't let this chance get away. You two deserve some happiness." She sat on the edge of the bed and took his hand. "Life has dealt all of us a crappy hand lately. Let's change that."

Josh's eyes glossed over as he tried to find the answers. "Are you okay now, shrimp? Has this Elliott guy finished with you?"

From behind the curtain, Elliott pushed to hear her answer, his growing erection ready to peak.

Tears welled up. "I don't think so. Josh, I'm afraid of him, even though Amanda and Rachael are always around. He's smart. I don't know if he wants to just rape and torture me some more, or if he wants to kill me and my family now. He's been so close. He can almost anticipate our every move. Honestly, I'm scared of the bastard." She dropped her head forward, and her wavy blond hair cascaded over her face.

"Come here, twerp. It's hug time."

Meg snuggled up on the bed with Josh and felt the rush of safety, like on Catalina. "I think I need to go back to the island again."

"That's a date." As she nestled into his strong arms, a scant vision of their encounter in the golf cart tumbled in and out of his memory.

17

The searing sun drifted a little west, increasing the temperature to over 115 degrees. Sand, a few drought-starved scrub bushes, and a lazy buzzard soaring overhead added a touch of despair to the situation. The area was desolate beyond the human imagination, and Grace and Amanda took turns shading each other by scooting around in the scorching sand.

"Your turn, Mom. Lean your head this way. Your face is beet red." The perspiration continued to drip into her eyes, and she squeezed them shut to minimize the sting. Her blouse and pants were stained with sweat. She wondered how long Grace would be able to tolerate the heat but didn't bring it up. Mom is a tough old cookie. She wouldn't want me fussing.

"Should have put on more sunscreen this morning. One can never anticipate how the day is going to go," Grace said with a laugh.

Amanda shook her head in amazement. "Your sense of humor escapes me. By tomorrow at this time, we'll be toast." The thought, the realization, shook her. She stared at her mother's lovely face. She must have been a real beauty. "Guess I shouldn't let the time pass without telling you what an awesome mom you've been." Her voice broke. Watching her mom die a painful death in front of her was unthinkable.

"Oh, for pity's sake. If I had known this would be my last day, I would've worn something more appropriate." She laughed again. "While we have time, I would like to do some confessing, but not the last rites sort of thing."

Amanda scoffed. "Secrets? Mom, you're an open book."

"Well, tell me, smart-ass. Give me the short version of *This Is Your Life*."

Amanda decided to play along. She took a deep breath and spurted out the history in one elongated gasp. "Born in Downey, married your high school boyfriend, was a classical ballet dancer, had three daughters, got a degree from Fullerton University, taught school at Esperanza and Valencia High, was an early widow, sold real estate, and then retired to become a writer. How's that?"

"Oh, Amanda, you missed one huge part."

"How so?" Amanda wrestled with the duct tape on her wrists. She had learned a trick while training at Quantico, but she had to be standing to do it. *Duct tape to the wrists, in front, hands to the chest; thrust both hands down and out at the same time. The tape will tear.* "Mom, I'm going to stand. I think I can snap the tape." She tucked her legs under her to get to a kneeling position.

"Just relax. No hurry." She continued with the subject of her background stint, hoping to engage Amanda. "You'd be surprised by the untold history, I'm sure, and probably wonder how I had the gall to dictate behavior to you and your sisters. Tell you how to run your lives and the like. Move around a little to the left. I want to see your reaction."

Amanda gave in. "Sure, why not? Apparently standing is not an option." She brought her knees to her chest and pushed with her heels and butt until she negotiated the turn.

"Well, here we go. When you were nine and Rachael seven, I was teaching at Esperanza, like you said. We buried your father earlier that year, and my mourning ritual was interspersed with the anticipated arrival of the baby, your sister, Meg. No one questioned my emotional outbursts, but no one really understood the truth. Here's the clincher." Grace paused, ignoring the sweltering heat and discomfort of the sun's merciless rays, and gave way to her emotions.

Amanda was surprised at the now-serious tone. "Mom, you don't have to do this. If you've been carrying a secret for all these years, maybe you should leave it alone." She leaned over and wiped her sweaty brow on Grace's shirtsleeve.

"No, Amanda, it's time. I'll throw this one sentence at you. Let it soak in for a minute. Reflect back on all of the weird vacations we had when you were young, the midnight phone calls, and any other questionable activities that went on in our house."

"You always had a reasonable excuse for them, as I recall. I didn't think a thing about it, but okay, shoot." Amanda switched around in the sand so that her mother would be looking at her with shaded eyes. She dropped her head to protect her eyes from the intense sun.

"I'm a retired CIA agent."

Amanda's eyes popped open. She drew in a quick breath and straightened. "What?" Hence, France? Germany? Russia? Sweden? South America? "Mom. Wow, speaking of keeping secrets. I can't believe it. Did Dad know? Do Rachael or Meg know?"

"No to all questions. I told your dad I was doing research for the school district, and he seemed to buy it. He was busy with his own budding career. You kids didn't mind because it was always an international adventure to tell your friends about when I dragged you around the world."

"Were they dangerous missions? Were you ever shot or compromised?"

"Yes to both. That one time in South America, I had to go to the hospital. Remember?"

"Yeah. You had to have your appendix out. No?"

"No. Gunshot wound, left thigh. I showed it to you one time."

"You told me that scar was from chicken pox." Amanda's mind was reeling with this new earth-shattering information. "God, you really had us fooled. But now what? Retired?"

"Yes, but I still have a few connections." Grace paused. That was the easy part of the history lesson. Easy to accept and laugh about. "Amanda, there's more to the story."

"Well, nothing could surprise me more than this." She was oblivious to the agonizing heat and dehydration that was taking its toll on both of them, momentarily swept away by the startling news.

"Have you noticed that I often use the number twenty-eight on passwords and codes? Well, there's a reason for that. Just a little reminder to me about a wonderful age in my life. The year I fell in love with Meg's dad."

It took a minute for the statement to sink in. Amanda's eyebrows shot up, and she leaned forward. "What do you mean, Mom? Meg's dad? What are you talking about?"

Grace turned her head upward into the cutting sun, searching. "Shouldn't be too much longer, hopefully." Explaining further was going to be painful.

"Mom, spit it out. What…" Amanda feared heat exhaustion was setting in, and there was no way to help her. No water, no shade. "Tell me. What do you mean? Meg's dad? Who do you mean?"

Grace paused. The moment had finally come to share her well-kept secret.

Grace was not known to cry, so when tears welled up in her eyes, Amanda's curiosity changed to concern. "Mom?"

Grace straightened, pushed back the tears of regret and sadness, and assumed a detached attitude."Your dad had been ill for several years, as you recall. I was his caregiver except for when we had to leave the country for my CIA assignments. During one of those ops, I was paired up with Luke." A distant noise diverted her attention from the story. Again looking up, she spotted the helicopter, feeling immediate relief from her storytelling. "Well, I'll have to tell you the rest later. Looks like we're going to be rescued." She smiled.

Amanda watched as the speck in the sky took shape. A private helicopter, landing within a quarter mile of us? The heat rising from the desert sand made the unfolding scene look like a mirage. "Mom, what's going on?" She twisted around in the hot sand, switching her attention between her smiling mother and the approaching aircraft.

When it touched down, two men jumped from the chopper and sprinted toward Grace and Amanda. The taller of the two yelled instructions as they approached. "Take care of the brunette. The other is mine."

Amanda couldn't take her eyes off her mother as the man gently cut the duct tape from her hands and feet. She could sense their bond, the careful love the man displayed to her mother. When he stood her up, she laced her arms around his neck and whispered something as they started walking toward Amanda.

"Amanda, I'd like you to meet Luke Wilson, Meg's father."

18

Meg rejoiced in the security of Josh's arms. Reluctantly she broke loose, gave him a final sisterly kiss, and flopped back into her wheelchair. She kicked the footrests out of the way to let her feet navigate and give her shoulder some rest from pushing the wheels. "Thanks, I needed that. Getting a little tired. Don't want to overdo it, 'cause then the doc wouldn't let me go. Be back later." She struggled with the wheelchair but finally got it started toward the door.

"Damn right you will; too many unanswered questions." Josh wanted more background to fill in the voids but realized he, too, was exhausted. He rolled over, closed his eyes, and struggled to fit Rachael into the last six months, the forgotten phase.

Behind the curtain, Elliott turned, grabbed his cell phone, and quickly called Derek. He whispered into the receiver, "She's leaving around four. Friends are taking her home. Watch her from the empty foreclosure house across the street, and when everyone's gone, grab her."

"What about you? When can I pick you up?"

"Did you help Marisa close down the house?"

"Yes. She packed up and left before I did."

"Good. Call me when you get to Bullhead, and we'll figure the logistics. If I don't answer for any reason, abort the mission."

"But—"

"Something could still go wrong. If I don't answer, call our attorney. Means they have caught me. I already have a plan for that. Just call the attorney." Elliott closed the phone before Derek could argue.

***

Meg forgot her phone when she was leaving Josh's room, so she wheeled back, stopping abruptly when she overheard part of Elliott's whispered conversation. She recognized his voice. Panic. She rolled forward, moved to the right side of Josh's bed, and was glad to see he was sleeping. The privacy curtain was the only thing separating them now. She closed her eyes and let her senses work. She could feel him there. *It's Elliott! Oh my God.* Meg experienced an immediate stabbing pain from the hurt he had inflicted on her. She had to keep it together but was now on the verge of vomiting. Turning the chair, she headed toward the door, grabbing the waste paper basket in the corner before she retched. Wiping her mouth on her hospital gown, she rolled down the hall and dropped the basket in the open elevator. Once inside her own hospital room, Meg called Rachael. "It's him, Rach. It's him!"

"Calm down. Who's him?"

"Elliott," she whispered.

Rachael strained to listen. "What? Are you sure? Where?"

"Absolutely. He's in the room with Josh, for God's sake."

"Keep an eye on his room but don't go back in. I'm on my way." Rachael chastised herself for not following through with the investigative officers. Big mistake. As she drove her Mustang from headquarters, dodging in and out of the slow traffic on 95, she dialed Amanda's and Grace's numbers. Still no answer.

Meg was waiting for her when she finally arrived back at the hospital. Her sister's anxiety was apparent.

"He can't be armed, so it'll be an easy takedown. I'll walk in like I always do when visiting Josh, go between the two beds, pull back the privacy curtain, and cuff Elliott to the gurney before he knows what hit him. You call security for backup. He's wounded. No problem. We've got him, that son of a bitch."

"You should wait for help. For God's sake, don't underestimate him. It's Elliott."

"How sure are you? Did you recognize him?"

"He's had plastic surgery, but I know his voice, and I know what I heard. It's him."

"Stay outside and wait for backup. No heroics."

When Rachael entered the room, Josh was sleeping. Cuffs were in her left hand as she slowly pulled the privacy curtain back. Elliott was not in his bed. Rachael could hear the fan running in the bathroom and pulled her gun as she approached the door. It opened.

Elliott pulled back, shocked. He lunged forward, knocking the gun from her hand. "Bitch." He grabbed for her throat.

Taken off balance by his quick move, she lifted her knee in his direction, but he feigned right and grabbed her arm, turning her. His choke hold paralyzed her.

"Bastard." She stomped down on his foot.

He absorbed the pain and held on. The scuffle escalated, and they crashed to the floor.

Josh woke. "Rachael?" He yanked out his IV and tried to untangle his heart monitor, yelling for help. The bedside tray overturned, breaking the mirror.

Elliott rolled over, grabbed a shard of glass, and slashed at Rachael's face. She ducked. He grabbed her again.

Meg wheeled around the corner of Josh's room and reacted. She leaped from the chair and with four giant steps jumped on Elliott's back, grabbed a handful of hair, and yanked his head back. He released his grip on Rachael.

Josh rolled out of bed and kicked the gun to Rachael as she scrambled to a standing position.

"Stop, Elliott, or I'll shoot. Don't give me a reason." She steadied the gun with both hands and pointed it at his head.

"Kill him, Rachael! Kill the son of a bitch!" Meg screamed as she untangled herself from Elliott.

Elliott slowly moved to his knees, putting his hands behind his head. "Looks like you won this round, Rachael." He smiled and relaxed. "Can't shoot an unarmed man, can you, detective?"

"On your stomach, Elliott. Hands behind your back." Rachael shook from the anxiety coursing through her. She handed her Glock to Meg and cuffed Elliott.

"Oh, Meg, darling. You look wonderful. I've been listening to your voice for two days now. Our friend here has been hard when he hears you. Wants to say hello. Why not shoot everyone? And we can get out of here, darling."

Meg cocked the gun. The room went silent.

"Meg."

Her hand started shaking. The desire to end it, to kill evil, was overwhelming. Her hatred engrossed her. The shaking became more violent as Rachael put her hand over Meg's. "Rach. I want him dead."

"I know. But not this way." She slowly removed the gun from Meg's grip.

A weak voice pierced the tension. "A little help here…"

Josh's body lay crumpled in the corner. Fresh blood seeped through his bandages. Meg rushed over and applied pressure. "Help. We need some help here!"

***

Derek dialed Elliott's phone per the plan. Somewhere in the debris, under the bed, the ringtone persisted into a now-empty hospital room. When it switched to voice mail, Derek pulled the car over to the curb. *Not a good sign. It'll be easy to trace all of the calls. Damn.* He pulled the SIM card from the phone and tossed all the parts out the window at various intervals, watching through the windshield as the fast-moving traffic crunched them. He located his Walmart phone and called Marisa.

"Something's gone wrong. Elliott didn't pick up the phone. I'm near the hospital, but it's too risky to go there."

"What are you going to do?"

Derek hesitated. He'd never made decisions for Elliott. "You finish up with the San Clemente project. I'll switch the drug run to Catalina, starting in ten days. That'll give me time to get to the island and set up the business."

"Do you have contacts for all the pilots and drug suppliers? Shit, this is a mess. And what about Elliott?"

"I have most of his contacts. That'll have to do for now. He said his attorney had the means to bust him out, so I'll call him and get started on the plan."

She paused and then asked, "Derek, is he okay? I mean, mentally? His obsession with Meg is really interfering with business. And I'm not into killing people. This Amanda and Grace thing went way overboard for us. What do you think?"

"I've been wrestling with it, too." An audible sigh drifted through the phone. "This Meg fetish has been going on for over a year. You're right. Business is suffering, and the killings? Well, you know I'm against that. We'll have to talk about it later, sis. I'll be in touch with an update, whenever there's any news."

"I'll start shredding documents. Nothing is unpacked yet, so if I have to make another move, it should be easy."

"Good. Shit, this is a mess. This is a new throwaway phone. Use it to contact me. Destroy the phone you've been using. It's traceable. Get a new one."

"Listen. Elliott's got me all freaked out. Maybe I should hold off on San Clemente. Can we handle the business without him?" Marisa asked.

"I'll do the drugs and money laundering but not those damn body parts. Too hard to find donors on the Tijuana streets."

"I'm with you on that. What about this new angle? Human trafficking? Has he talked about it?"

"Another quick turnover, I think. He hasn't told me the details. Look, I gotta go. I've got to call the attorney and make plans for Elliott's release, if he's been caught."

Monsoon-like clouds were gathering toward Havasu, and the preemptory winds sent bursts of dust and refuse across the boulevard. Derek spun the car into a quick U-turn and crossed the bridge to the casinos. Realizing by now that his identity was compromised and that photos might be passed around to the alphabet agencies, he took the side streets. There were too many cops around who might recognize him, so he settled on a sleazy motel off the strip.

***

Marisa said good-bye, reached for her glass of wine, and stared into space. Her mind raced through bloody scenarios that soon would be a part of her life. Human trafficking? Young girls from Mexico? Selling them into sex slavery? Twelve-year-olds? What's he thinking? How did our family get so screwed up?

19

Grace and Amanda eagerly accepted help into the chopper and grabbed the water bottles before they sat down. Since they were both at a serious level of dehydration and heat exhaustion, cold compresses were applied to their faces and arms.

Amanda glanced over at Grace, who was actively engaged in conversation with Luke. *What the hell is going on? This mystery man drops out of the sky, saves the day, and Mom doesn't have time to finish the conversation? Ignores me? I think not.* Amanda tried to listen to their conversation, but the whir of the helicopter gulped their words.

Amanda could stand it no longer. She gave Grace a hard bump on her shoulder to get her attention and yelled, "Okay, Mom. Let's hear it. Who is this guy?"

Luke smiled at Grace; his smile always had a quizzical smirk at the end of it. Releasing her hand, he tilted his head and said, "Looks like you got some 'splainin' to do, Lucy."

Grace never took kindly to anyone pushing her. "Don't get smart mouthed with me, young lady. When the time is right, you'll hear the rest of the story… And that will be after we've had some time with Meg. Now get on the phone and let Rachael know we're okay. They have to be worried sick." Bossy Grace was in charge again. She turned back to Luke.

***

When Rachael's phone went to voice mail, Amanda tried Meg's number again. The line connected as Meg entered Josh's room. "Mandy. Oh my God, Mandy. Where are you? Is Mom with you? Are you okay?"

"Slow down, sis. We were kidnapped, but we're fine. On our way to Bullhead now. I need to bring Rachael up to speed about Elliott and Derek."

"What? What the hell is that noise? Kidnapped? Huh?"

"Just listen."

"Me first. Rachael just cuffed Elliott. He was here in the hospital with us. Can you believe that? She dragged his sorry ass downstairs. Transporting him to Bullhead jail for the night."

"Thank God." Amanda turned and gave a thumbs-up to Grace.

"Hey, but what do you mean—Derek and Elliott?" The unusual combination of people finally registered. "In the same sentence?"

"Try to reach Rachael. Tell her that Derek is Elliott's brother and accomplice."

"What?" Meg was almost speechless, but she managed to continue. "That lying son of a bitch. He was using me the whole time he was dating me? Setting me up for Elliott?"

"Look, Meg, we should be landing on the hospital roof in fifteen minutes. Rachael needs to get a heads-up on this information. It's important." Amanda glanced back at Grace, who was smiling at Luke. Dear Lord, what's going to happen next? Poor Meg. She's really not in any shape to hear about this. New father? "Can hardly wait to see you."

"Me too. Oh, tell Mom that Josh helped catch Elliott, but he's bleeding again. Didn't have to go back to surgery, thank goodness. Doctor says he's fine, but Rachael's wiggin' out. She'll really be stretched when she hears the latest." Meg paused and stuck her head out of Josh's room, searching for the source of a loud commotion. "Wait a sec, Mandy. Some loudmouthed woman is pushing her way down the hall. I'll call you back in a minute." Meg shoved the phone in her pocket and started for the door.

The security guard stopped a wiry redhead, who was rushing down the hall. She showed some ID, pushed by Meg, stormed inside, and headed directly to Josh, who had dozed off. She walked over, looked for a chart, and then stomped to the head of the bed. Leaning over, the woman whispered something in Josh's ear and then kissed him hard on the mouth. His eyes opened, and he pushed her back.

Meg took an immediate dislike to the woman and attacked. "Excuse me, but what do you think you're doing?"

The stranger looked up. "Kissing my fiancé. What's it to you?"

20

Rachael rode shotgun in the van, transporting Elliott to the Bullhead Police Headquarters. She refused to lose sight of him until he was booked and conveyed to the custody of the Kingman jail.

"Print him and book him," Rachael said to her fellow cop. "Finally got the bastard."

"Good catch, Rachael," yelled her captain as she entered the squad room. Five fellow officers were in the room and gave her a standing ovation. "Anyone hurt in the scuffle? You've got blood on your shirt."

"Josh got pushed around, but he actually saved my life by kicking my gun to me. He's okay, just roughed up a little." She flopped into her swivel chair, exhausted.

"Well, when you get Elliott to Kingman, maybe you can play nurse for a while."

"Was going to talk to you about that. Might need another week or two in Catalina."

Rachael immediately regretted her comment. She knew Elliott collected tidbits of information like that to use later. She stood, went back to booking, grabbed Elliott by the cuffs, and shoved him into the interrogation room.

"I'd like to make my one phone call."

Rachael shook her head. "Maybe when we get you to Kingman."

"I know the law. You are obliged to let me contact my attorney." His arrogant air had returned.

The captain nodded to Rachael.

She shook her head. "Shit." She walked to the captain and whispered, "He'll lay out an escape plan if we let him talk to anyone. Just this once, say no, Cap."

The captain leaned over the interrogation table and handed a phone to Elliott. "Make it short."

"When am I being transferred?"

"No need for you to know."

"On the contrary, my attorney will need to know where to come and when."

"Too bad. Come on, Rachael." The captain left the room to make arrangements for transport and jail accommodations in Kingman and to give Elliott his moment of privacy.

Elliott leaned back and smiled. "Well, Rachael. You'll probably get a promotion for catching me. I hear I made the FBI's Ten Most Wanted list." His conceit irritated her. "By the way, how do you like my new look? Lost twenty pounds, have a new hairline and a more Grecian-style nose. I'm sure Meg liked it."

"You sick son of a bitch. If Meg gets anywhere close to you and I'm not around to stop her, she'll filet your face." Rachael shot him a disgusted look. "I should have killed you when I had the chance or let Meg do the honors. But watching you struggle for your last breath when the needle is stuck in your arm will be reward enough. I'm sure Mom will organize a party, and we'll all have shots of tequila as you die."

"Not going to happen, dear friend. Perhaps you haven't noticed that Grace and Amanda are missing." He leaned back as far as the chair would allow. A smug look registered on his face.

Rachael stopped and turned to him, faking a surprised look. She had finished the conversation with Meg and knew the situation, so she decided to play along with Elliott. "What? They're on their way back to Bullhead. Left the Ontario airport an hour ago."

"Oh, so naive. Sorry, pumpkin, my brother is holding them captive until my release has been negotiated. That will be the first item on my attorney's agenda." He watched, looking for some response. Not surprised by the news?

Something's gone wrong. How did she find out? Does she know about Derek? Elliott experienced a moment of alarm, a hairline crack in his foul foundation.

"Sorry, that'll be a short conversation. There's nothing to negotiate." Rachael smiled. *If it's sparring you want, bring it on,* she thought.

"Really? Didn't think you'd sacrifice your loved ones so easily. You know the kind of torture I can dish out." His malicious leer returned. "I'm amazed at that." Though he was outwardly projecting his usual superior attitude, inwardly he knew something was amiss. *What does she know?*

"You're little plot was foiled. Mom and Amanda should be landing on the hospital roof as we speak. Sorry, asshole. Missed again. When are you going to learn?" She leaned across the interrogation table and smiled, glaring into his soulless eyes. "Pennington women always win."

Elliott reared forward, rage registering on his face. *Derek, you stupid fool. What have you done?* "I'm going to kill you."

Rachael, not backing down, generously sneered at Elliott's frustration. She turned, distracted by the sound of the captain shouting from the squad room. The captain slammed into the room, yelling. "The media's all over the fuckin' station, and Elliott's attorney is already here, demanding to see him. How the hell did this leak out? No coverage. That's what I told everyone: no coverage till we transfer him. Shit!"

Elliott regained his composure, leaned back in his chair, and grinned again at Rachael; his newly capped teeth reflected light off the fluorescents. When he recognized her frustration, he immediately grabbed the upper hand. "My attorney—how fortuitous. Send him in, by all means."

Rachael was livid and wanted to smash him in the face but held back. She stood aside as the robust attorney barged into the room. "We'll be watching through the window. Don't touch the prisoner at any time. Got it?"

The attorney brushed by the captain. "Have you taken pictures of the bruises and cuts on my client's face?" He slammed his briefcase on the table and yelled at Rachael.

"Those are left over from his boating accident. Call the hospital if you want to verify. I'll leave you alone with your client." She slammed the door as she left.

The portly attorney wiped sweat from his brow and pulled out the chair. Yellow stains marked his wrinkled pinstripe shirt, and he loosened his rumpled tie as he sat down. "Elliott, you okay?"

"Never better now that you're here. Did Derek fill you in on the plan? Did you bring the goop?" he whispered.

The attorney reached into his pocket and retrieved a small tube, hid it in the palm of his hand, and kept on talking. "The cops searched me coming in, but the medicine is in a Neosporin tube. Clever, huh? I'll squeeze some of the ointment onto the table as I leave. When I'm gone, push your cuffed hands over the spot, and you'll have a convulsion within five minutes. It'll be slight, so they won't have to take you to the hospital. Paramedics can handle it. Lethal shit if you use too much—be careful."

"Good, then my transport to Kingman won't happen until tomorrow morning, and Derek will have time to finalize the rest of our plans. I'm sure Rachael will go with her pilot friend in his helicopter, tracking us overhead. So, Derek will—"

The attorney cut him off. "Don't tell me the plan. I don't want to be complicit."

Rachael watched through the one-way mirror, trying to read lips. Whatever he's cooking up, I'll be ready.

21

Meg wasn't going to be dismissed by the red-haired bimbo who had stormed into Josh's room. She rang for a nurse and stood guard on the other side of his bed. "You have no right to be here," she snarled, adjusting Josh's pillow at the same time.

"Says who?" Dressed in cutoff jeans and a Grateful Dead T-shirt, faded by time, the Medusa ignored Meg's interference and then seemed to hiss at her. "Josh and I are going to be married. I'm here to take him home and nurse him back to health. Don't get in my way." She stomped up to the opposite side of the hospital bed and yanked at the sheets.

"Bullshit. Just wait till Rachael hears about this." Meg grabbed a handful of sheet and tugged back.

"Rachael? The old summer girlfriend of his? She dumped him last summer when we were split up. Hell, it only took a week for him to get over her and come back to me."

"More bullshit. He's never even mentioned you."

Josh was picking up on part of the conversation but was still a little drowsy from the medication. He blinked hard and tried to concentrate, to focus on the present problem. "Stella, is that you? I was just talking to Rachael about you."

"See, smart-ass. Of course he knows me." Her tone changed, and she snuggled up to Josh. "Hi, darling. Yeah, it's me. I've come to take you home, sweetheart." She was purring.

75

Again, he tried to adjust his vision. She and Meg looked stringy to him, out of focus. Leaving the hospital sounded good, so he managed a few words of agreement. "Great. Want to work." He mumbled something else and closed his eyes.

"Look at him," Meg insisted. "He's not ready to go home. Get the hell out of here before I call security."

Stella snarled. "Out of the way, bitch." She yanked the sheet back, shut off the IV, and retracted the needle. Grabbing his head and legs, she propped him upright. Ignoring Meg, she adjusted his hospital gown and rubbed his groin area. "I've missed you. Discharge papers are signed. A wheelchair's on its way."

"Are we going home? To Catalina? Now?" Josh pushed her hand away.

Stella looked at Meg. She smirked. "Honey, that's our business. I'll tell you where we're going after we leave. No need to let this snarky blonde know anything."

"Snarky? You'll think *snarky* when Rachael is through with you. Josh, what the hell are you doing? Wait for Rachael." Meg was prepared to take on this nuisance if necessary. She considered the redhead's size. She outweighs me, she thought, but with my Krav Maga training, she doesn't have a chance.

"Oh yeah, Rachael. Should talk to her. Where is she?" He sat up straight in bed and waited a minute while his vertigo subsided. "My robe. Stella, get my robe."

"She's taking Elliott to the police station for booking. Come on, Josh. Get it together."

"Who's Elliott? Oh, yeah. I remember him. He's…he's…Is she coming back?"

"She's busy till this afternoon. What's the hurry? You need more rest." Meg, stalling and pleading at the same time, blocked the doorway. Her keen instincts were screaming that this strange woman was a major threat.

"Don't want to wait, Meg. Sorry. Need to go home." He stood by the bed, and Stella finished tying his robe, constantly reaching for his bare skin at the same time.

"Josh, please. Don't be an asshole. Talk to Rachael. She's your woman, not this Jezebel."

Josh made no reply. The meds, still coursing through his mind, left him in a confused state. Why was everyone fighting?

Stella interjected, "Well, how melodramatic of you. We're going." She tossed her wild red hair back and sneered. She spewed out the words, revealing teeth, yellow from neglect.

"Like hell you are." Meg started for the other side of the bed but stopped when a nurse came in with a wheelchair.

"Here's your carriage, Mr. Meyers." Josh sagged into the chair, overwhelmed by the drama.

"Stop. You can't do that. It's too soon to be discharged."

"Don't listen to her. Here are the signed orders." Stella shoved them to the nurse.

"Come on, Meg. It'll be fine. I want to go home." He motioned with his hand for Stella to push him forward as the nurse watched in wonder at the unfolding scene.

Stella whisked him out of the room without further comment and headed for the elevators.

Meg snatched her cell phone and dialed Rachael. "You need to get back here, now."

"Meg, I have to finish booking Elliott. His attorney's with him. I can't leave." Rachael had her hands full at the station and didn't have time for Meg's hysteria.

"Rach, this redheaded bitch just showed up—Josh's old girlfriend from Catalina. And she's leaving with him right now. She's off her rocker, but he said yes."

Rachael sighed. She wanted to cry. The battle on the boat dock and the recent scuffle in the hospital room had left her physically and emotionally spent. Deciding to leave her cop hat on instead of following her heart was a tough decision, but she had to take the chance on handling the bitch situation later. "Meg, I have to stay here and follow up with Elliott. Do what you can. Handle it."

"Like that's going to be easy. Shit, I'll grab Amanda, and we'll follow her."

***

Loud screams came from the interrogation room down the hall, and Rachael started running toward the commotion.

Someone yelled, "Get a medic! The perp's having a seizure!"

Rachael bumped into Elliott's attorney on his way out, pushed past him, and dashed into Elliott's interview room.

Elliott, lying on the floor, screamed when his vocal cords seized. He lost consciousness and then developed violent muscle contractions. His eyes rolled up, with only dead white filling the cavity.

"Shit. Now what?" Rachael stood back and watched, not willing to pour any more energy into the feat. She put her hands on her hips, shook her head, and didn't try to help. "Let the bastard die."

22

Amanda smiled at the attendant. "Thanks, that lotion really helps the sunburn." Even her eyelids hurt when she closed them.

Adjusting the IV drip, the attendant stood back. "You look one hundred percent better. A day or so of rest, and you'll be on your way."

Meg popped through the hospital room door. "You and Mom look like lobsters. Just how perverse was Derek?" She had graduated from using the wheelchair, and she stomped into the room. Her hospital gown had ended up in the trash, and Meg was in her river attire—purple crop top and fringed short shorts.

Amanda could see Meg's impetuous nature was in charge. "Not as bad as Elliott, but no hero either. Meg, there's so much damn stuff going on right now. Mom—"

"You think?" Meg interrupted her sister. "This creepy redhead showed up and kidnapped Josh right out of the hospital room. Can you believe that? Let's unhook all this shit, and you come with me." She started for Amanda's bed. "We have to follow her and find out what's going on. Josh isn't in any condition to move, let alone fly back to Catalina. Come on, help me." She started struggling with Amanda's finger clamp.

"Wait." Amanda shook her head and sighed. "Is there no stopping you? I need some rest; so does Mom. And you? You're probably still in shock and don't know it. Heard you had Elliott at gunpoint."

"Should have killed the SOB." She pulled back from the bed, realizing Amanda wasn't ready to help in her conquest.

"Why not stay another day in the hospital with us? Then we can go back to the house together tomorrow and get organized." Besides, little sister, she thought, you have another big surprise, or two, coming. Mom, a retired CIA agent, and a new dad.

Meg paced around the room, not willing to give up on a good battle, but she knew her limits. "You're right." She plunked down in the chair. "God, you're getting more like Mom every day."

"Thanks, I think."

"But me, ha. I'm fine. Just need a few hours on the river."

Amanda recognized Meg's flippant answer. Typical for hiding the truth.

Meg didn't want to tell Amanda she knew she was suffering from emotional stress. The last encounter with Elliott had been more traumatizing than she'd showed. Still, the long nights of no sleep, fearing he would return and hurt her again, were taking their toll. She felt that helping Jessie through her traumatic maze might be cathartic for her. Taking on a more serious note, she continued, "Mandy, I mentioned this to Rachael but haven't told you and Mom. I need to get away from Bullhead. Jessie and I are talking about going to Catalina." She paused and fiddled with a string on her shorts. "I'm going to call the Conservancy about a job tomorrow."

Amanda knew it was unlike Meg to run away from problems. Meg was a pit bull. She wondered how deep her sister's trauma had gone. Outwardly, in the last six months, she had returned to partying with friends, working, and playing. The old Meg. But this turn of events was bothersome.

"Good idea. If what you say is true about the schizophrenic redhead, I'll bet Rachael ends up in Catalina, too. I think she wants to get married."

"Ya think?" Meg said with a huge smile, but inside she was worried about the redhead.

Amanda wanted to tell Meg that Grace had some startling news, but she knew it wasn't her story to tell. Moreover, Meg was probably too delicate to handle it with everything else that was going on. Grace should be the one. Grace, the Creator. "When I'm off the IV, I'll head up to your room to meet Jessie. Is she fun?"

"Could be, I think. She's a barrel racer with the rodeo, part time, and also in the movies. Loves it. Has a cute brother, too."

"Oh, here we go again."

23

The captain reached Elliott first and tried to grab him as he thrashed around on the floor. "Turn him on his side but don't hold him down. Protect his head. For God's sake, give me some help here." Elliott flailed around like a madman.

Against her emotional response to let Elliott die, Rachael shoved the interview table out of the way and watched as Elliott continued to flail about the floor. There was nothing to be done; they could only wait. "What happened?"

"Don't know. The attorney yelled, 'Help him' and then bolted."

Elliott's cuffed hands flew sideways, clipping the captain and knocking him against the wall.

"Son of a bitch." He quickly recovered and grabbed Elliott again. "When I came in, he was having weird muscle contractions. Arm and leg spasms, like now. Slurred words. Fell to the floor. Seizure?" He panted from the exertion as he tried to hold Elliott down.

Elliott reared back, and grotesque facial expressions spread across his face as if a 9.0 earthquake ravaged him. His body stiffened.

Rachael and two other cops held him down. "Get the paramedics. Stop the attorney and search him."

"Medics are on their way. Attorney skipped out."

Elliott's body seemed to relax, but he started convulsing again as the paramedics arrived. They quickly administered Dilantin. His attack subsided.

"We can't transport him to Kingman until tomorrow. It's too far." The medics lifted him onto the gurney. "Warmcy is full, but we could try to find a room. You want us to take him back to the hospital?"

"No, for God's sake. He'll get away again. We have to keep him here. Okay to restrain him?" Rachael, totally frustrated by the setback, pushed for an answer.

"For now, yeah. But when he comes around, that shouldn't be necessary. Does he have a history of epilepsy?"

"Who the hell knows?" Rachael had no empathy. "Could he be faking this?"

"No. Doesn't look like it."

"Are there any meds that could cause this? Review the tapes. See if the attorney handed him anything."

"Shit, Rachael. You were watching through the window. He didn't swallow anything?"

Rachael looked at his mouth and nose. "Nothing other than spit." She checked his neck and arms. Nothing. "Wait," she said as she turned over his cuffed hands. "There's a substance on his right index finger." She put on some gloves and took a sample. "Run this by the lab. Don't let it touch your skin."

The paramedics rolled him into a cell and transferred him to the cot. "He's all yours."

"Great." Disgust accompanied the words. "We'll need a twenty-four-hour suicide watch assigned." Rachael looked over at Elliott. "I know he was faking this. It's part of a plan."

"Nah. He has the typical symptoms of a seizure. Be sure to inform Kingman jail about his condition so they can keep an eye on him." The paramedics checked Elliott's vitals, transferred him to the cot, pushed the empty gurney through the cell door, and headed for the ambulance.

Rachael peered down at Elliott, who was now cognizant of his surroundings. "Too bad you survived your attack. Would have saved the state some money. Wish we had Old Sparky. I'd be all dressed up with the family, smiling, as you turned to toast."

Elliott's eyes finally focused and he mumbled a quick reply.

Rachael leaned forward to hear him.

"I'm going to kill your family."

She tried to hide her shudder. She had sparred with many crooks, murderers, and rapists, but no one affected her like Elliott. Because he'd come so close? Because she had witnessed his brutality? She leaned in closer so the paramedics couldn't hear her. "No way. I have friends in the Kingman jail. You won't last a week."

***

The storage unit off Highway 95 hid the van. Derek finished spraying the insignia on the doors with a color that matched the Bullhead police transport, stenciling the number 929 on top, and inside he placed ten orange road cones. From the air, the van could easily pass for the Bullhead PD vehicle. A college student, Buzz, had been hired to drive it.

"We're shooting a movie outside of Kingman," Derek said, "and you'll get paid one hundred fifty dollars to drive the van from an underpass on Ninety-Five to the Kingman jail."

Derek planned to pick up Buzz at 7:00 a.m. the next day at the Laughlin Bridge. Buzz would make his own arrangements for his return home. Nothing tricky. The kid was ecstatic, especially when informed that his name would appear in the credits.

A used silver Honda Accord was purchased with cash and incorporated into the escape plan. One of Elliott's seaplanes would fly to Katherine's Landing from Mexico and wait for the arrival of the escapees. All was ready.

***

Elliott spent a restless night in jail, and Rachael watched his every move on high alert. She was exhausted. When almost nodding off, she would recall vivid images of Elliott's method of torture and suddenly jerk to a vigilant posture. Adrenaline was pouring through her. She needed to get Elliott to Kingman, where security was tighter. Since Elliott was tucked in for the night, she decided to call Meg and get the details of the strange redhead.

"Hi, sis. Really tired but need to hear about Josh. And before I forget, would you call Catalina and make reservations at the Mac Rae Hotel for a week? Oh, and ask the sheriff's department to call me when they have time."

"Sure, no problem."

"Get as much background info on this Stella person as possible. Especially any gossip about their relationship. Catalina's a tiny community. Call your friends."

"Jeez. Who am I? Your personal secretary? I've got Mom and Amanda to take care of and also my new best friend, Jessie. I'll do what I can."

Rachael backed off. Meg could be pushed only so far. "Thanks. I owe you. Gotta go. Captain's calling."

Meg said good-bye to a disconnected phone.

Final preparations for Elliott's transfer were falling into place. "Can we get someone to ride shotgun?" she asked the captain.

"Come on, Rachael, you know we're shorthanded. You've got it covered by air. What's the problem?"

"Guess I'm just a little nervous. You're right." She heard the sound of the helicopter and grabbed her gun, badge, and purse. "Well, here we go."

As forecasted by the *Mohave News*, a monsoon had gathered overnight, and the threat of rain was imminent. Rachael dashed over to Chris's helicopter. "You okay to go in this weather?" The wind whipped mini funnels of sand across the open field. Rachael's hair wrapped around her face, obstructing her vision as she wrestled with the helicopter's door.

"Checked with Havasu. The rain's starting now, so we have a good two hours before it reaches us. Shouldn't be a problem. I've flown in worse conditions. Ready to go?"

"Soon as I settle Elliott in the van."

Elliott was led to the back of the van. Despite the wind and his resistance, Rachael and the driver managed to shove him inside. Rachael checked his ankle manacles and attached his handcuffs to the overhead bar.

"What's the matter, Rachael, dear? Don't trust your partners? You know, sometimes I get so sad. If you hadn't caught me last year, well, Meg and I would have had our firstborn, and you would be an aunt. Tsk-tsk. What a loss."

"Look, you sick bastard, Meg would have flushed any of your offspring down the toilet. You're the most despicable version of a human being I've ever met. Sorry I only winged you during the gunfight." Come on; don't let him get to you. She gave the cuffs an extra tug, jumped out of the van, and, with the help of the wind, slammed the door.

She heard Elliott chuckle as the doors closed. Rachael was furious with herself for letting Elliott annoy her, for joining in a verbal sparring contest with him. Shaking off the moment, she stopped by for one last word with the driver. "If you have any problems and the communication system is out, flash your lights and swing back and forth on the highway. We'll land ASAP and help. Elliott is being too cooperative. Something's amiss. Stay alert."

"It's okay, Rach. I've done this a hundred times."

"Not with this sick bastard and his friends." She masked her concern. Banging on the side door twice, she started for the helicopter. Chris, what a loyal friend. Civilian yet the best chopper pilot around, and he's always ready to help me. Too bad he's married. Would be a good catch for Meg.

"Hop on board," Chris yelled as Rachael climbed into his helicopter. "Good thing I had the day off. Wouldn't want to miss delivering the asshole to jail." He powered up the machine. "Is Amanda doing okay? I really felt bad that she was kidnapped during my watch."

"She's fine. Roughed up a little. No biggie. And most important, it wasn't your fault."

"I know but still."

"No worries." Rachael climbed into the sleek helicopter and strapped in. "Wow, when did you get this new toy? It's beautiful."

"Just delivered last week. It's a 1991 Bell two oh six-B. Cost me a pretty penny, but it's worth it."

"We'll party tonight. Drinks are on me. Let's go." She projected a light-hearted attitude, but her stomach rumbled with apprehension, and she knew the anxiety would prevail until Elliott called the Kingman jail "home."

"Regular route?" Chris pulled back on the stick and maneuvered the chopper through the dust storm.

"Yeah. Direct to Kingman. Don't let that van out of your sight for one minute. You know who we're dealing with."

Derek picked up Buzz per their arrangements. A quarter mile before the underpass on Highway 95, he pulled the car over. "Help me set up the orange cones. We want to direct traffic into the right lane."

"No problem." The wind from the monsoon was picking up, so they added small sandbags to the cones before heading back to the car.

"Here's the cop uniform you need to put on. Do you remember what to do when I say, 'Action' into the walkie-talkie?" Derek pulled the items out of the trunk.

Buzz ducked behind the car, dropped his pants, and pulled on the uniform. He struggled with the tight shirt. "Yeah. The cameras will start rolling when the other van approaches. When you say, 'Go' into my headphones, I take off for Kingman. Drive the speed limit and stop in front of the jailhouse." He ran his hand across his blond hair. "My hair look okay?" The wind had played havoc with it. "Any close-up shots?"

Derek looked at the kid and hid his aversion. "Hair's fine," he replied. "Listen, our helicopter will be filming some of this overhead, so probably no head shots. Keep your head inside. But you've been a good sport, so I added an extra fifty bucks. Stop at the Cracker Barrel for breakfast, 'cause we'll need a little more time to set up the cameras before you arrive at the jail."

"Hey, thanks. Anytime you need another walk-on, just let me know. I can do stunts on the water, and the girls think I have a great profile. What do you think?" asked Buzz as he muscled up his best Channing Tatum stance, turning slowly to the right.

"Sure, sure." *Idiot.*

"Say. How am I going to get home? Drive the van back?"

Shit. "Someone will pick you up. Take you back to Bullhead. Hurry up." Derek wondered whether he should have hired someone with a higher IQ but dismissed the thought since there was no time to change.

Derek knew timing and precise execution were essential for Elliott's escape. Through all the years of dealing with his brother, he'd never been asked to kill anyone until now. Amanda, Grace, and now a cop? He didn't like the thought of killing, but he knew his sister was counting on him. *Maybe I'll just wound the driver. Don't want to kill a cop. Maybe tie him up. Shit…*

The change of wardrobe was complete, and the two men drove the short distance, stopping half a mile from the tunnel where the van was parked. The early morning traffic had dwindled down to nothing, which was an essential element for the plan to succeed. "Get out. I'll lead the way to the underpass; you follow my car. Then, I'll do a U-turn, park across from the van, and get the cameras ready."

When they arrived in the dark tunnel, Buzz was concerned. "Don't you need some lights?"

"Camera will cover it; don't worry. Now get in the van and start the engine. They're moments away."

It felt like an eternity, but Derek got the signal from his well-paid lookout. "Okay, be on the ready. Start the van now. Cameras are rolling."

The small light came on from the camera, and Buzz gripped the steering wheel. He was vacillating between looking tough and smiling.

"Ready? Go!" The faux cop van took off per the plan as the police van entered the underpass.

A nail strip, which had been placed after the last orange cone, penetrated the PD tires, and the van swerved, coming to an immediate stop inside the tunnel. Derek stepped from behind the car and dashed toward the driver's door.

The cop, wrestling with the steering wheel as the vehicle came to a rest, saw the man approach. Armed. Panic hit. He reached for his gun.

Derek fired one shot that smashed the safety window and grazed the driver's forehead. The driver dropped his weapon and fell forward as Derek used his Glock to smash the shattered window; he reached through and cold-cocked him. He immediately unlocked the door and pulled the driver to the ground. Minimal blood was seeping from the wound.

The cop moaned. "Don't kill me. For God's sake, man, don't kill me." He cowered and tried to roll under the van.

Derek hesitated, knowing he should put a bullet through the driver's head, but instead he belted him again with his gun. Finding the keys, he rushed to the back, looking through the tunnel to ensure Buzz was playing his part. He was. Perfect.

"Nice job, little brother. Be careful with the bandaged arm. That bitch took pleasure in locking my hands overhead." Elliott massaged his hands and shoulder as Derek unshackled his ankles. "Good. Now go look outside. If the helicopter has passed over, we're in the clear." He gingerly stepped down to the pavement. "I'll get in the car." As he rounded the back fender, he paused and stepped over the unconscious cop.

"It's all clear. The chopper is out of sight. Let's go," said Derek, readjusting his eyes to the darkened tunnel.

Elliott hesitated. He knew the answer but asked the question. "Is he dead?"

"No, but he's out. He won't interfere with the plan; let's leave him." Even as he spoke the words, he knew the cop was history.

"Pussy. Give me the gun." Elliott took the gun, pointed it down at the wounded cop, and fired two shots. Typical mafia double tap to the head. Gray matter, blood, and bone fragments careened across the pavement and up the side of the van as life oozed out of the cop. "Next time, finish the damn job." He shoved the smoldering gun into the waistband of his orange police jumpsuit.

Sounds of the helicopter faded, and the two brothers headed down the highway in the opposite direction, toward Katherine's Landing.

***

Twenty minutes later, Buzz pulled up outside the Cracker Barrel restaurant, slammed the door, tried in vain to fix his hairdo, and waved to the helicopter flying overhead. He felt sure that he would be headed for Hollywood if they caught a good shot of his face. He smiled.

"What the hell is going on?" yelled Rachael over the din of the rotor blades. She reached for the binoculars. "Idiot. He's stopping for breakfast. Did you get a look at his face? Is that our driver?"

Chris didn't look. The mounting monsoon was playing havoc with the chopper. "Shit, Rachael. I don't know. Is this part of the plan? Breakfast? What do you want me to do?" Not waiting for an answer, Chris searched the area for a spot to land.

"I tried to call the van, but he doesn't answer. Something's gone wrong. He wouldn't leave Elliott in the van by himself. Shit. Can you land?" The binoculars were useless, so she dropped them and checked her gun.

"Empty field about a quarter of a mile south." The wind subsided once they had cleared the foothills, but it still played hell with the chopper. "Good enough," he said as he motioned toward the vacant field.

"Do it. I'll call headquarters."

By the time the helicopter landed and Rachael and Chris sprinted the quarter mile, Buzz was on his second cup of coffee, waiting for his blueberry waffles. Chris headed for the van, while red-faced, sweating, and worried Rachael entered the café, walked through the gift shop, stopped at the hostess desk, and flashed her badge. "I'm looking for a cop. Should have come in here about twenty minutes ago. Where did you seat him?"

"Is there a problem?" The girl acted frustrated. The restaurant was overly crowded, and she didn't want to be responsible for a scene.

"Where did you seat him? I don't have time to explain. I'll keep it down."

"Third table next to the windows. You can't see it from here. Behind the fireplace."

"Thanks." She grabbed her two-way. "Chris, check in."

"Van's empty, Rachael. Shit. It's not a Bullhead van; it's a knockoff."

"Damn. Come back in the restaurant. The hostess will tell you where I am. Be my backup."

"I don't have a gun. Shit. Don't worry. I'll stop him somehow if he gets past you."

"The owner will lock down the kitchen area. His only other way out is the front. You cover it. I can see him from here. He's in a rent-a-cop uniform." Rachael walked to Buzz's table, pulled out the chair, and sat down.

"Hey, hi, pretty lady. If you're looking for company, sorry, I can't help. Still working." Buzz took a bite of his waffle and grinned, hoping this might be another scene for the movie. He looked around for a camera. A talking part maybe? He straightened, picked up his napkin, and dabbed his mouth, a sophisticated move he'd seen in *Dial M for Murder,* an old Ray Milland movie.

Rachael was astonished to see such a young kid. Eighteen maybe? "You driving that police van parked outside?"

"Yeah. Are you part of the gig?" He brushed back his hair and looked up at the corner of the room. His best profile exposed. "You playing a cop, too?"

"I *am* a cop." She showed Buzz her badge. "What gig are you talking about? Where's the prisoner? When did you change vans?"

"Huh, what prisoner? All I was supposed to do was drive the van from the underpass to here, have breakfast, and then drive to the jail. Is something wrong? Do they need to do another take?"

"What take?"

"The movie. Got paid a hundred fifty bucks and breakfast to drive the van. What's going on?"

Rachael grabbed her phone, now ignoring the kid. "Captain. Elliott's escaped. They did a switch under the Ninety-Five overpass. Had a duplicate van waiting."

Buzz interjected, "He was driving a silver Accord, if that helps. The guy who was shooting the movie."

"Describe him."

"Tall, six foot one or so. Blondish hair, good looking. Probably could have been a movie star. I was kinda jealous."

"What else?"

"Oh, nice manners. Smart. Think his name was Dennis or Dwayne."

"Could it have been Derek?"

"Yeah. Derek. That was it."

The captain had been listening in. "It's a cinch they started in the opposite direction. Half-hour lead. Maybe back to the river?"

"Elliott has float boats and seaplanes he uses to smuggle drugs. Alert Katherine's Landing and Davis Dam to watch out for him. Alert everyone as far down as the wide section of the river, by Avi. We may get lucky: if the monsoon picks up again, they'll be grounded. If they're spotted, shoot 'em down if you can. Send a squad car to the underpass to pick up the van. Paramedics, too. We probably have an officer down."

Buzz listened in total confusion. "Uh, lady. Am I under arrest? Really thought it was the best gig I ever landed." His posture had taken a sudden downturn, along with his smile.

Rachael shook her head in disbelief. Dumb kid. Thought by tomorrow he'd be a movie star. Can't fault him for that. "No, you're not under arrest. You can't get back into the van. Evidence, you know. Stay here until someone comes to get you. If everything checks out, you can probably leave."

"Swell." Buzz took another bite of waffle and looked around the room. Seeing the attention he was drawing, he decided to continue the role. He stood very straight, stretched out his hand, and reached for Rachael's. "Thanks for the update, officer. I can take it from here."

"Asshole," she mouthed to him and then gave him his moment. On the way out, she made a quick call to Amanda and Meg to warn them to be on the lookout for Elliott. "I don't think he's stupid enough to hang around. But who knows? He has such an elevated ego. I'll come to the hospital when I get back, and we'll decide what to do. What's happening with Josh? How's Mom?"

"The sicko redhead left the hospital with Josh. You'll need to call his captain at Catalina; I couldn't get through, but I know that's where they're headed. Mom is well. Dehydrated and sunburned like me," said Amanda. "When she hears that Elliott has escaped again, she'll probably have a shit fit and call Luke."

"Who?"

"Long story."

24

The seaplane circled, fighting the strong wind, and finally made a rough landing at Railroad Cove, adjacent to Katherine's Landing. The pilot studied the waves and taxied toward an opening on the sandy beach to wait for his passengers. Fishing boats, day cruisers, and personal watercrafts dotted the shoreline, their owners manually holding the tie lines, fighting the wind. Boaters always assist other boaters when help is needed, and that axiom stretched to the seaplane. A larger opening was made for the plane as it approached. Mini whitecaps sloshed over the pontoons as curiosity trumped the weather conditions and kids and adults flocked to the plane. Not wanting to create more interest, the pilot allowed the intrusion until he saw the Accord approach.

Derek drove the speed limit until they reached the dirt road by the dam and then tromped on the gas. Time was inching by.

"Take the bags to the plane, Derek," Elliott said as they pulled to a stop at the edge of the water. Again feeling the effects from his loss of blood, Elliott could only bark orders. He barely had strength enough to lean against the car and wait for help. Dehydration was taking over again. "Get me some water." He hobbled toward the plane as the wind whipped sand across his face and the cold water snaked around his ankles. "Hurry up."

"Jenny, come away from that plane," yelled a worried mother.

"Fire it up, asshole!" Elliott screamed at the pilot. "Out of my way, you fuckin' brats."

Parents rushed to grab their kids as the foulmouthed man dressed in jail-issued clothes waded into the water. Elliott shoved a lingering teenager sitting on the pontoon.

A burly man roared as he approached Elliott. "Hey, watch it!"

"Manuel," yelled Elliott. The pilot held out a hand and helped him onto the pontoon. Elliott held onto the wing, and with the other hand, he pulled the gun from his waist and fired two shots into the air. He felt smug as the crowd ran for cover.

The force of the wind made it difficult to turn the plane, but with Derek's help, it was straightened out, and the pilot fired up the engine. With the wind reaching dangerous proportions and the lake riddled with whitecaps, the pilot's skills were challenged, but he finally muscled back the stick, fought nature, and accomplished liftoff.

Once airborne, Derek decided to take control of the conversation. "Okay, fifteen minutes. That has to be a record getaway for us. Buzz should be having breakfast, and Rachael should be aware of the switch by now." Derek tried to steer any discussion away from the dead cop. "If she takes fifteen minutes to land and find Buzz, then we should still be okay." He was clicking off the time frame. They were flying over Katherine's Landing now and clearing the Lake Mohave and Davis Dam area. Below, the river narrowed, with statuesque casinos dotting the shore. "If the damn weather doesn't get any worse, we should clear the desert in twenty minutes."

Elliott wasn't interested in Derek's idle conversation. He knew he was trying to cover his ass, so he ignored his brother and started making calls. "Marisa, have you set up operations in San Clemente yet? How many planes and boats?"

"Handled. We'll discuss it in person, not on the phone. No more phone calls." She disconnected the call without further conversation.

"Who the hell does she think she is?" He was furious with being dismissed. "Your sister needs a few manners." His eyes narrowed as he selected a solution to that problem.

Still waiting for flight instructions, Manuel headed toward California. Being one of Elliott's regular pilots from Mexico, he knew better than to interrupt the one he knew as "El Jefe."

Overcoming his annoyance with Marisa, Elliott flip-flopped back to the quick escape, the execution of his masterful plan, and he complimented Derek on his contribution. Now it was time to discuss his failure. A verbal reprimand for not killing Amanda and Grace wouldn't be enough. On the other hand, execution would be overkill; he needed both Derek and Marisa to cooperate and contribute to his new business. "Derek, any problem handling the two Pennington women? Everything go as planned? I can see them. Shriveled-up bitches."

Does he know I didn't shoot them? How could he? Middle of the desert, no water? They're probably dead by now. "No hitches. Marisa was a big help in all of this."

Elliott was sitting behind Derek in the plane. "You didn't follow my orders, did you?"

Derek was close to panic. "What do you mean?" He was afraid to make eye contact, so he focused on the mountains looming in front of him and reached for the sissy bar.

"The driver. I told you to kill him. No witness. But you're such a fucking wimp, you couldn't do it." Without hesitation he leaned forward, grabbed Derek's head, and slammed it against the cockpit window frame. "Never again. Do you understand?"

Derek was dazed and mumbled, "Yes." *Bastard. He knows I can't protect myself here.*

The roar of the plane's engine filled the void in conversation.

Steepling his fingers, Elliott began to hum, a different man appearing. "You deserve a nice vacation, Derek. As soon as the money starts rolling in from the drugs and coyote activity in Mexico, just tell me where you want to go. It's covered."

Derek had a blank expression on his face. He wanted to wipe off the dribble of blood on his head, but he wouldn't give Elliott the satisfaction. *Crack my head one minute and bribe me the next?* He knew Elliott had millions hidden offshore, but Elliott said he needed more to send him to France? *I think not, you prick.* He found his subdued voice and said, "You should probably let the pilot know where we're going. Where? Catalina?"

"Of course. Meg is headed that way. I have unfinished business with her."

"Elliott. That's not the smartest thing to do. Every law enforcement agency will expect that. Let's stop at San Clemente and spend some time with Marisa, set up some new drug drops. The business needs your attention. Meg will always be around."

"Back side of Catalina," he said to the pilot, ignoring Derek's input. "How's the activity been at Cottonwood Canyon? Coast Guard still hanging around?"

"*Si*, senor. Best to land by China Point for tonight. Nice cove there. Deep."

"Do it. Derek, call ahead to Two Harbors. Have José take supplies to our hideout east of Cottonwood. We'll set up shop there until we finalize our permanent arrangements. Discussion closed." He leaned back in his seat and watched the desert disappear into the background and Barstow take form on the horizon. "We beat the monsoon. Good omen."

Derek knew by watching that Elliott was already formulating plans, which would necessitate his help. *I need to get away from him. I might be able to have a normal life...well, normal for a supposed gay guy.* He smirked. *Little chance for either Marisa or me if we continue on this path.* "Elliott, I'm thinking about heading for San Francisco. Maybe change my whole identity. I can practice law...I'm thinking estate planning or something that won't draw attention."

Derek regretted his honest words the minute they were spoken. Elliott's eyes narrowed; the furrow between the brows deepened. "You mealymouthed pansy. Move to gay land? Maybe adopt a baby with your boyfriend? Do you honestly believe I will ever let you go?"

There. He'd said it. Derek knew the answer, but the magnitude of the situation finally hit home. Unless Elliott was dead, Derek would never have a life. *Do I have a choice?* He glanced out the window, watching the remaining fleeting clouds drift over the Big Bear area and beyond to the blue Pacific, which brought him no solace today. *Is this yet another flight toward disaster?*

"I have a new enterprise that might entice you. There is a huge market for human trafficking, and we have all of the contacts and equipment to make this a lucrative business. By the time we reach Catalina, I'll have a plan. Think about it. See if you can add anything to the equation." He leaned forward and grabbed Derek's shoulder, squeezing to the point of pain. He laughed, released the grip, and closed his eyes to nap.

After a few minutes of quiet, Derek turned and looked over his shoulder, watching Elliott sleep. His brother had cared for Derek and Marisa during their childhood, keeping the family together when the social workers had come calling, and sibling loyalty had glued them together for fifteen more years. But now was the time to end the foul life—to be free, to be a normal person. Derek faced front again, turning his back on Elliott in more ways than one.

When Meg was wheeled to x-ray to reexamine her shoulder, Jordan pushed her call button. "Help me into the wheelchair. I want to go to the morgue," she barked as soon as the nurse arrived.

"That's not possible," the nurse replied as she smoothed the bedding.

"Make it possible. I want to see my sister. Now." Jordan was in no mood to play nice.

"I'll have to check with the doctor. Wait a minute." The nurse left the room, and Jordan felt a lifetime crawl by before she returned with a security guard.

"This is highly irregular," said the guard as he pushed Jordan toward the elevator, "but the director said the circumstances were unusual, so she said okay for five minutes."

The morgue was small, like any other hospital morgue, with only room to handle six bodies. Because of overcrowding, nineteen bodies had been transported to the funeral home across the street, but Jessie's body was still in the basement. The makeshift room was near freezing, with the air-conditioning cranked down all the way. The guard checked the toe tags, and once Jessie's body was located in the foul room, he pushed Jordan's wheelchair close to her sister's head.

Jordan asked to be left alone. "I'll only need a minute. Really want to tell her good-bye alone. Please."

The guard hesitated. "Sorry, not supposed to do that. Hospital procedure and all."

Jordan's typical aggression poured forth. "What? You think I'm going to hurt her body? For Christ's sake, she's dead."

The guard mumbled something under his breath and left the room.

Jordan touched the white sheet. The frigid temperature startled her. She slowly dragged away the sheet to uncover her sister's face and stared down. Jordan wasn't prepared for the gory sight before her. A short gasp escaped. Acrid blood caked Jessie's parted lips. Some teeth were missing, glass slivers protruded across her forehead and cheeks, and dried blood encased her eyelids. Her nose was sideways, and the rest of her face was charred. She pulled the sheet farther down and looked at her white, lifeless body. Very little remained of skin tissue, and her hands were so scorched that the skin was falling off her fingers. So this is what death looks like. She had no tears.

Jessie, the good twin, dies, and Jordan, the bad seed, lives, and everyone believes the opposite. Is that irony or what? Memories drifted by of their life together: how happy they'd been to share their birthdays and everyday identity. Happy times until they weren't. Swapping clothes, misleading teachers, deceiving boyfriends, making Payden's life a living hell with their pranks—everyday twin stuff. There wasn't a mean bone in her body. I got all the mean. When did my mean show up? When did we stop being friends? Everyone loved Jessie. Everyone put up with me. And here I am, playing our twin game again. Everyone thinks the good twin survived, as it should be. What if I never tell them the truth? Could I get away with it?

Jordan mentally moved back to the day of the accident. She leaned over to touch Jessie's cold face. Why did you stay behind? Why didn't you come inside with me? Why are you dead? Touching her opened up the little space in Jordan's heart. What am I going to do without you? Now the tears came.

Jordan turned away from Jessie's body, and a sound of grief only a few people would understand or feel erupted from her. The unrecognizable sound passed upward through her body, and she opened her mouth and emitted a wailing noise.

Payden entered the room, stopped, and felt that heaven had never heard such a sound. He gently held her and let her sob until she stopped. Now there were no tears, and Jordan's transfiguration to Jessie was complete.

As Payden embraced his sister, a sudden chill ran through his body.

26

Around three in the heated afternoon, the Pennington women were discharged from the hospital, but Jordan had to stay an extra day. Meg's car was still at the Oasis Casino from two nights ago when the violence had occurred. Since Rachael had the only set of wheels, they decided to head home in her car, stopping at Earl's Castle for an early dinner. Hearts were heavy, but they managed a laugh as they passed through the double doors to the bar, ready to relax, eat, and drink. The persistent monsoon wind whipped around them, slamming the doors after they entered.

A favorite restaurant with the locals, the Castle was only a block off 95 and adjacent to the community park. Featuring a home-cooked meal of meatloaf, chicken fried steak, or daily specials, the small café was usually busy but not at this hour. Town news and gossip were also served to those sitting at the bar.

Earl beamed his abundant smile as his favorite family entered. "Oh, look what the monsoon blew in. Must be a huge celebration when the whole gang shows up at one time." He dried his hands on his apron and gave Grace a hug. "What'll it be?"

"Let's sit at the bar. I need a long straw to the nearest vodka bottle," said Meg.

"Any long table will be fine, Earl," Grace answered. Iced water came, lunch was ordered, and instant chatter filled the room. Everyone was excited to be alive and together as a family.

Before the salads arrived, Grace felt her phone vibrate. Annoyed at the intrusion, she glanced at the display. "Take cover…Duck. Now."

Meg stood and banged her fork against the glass of her Long Island iced tea. "Hear, hear. Let's raise our glasses. All is well in Bullhead. It's about time. We sure as hell need a break."

As Meg lifted her glass to drink a resounding toast to life, Grace jumped up. "Take cover!" she yelled, tipping the long dining table over with one move. She grabbed Meg on her way down and pulled out her Beretta.

Meg went flying for cover. She kept her head down but finally looked up at Grace, who was peering around the overturned table. "Mom, what the hell are you doing? You've got a gun?"

Grace grabbed Meg's head. "Keep down."

Glasses went flying, along with the silverware, plates, and napkins. Rachael and Amanda ducked behind the other table. They grabbed Earl on the way down. The south wall exploded as an out-of-control car smashed into the restaurant. The wood paneling splintered into a million pieces, followed by the merciless wind. The solid exterior had saved everyone from annihilation.

Meg crawled over to her mother. "You see anyone?"

A quick look. "It's a car." She took another quick look. "Kids running away."

Amanda and Rachael pulled their guns and took turns peeking around the overturned table. "You go left, Rach. I'll cover Earl."

Rachael peered around the table, and through the rubble she saw three kids running from the scene. "Looks like teenagers running."

Another text. Grace grabbed her cell phone, which displayed,

You okay?

Grace returned the text to Luke.

What the hell was that?

Kids joyriding. I'll take over. You go home. No threat.

"Stay down, Earl," Rachael said as she and Amanda carefully stood and brushed the debris from their clothes. He obliged. "Put your guns away. All clear," she said as the two investigated the wrecked vehicle. She helped her mother to her feet. "What the hell are you doing with a gun, Mom?"

"Yeah, what's with that?" chimed in Meg.

"A new toy I picked up at Big Lots. Why should you girls have all the fun?" Grace straightened her shirt, helped Meg return the table to its upright position, and then with her motherly voice said, "It's time to go. What a picture we make. Well defended against a runaway car. Let's pray this isn't an omen sent by Grandma Pauline. Let's go home." She walked over to Earl, who was standing in the middle of his ruined restaurant, shaking his head, and hurling obscenities.

"What do you mean, 'Go home'? We need to find out if this is part of Elliott's doing," insisted Meg.

"It's not."

"How can you be so sure?" This was Rachael's town, and she was a cop. "I need to investigate." She started outside to check on the car. The subsiding wind greeted her with a gust, giving her an eyeful of grit.

Earl walked through the wreckage, stepping over remnants of broken tables, booths, and food, and finally gave in to the absurdity of the situation. With a smirk, he asked the family to stay for lunch on him. "I'll even dust off the table for you if I can find one. Only in Bullhead do you get this kind of kinky offer."

The Penningtons declined the sarcastic proposal and headed outside. Picking fragments of brick from their clothes and hair, they headed into the heat as Amanda holstered her gun.

"Helluva day," Meg said. "Mom, who sent the text? How did you know to take cover?"

"A guardian angel." She didn't offer any more.

Amanda leaned over and whispered, "Named Luke?"

"Mind your own business." Grace gave her a bump on the hip and a "Be careful" look.

Rachael was staring into a driverless car when they joined her. "Looks like it's been hot-wired. Probably some kids from the trailer park." A blue-and-white patrol car pulled up as she prepared to call it in.

"Hey, Rachael. Looks like danger follows you around these days. We've got this."

She greeted her fellow officer with a nod. "Thanks. Since Elliott didn't have anything to do with it, it's all yours. I'm hoping to get rid of this black cloud as soon as I get into the river. You know how that goes."

"Right on. Catch you later." They were river cops and knew the healing powers of the Colorado.

The four women silently climbed into the car and headed home, happy to be alive but tired of the drama.

The single-story, three-bedroom home was waiting for them. Grace had purchased the house years ago, when the girls were small, and it was always their magical home, their summer retreat. Small, but not too small, the kitchen and living room displayed a wall of windows with a sliding door leading to the expansive covered patio deck. Spiral stairs led down to the lower deck, which was only steps from the blue Colorado River. Grace had paid to have a boat dock installed, and the family spent hours sitting on the dock, watching life float by. Everyone piled out of the car as the electric garage door closed behind them.

"Turn on the swamp cooler. The house is hot!" yelled Rachael as she headed for her bedroom.

"Too much humidity. Won't work," replied Amanda. The house had been empty for four days, and it felt as if an incendiary bomb had been set off.

Immediately after kicking off her shoes and putting on some shorts, Rachael took a jug of white wine out of the refrigerator and grabbed four plastic glasses and her gun. "Meet you guys down at the dock. I've got the wine." Nothing could be done about Elliott or Josh for the moment, so the time was right for a little family bonding.

Eight legs dangled over the edge of the boat dock. At four thirty, the temperature had dropped to 108 degrees, which was cool for an August afternoon, and only a few wisps of wind penetrated the afternoon. The water showed few signs of the monsoon that had ripped through the area and reluctantly moved on, and the WaveRunners weren't out yet to screw up the almost-flat water. Quiet. Peaceful.

Beside each woman was a glass of wine, and a Glock and a .22 sat between Rachael and Amanda. Meg stood, grabbed the dock pole, leaned over, and kicked some frigid river water at Rachael.

"Hey, watch it. Don't dilute my wine."

"Don't you girls get tired of lugging around those weapons?" asked Grace.

"We're never fully dressed without a gun. Is that from *Annie?*"

"That's a smile, idiot," said Meg, and then she sang a few lines of "Tomorrow." They laughed and begged her to stop. The river calm was taking over.

Grace continued, "Looks like this is it for a while." She glanced down at the row of her beautiful daughters. "You kids are headed in different directions and for different reasons. Say good-bye to your Grandma Pauline. I'm sure she's sitting on that cumulus cloud up there." They all looked up and nodded. "Probably will shed a few raindrop tears before you leave tomorrow." Grace belted out the first stanza of "Raindrops Keep Falling on My Head," much to the dismay of her daughters. Family tradition required breaking into song whenever a sentence came anywhere close to a musical.

Meg piped up. "Stop. Please. Don't torture us anymore. You know, Mom, everyone thinks I'm nuts when I talk about the clouds and Grandma Pauline. It's really nice to be here with you guys who understand."

"Amanda, where are you headed?" asked Rachael as she kicked some water at an inquisitive duck that was getting too close.

"FBI is sending me to San Diego. Might go undercover on a cruise ship. Dancer, maybe? Guess those dance lessons are finally paying off, Mom. If any of you end up in Catalina, the ship does an eight-hour layover there. We'll connect."

"For sure, I'm going to Catalina. Cleared a six-month leave of absence from the PD. Got to find that bitch who kidnapped Josh and fix her little red wagon. Might have a job lined up with the Conservancy. Security guard." Rachael turned away from her sisters and let her gray matter float on the nearest cloud, taking a trip into a rocky future.

Meg was getting antsy. "I don't have a job yet, and the high season is coming to an end in Catalina. Otherwise, I might be able to teach scuba diving or some other water stuff. Jessie's decided to go with me. She'll talk to Joe at the stables and see if she can get a job. I might have to bartend."

Rachael changed her aim and kicked some water at her. "What if...Say that doesn't work out. How about college?"

"You know, Rach. I don't really care right now. Life is so screwed up. Bumming around Catalina might be what the doctor ordered. I can always stay at Mom's and go to Cal State if I ever get motivated again. Or go back to Mohave Community."

"How well do you know this Jessie? She made a really quick decision to move in with you...kind of spur of the moment. How rational is that?" said Amanda. "Seems like she tripped through the mourning period pretty damn quick."

"I know she's just running away from facing her old life. Her brother and I have talked about it. But he says she's funny, reliable, and good natured. So that all fits in with my lifestyle. We'll know after the first few weeks."

No one had addressed the underlying problem of Elliott. None of the women wanted to spoil one of the few moments the four had together. Bonding was a fundamental tenet of the family.

Footsteps echoed on the boat ramp, and the conversation stopped as all heads turned toward the sound. Amanda immediately recognized the man. Meg looked, worried it might be Elliott, then turned back, totally disinterested. She drank some more of her wine, while Rachael reached for her gun.

"Afternoon, ladies," said Luke. "Mind if I join you?" He'd kicked off his shoes. He had on a bathing suit and a tan-colored wifebeater. Everyone noticed his penetrating blue eyes as he approached.

Amanda reached over and touched her mother's hand. "I'll take Rachael upstairs and tell her. Now's a great time to come clean. Let Meg know," she whispered. Amanda jumped up, gave Luke a halfhearted hug, and whispered, "Welcome to the family. Good luck with your daughter. She can be a pistol." She reached down and picked up her gun.

Amanda's gesture surprised everyone.

"Rachael and Meg, this is Luke, Mom's friend. Luke, Rachael and I would love to sit and talk for a while, but we have packing to do." She slugged Rachael on the shoulder. "Get your gun and come on."

"What are you talking about? Who is this guy? Mom?" Rachael wasn't going to be dismissed that easily. "Let go of me, Amanda." She slapped her sister's hands as Amanda tried to pull her to a standing position. "I haven't finished my wine. What's with you?"

Amanda reached down and poured the rest of Rachael's wine into the river. "There. Now the fish can enjoy their afternoon swim around the dock. Come on, sis. We need to get started." She turned her head so that only Rachael could see, made an ugly face, and spoke another "Come on" with threatening overtones.

Rachael stood up and looked at her mom. She had too many questions and wouldn't leave.

Grace recognized that the stubborn side of Rachael was appearing, and with a stern look, she addressed the situation. "Amanda will answer all of your questions upstairs. At least she'll try. I need to speak to Luke and Meg right now. Please."

Rachael saw that her mother was uptight. Totally not like Mom to let anyone see her unnerved. "Okay, I can tell when I'm not wanted. Nice to meet you, Luke, I think?" Rachael was reluctant to leave, so Amanda grabbed her free hand and yanked her up the boat ramp.

"Nice to meet you, too. I know." There was a spot to sit next to Grace, so he took Rachael's left-behind glass, filled it with wine, leaned over, poured more into Grace's glass, and joined in the foot soaking.

"Mom, what's this all about?" Meg nudged her mom on the shoulder and shot a quizzical look her way. "You been holding out on us? A beau, at your age?"

Grace sighed and thought. I guess this is the right time to tell her. For her to meet her father. Was I right in keeping this from her for all these years? Will she understand? "Meg, darling, finish your wine and take a deep breath. We have a story for you."

Luke leaned back and watched the cirrus clouds float by. Good luck, darling.

"Twenty-three years ago..." Not the way to start the story. She took another sip of wine and waited.

27

History had repeated itself each summer on the magical island of Catalina. Grace would rent the same bungalow for four weeks and take the girls vacationing, to their delight. Josh, a full-time resident, would check with the rental office in town and always be waiting on the dock as Rachael and her family stepped off the *Flyer*. It was obvious to all that Rachael and Josh's summer romance would continue where it had left off the year before.

When it all began, Rachael was an eight-year-old, flat-chested tomboy, but the two played the growing-up game until that last year when Rachael had teased him, saying, "If you get lucky, I might flash my thirty Cs at you." Rachael loved him intensely with a summer love that had carried on for ten years, but when Rachael was eighteen, the family no longer vacationed on the island. That's when Stella made her move.

During the winter months, Josh dated every available girl on the island, and finally Stella nailed him. The sex was different, unusual, and their relationship lasted for six months until he realized she was psychotic as hell and tried to break up. When Josh dumped her last summer and took up with Rachael again, Stella hoped it was just their usual summer romance. She heard that the two had a falling out, and when Rachael left Catalina and headed back to Bullhead, Stella tried to make her move. Josh was friendly but wary, and he stayed at arm's length. Stella pleaded with Greg, Josh's partner on the PD, to fix the problem, but he refused to get involved with her shenanigans. When Stella heard Josh's memory was impaired from the shooting in Bullhead, she swooped in. It was her final chance.

She hired a private plane from the Airport in the Sky, flew to Bullhead, grabbed a taxi in the intolerable heat, and found her way to his hospital room. Entrapping him had to be accomplished before his memory of the last few months returned. Once married, she felt she could convince him to stay with her, especially if she were pregnant. Screw Rachael. He'll get over her. Handling him, guiding him, and nursing him were going to be risky, since it would be necessary to hide him from his friends at the sheriff's department and keep him sedated for a week.

She needed a refill of Cialis or a more potent prescription for erectile dysfunction, and she also wanted some Versed and GHB to control Josh. *I've still got those forged script pads from the hospital. Can't fill them on Catalina. Maybe the Internet. Need my black-market contact. His name? What's his name? Need his name.* Her frenzied, schizophrenic mind was whirling as she dug through her purse. She had forgotten to pack her bipolar medication when she left Catalina, and the results were exhibited in her neurotic behavior. *Shit. Control, control. I've got to keep it together.*

That snarky blonde marred the first part of the abduction, but here he is in the taxi with me. "How ya doing, honey?" Stella asked as she glanced over at Josh. "A couple of miles, and we'll be at the Bullhead Airport. Then off we go to Catalina." The cab was winding through the slow traffic on 95; everyone was pulling boats and WaveRunners to the dam. She yelled at the driver, "Honk your damn horn. Get those assholes out of the way!" She needed her meds.

Josh was still feeling the effects of the sedative the hospital had given him and could barely get out of the taxi when they pulled up to the unloading zone. "Come on, Stella, what's the hurry? You're acting like we're running away." His muscular frame and usual energy eluded him, and he leaned against the newspaper rack for support as Stella hurried to grab an available wheelchair.

"No, silly. Just anxious to get you home and back on your feet. Your captain called and said to take two weeks off. He's holding your job."

He shook his head and tried to blink through the mental fog. "I know this sounds dumb, but were Meg and Rachael fighting in my room? I remember bits and pieces of it. Were they fighting?"

Shit. "Oh no, I had *General Hospital* on the TV. I thought they looked a little like the sisters, too."

"But I got into the fight, didn't I?" He rubbed his biceps and felt instant pain in his rotator cuff from the stretch. "Did I fall out of bed and land on my shoulder?"

"Not really. You were sleeping. Probably had a nightmare." Her nerves were beginning to fray again, stretching the limits of control.

"Hmm. It seemed so real." Josh was still in the hospital gown and became embarrassed by his attire. "Where's my cell phone? I'd like to find out what's going on back home." He fumbled around, looking for pockets and his phone.

"It got smashed on the boat dock when you were shot. I've called and ordered you a new one. It'll be waiting for you when we get home. Department issue." *Stop asking questions.*

"I can't fly home in pajamas. Where are my clothes?"

Stella realized he was getting more agitated and tried to smooth his hair. He pulled away. "Too bloody to wash. I picked up some stuff at Walmart on the way to the hospital. It's in this bag." She dumped the bag on his lap. "You can dress here at the airport." *Too many questions.*

Josh seemed satisfied with the answers and closed his eyes to rest. Stella dialed her girlfriend in Catalina as she pushed him toward the restrooms. "Trish. Need a favor."

"Where are you? Man, one day we're eating lunch at Jack's. Next day you're in Bullhead. What gives?"

"Josh has been shot, and I'm bringing him home. Plane is gassing up, and we can leave in an hour. I've called my real estate agent and rented that tiny house on Eucalyptus. The one behind Flip's last place."

"What? Why? You own a house, and Josh owns a house. Why? You made out of money or something? What's goin' on?"

"Shut up and listen." Stella didn't have time to argue. "Have the utilities turned on in your name, not mine. Today. I'll reimburse you."

Trish became concerned. While she was a good friend of Stella's, she knew there were mental problems. Bipolar? Schizo? Stella had been in love with Josh for years. When he'd broken up with her, she'd stalked him, and he finally had to get a restraining order to keep her away. Trish really didn't want to get involved with one of her escapades, but she was afraid not to help. "What are you up to?" she said more forcefully.

Irritated and impatient, Stella didn't want Josh to overhear any of the conversation, and his meds were wearing off. "Damn it. Just do it." She slammed the phone shut. As she neared the men's room, a man held the door open for her to push Josh's chair through the entrance. "Sir, my fiancé has just had surgery and might need a little help changing into his clothes. If you wouldn't mind keeping an eye on him to make sure he doesn't fall, I'd appreciate it."

"No problem."

She pushed Josh's chair through the door and said, "I'll check on our plane. You change." Her mind was starting to drift. *Is this where the plane was going to be? Why is that man staring at me?* She checked her clothing since she felt naked all of a sudden. *I can't have an episode now. I have to marry Josh. Should have brought my meds.* She turned and leaned against the wall, pressing her head against the surface. Blackness was closing in on her. She felt someone taping on her arm. Wide eyed, she turned, ready to fight any demons that had found her.

"Hey, Stella. I've been looking for you. The plane's gassed, and we're ready to go. I filed the flight plan, but where's Josh?"

She tried to remember. "Josh?" *In the hospital, no...He's in the john... Yeah, in the john.* "Go ahead. We'll be right behind you."

"You sure he's okay to fly? He looks pretty sick. Saw him when you got out of the taxi. Hey, and you ain't lookin' too great, either. I don't want you guys to zonk out on the plane."

"Not your business, damn it. He's fine. We'll meet you in ten minutes." She was getting more frantic with each passing second.

When Josh walked out of the men's room, pushing the wheelchair, Stella rushed to his side. "You look great, honey." She kissed him. "Take my arm." She shoved the chair away, and it hit a man pulling a suitcase.

"Hey, watch it, bitch."

"Shove it, asshole."

The traveler took a closer look at Stella, and because of the crazy look in her eyes and the frenzied red hair, he decided to pass on an altercation.

Josh didn't return her kiss. Something felt wrong. He didn't want to kiss her, or marry her. No way. He shook his head again, trying to clear his mind, but nothing helped. He started to take a step, and the large muscles in his legs seized—a huge muscle cramp—and he bit back a screech. Realizing that Stella was his only hope for help at the time, he said, "I'd better sit down."

Stella twitched while she waited for Josh to rest, then abruptly pulled him to a standing position and pushed him toward the waiting plane.

After the Cessna took off, Stella began to relax. Her headache wasn't squashing her brain now, and she felt more in control. "It'll be dark when we land at Airport in the Sky. I've got a cart stashed. Quick trip home, and off to bed we go."

Searching for a sense of independence, Josh asked, "I'll be going to my house, right?"

Stella could feel that Josh was getting nervous about the arrangements. *Memory coming back? Shit.* "We'll see."

28

Amanda continued pushing Rachael up the circular stairs to the house. "Get going. Hurry up. We've got packing to do."

"Packing? Like hell. Quit shoving me. What the *F* is going on? Who *is* that guy?" Rachael glanced over her shoulder and saw Grace sidling up to Meg.

"First, we fix a double Jack and Coke, and then I'll tell you what I know." She grabbed two glasses, plunked some ice cubes from the dispenser, and poured two strong drinks. "Here, sis. Come over and sit by me. Bottoms up."

"Since when do we drink the hard stuff in the middle of the day?" She accepted the drink and took a long sip. "Wow. Strong."

"Since now. You'll need it. This is what Mom told me when we were stranded in the desert…"

***

Meg's curiosity was piqued over this new guy, but instead of being her impetuous self, she pulled an inner tube over to the boat dock and flopped in. She decided to play the game and wait for Grace to start the conversation. It didn't work. Grace just smiled, drank some wine, and stared across the river, idly splashing water with her feet.

When Grace and this man, Luke, seemed satisfied to ignore her and live in the minute, Meg finally gave up. She paddled the tube forward. "Okay, Mom. You should know I'm not ready for any more surprises today. What's going on? Who is this dude?" Meg stared up at Luke, and his penetrating blue eyes startled her. There was something familiar about him. When Luke returned her look, she couldn't hold the moment, so she switched her attention to her mother. "Well?"

Grace didn't know where to start. For twenty-three years, she had role-played this moment, but now that it was here, she couldn't find the words. She momentarily reflected on Meg's hideous year. A year that had almost broken her. She prayed Meg was strong enough to accept her real heritage but worried that their relationship would be marred forever. A chance she had to take. "Meg, I'll start with the bottom line, but I implore you to listen to the whole story before you get pissed off and leave. First, I love you. Everything I have withheld from you was to protect you." Before continuing, she looked at Luke, who patted her hand and then reached for his wine. "Luke is your birth father. In 19—"

"My what?" Meg's head snapped around to look at the man sitting next to Grace. Her father? He returned her look with an expression that changed between love and sorrow. "What are you talking about?" She grabbed the lead line tied to the inner tube and pulled close to the boat dock. "My dad…Amanda and Rachael's dad, our dad…died before I was born."

"Meg, listen, please. Luke and I were both with the CIA. I've been retired for a number of years, but he's still an active agent. He saved Amanda and me from the desert." Grace tried to pack in the facts before Meg could interrupt again.

"CIA? Mom, are you crazy? What are you talking about? But how? When? You're lying." She put her foot on the dock and pushed away. "Where the hell has he been all these years? CIA?" Questions were flying through her brain. Staggered by the news, she tried to untie the inner tube to escape.

"Wait, damn it. Listen." Grace had expected a scene and was prepared to fight. She yanked on the rope, pulling Meg back to the dock. "We were both married on an assignment in Brazil. Amanda and Rachael were with me. Luke's wife was an alcoholic. They had two children, a boy and girl."

"Ah, shit, Mom. What are you saying? I'm his bastard kid? I have a brother? And sister? Damn it. Mom, I'm so pissed off at you! How could you keep this from me?" The betrayal was so deep, she couldn't cry. She turned to

Luke. "And where the hell have you been…, Luke,…for all my life?" Meg looked at Grace, then at Luke, with anger welling up; she was too hurt to continue.

"Luke was separated from his wife. She attempted suicide when he asked her for a divorce. His kids were small. Meg, I know this is a lot to take in. I made up my mind that our love wasn't as important as his kids' future. I was afraid they'd hate me, and you, if we proceeded with our plans of marriage, so I broke it off. Luke didn't know I was pregnant. When you were one year old, I called him, and we discussed your future."

Meg crawled out of the tube and onto the rocking dock. She stood, holding onto the upright for support. Eyes fixed on the island. Shaking her head.

"When you were fifteen, Luke's wife died. We have been in love for all these years, but I made him promise not to interfere until I said it was time. I guess time has caught up with us."

"God, I can't believe this." Meg staggered as another wave hit the dock; she felt spent. Didn't know how to filter all the information. "So, Amanda and Rachael aren't my real sisters? How could you?"

Luke stood and blocked her way as she started for the ramp. The dock shifted again, from a second swell, and he caught her.

She looked at him, then at her mother, then at Luke again. "What am I supposed to do with all this? I don't know what to think." Near tears, she pushed away from Luke's hold. "I'm so tired of all this shit in my life. Let me go. I want no part of you."

"Meg, look at me," said Luke. "Your mother's love and secret should never be questioned. Her life has revolved around you and your sisters. Don't find fault with her now. It would kill her."

Meg started to cry. Heartbroken.

Luke tried to hold her. "I want to be part of your life, but that's your decision. It's totally up to you."

She put her hand against his chest and pushed him back. "Damn right, it's my decision. Now you're giving me advice? Go to hell. Both of you." She headed up to the house, emotionally numb. The foundation of her life had always been her family. Family had kept her sane during the serial killer year, and now to learn the base had been built on a lie was devastating. Her world shattered into a million questions.

Amanda and Rachael watched from the balcony deck as Meg ran across the dock ramp. At the top of the stairs, they tried to embrace her. "Hey, sis. Big day, huh?" A Jack and Coke was waiting for her. Rachael went for a hug.

"Don't call me *sis*. It'll never be the same. I don't need your hugs right now. You're not even my sisters." She hurried down the hall to her bedroom and slammed the door before the tears came crashing down.

***

Luke helped Grace to her feet. She put her head on his shoulder and moaned. "Oh, Luke. Did we do the right thing? How will this ever end?"

"She'll be fine. Just give her time. I love you."

She smiled and looked at him, into those deep, deep blue eyes that always intrigued her. "And I love you. I didn't think the day would ever come when we would say these words openly and not in secret."

"You like?"

"I like."

As they started up the boat ramp hand in hand, Meg reappeared on the balcony, rage registering in her eyes. "Hey, you. Give me the phone number for my so-called brother." Tears had given way to anger.

29

The seaplane made a rough landing on the far side of Catalina Island. Swells were almost two feet, leaving the pilot little room for error. The setting sun, cascading over the Pacific, painted Catalina onto an eerie canvas—a tiny, vulnerable spot of land plopped onto an endless blue ocean.

"Drivers will meet us. Rangers have gone home for the night." Derek felt fatigued and not only from the rescue of Elliott; he was becoming more and more apprehensive about his future. Mental fatigue transferred into physical fatigue. "Shouldn't be a problem going ashore." He busied himself with gathering the bags.

"The high season will last for two more months. It's a perfect time to build our stable of luscious women to sell. I'll prepare a questionnaire we'll send to our international contacts. We need to know how many blondes or brunettes." Elliott smirked. "Like, order a babe online. I also have a gem of an idea to fill the inventory. How about movie auditions at the beach for walk-on roles in our never-to-be-made film? Those blond whores will come flocking to us. Stunning."

He leered. Derek could almost see him salivate. Disgusting. "If you're making all of these elaborate plans just to capture Meg again, why the hell don't you just grab her now? We know every step she takes." He tried to act blasé about the whole matter.

"The intrigue of Meg is secondary, and I can wait. I have deflowered her, and she has rejected me. Now, I've decided to wipe out her whole family, but in the process, I'll make her suffer. I need to punish her again, and then…we'll see. Since you took Grace and Amanda out, that only leaves two to deal with." Elliott waited for a response.

"Yeah, right." Derek fidgeted. He hated Elliott's pompous attitude. He rubbed his head where Elliott had smashed it against the window earlier. He wanted to duck out of this conversation, so he opened the seaplane door and jumped off the pontoon onto the wet sand. A small wave crashed in, and the pilot helped him tug the plane to shore. "Use the tie-downs to anchor the plane to those rocks," he said to the pilot. "You'll have to take off before daylight. Otherwise you'll be spotted."

Elliott threw the few pieces of luggage to Derek, complaining about the constant pain from his gunshot wound. "Get me some pain pills. I might have popped a stitch." A trickle of blood showed through his shirt.

Get me this. Do that. Derek, tiring of the constant orders, questioned Elliott's ability to run the business. His obsession over Meg and her family was destroying a profitable enterprise. Is he finished with our money laundering and the pirated body parts? Derek headed up the steep climb where the Jeep was waiting, opened the back door, and crawled in.

Elliott watched his brother. Derek's newfound morality and dishonesty surprised him. Leaving Amanda and Grace in the desert and not following orders were paramount to mutiny. Placing the family in jeopardy was unforgivable. Elliott waited for his brother to come forward with the truth about the botched assignment, but Derek continued on with the deception. Elliott struggled up the hill, holding his seeping wound, grabbed the car door, and pushed for an answer. "Is there something you need to tell me?"

Derek looked away and tried to shut the door. "About what?"

Elliott's features turned dark. "Last chance." He turned, shuffled through the sand, and sat on a rock. Arms crossed, glaring, he didn't move.

"Nothing to tell." Derek knew he was close to a crash-and-burn scene.

"Let me make this easy on you. When I was in custody, Rachael gloated and told me that Amanda and Grace had been saved from their desert death. Sunburned and dehydrated but also alive and healthy."

Derek was frantic to improvise a believable story. "Let me tell you what happened."

"No. Let me tell *you* what happened before you exacerbate the problem. You left them where I told you but didn't shoot them. Idiot. Now they're back and can identify you and Marisa. You would be dead if you weren't my brother. No one survives betraying me."

"So, what now? Do I have to watch my back when we're together?" Derek found a brief moment of bravado. He climbed out of the Jeep and started for Elliott.

The pilot stepped in front of Elliott and handed him something, then moved behind Derek. An instant later, the pilot slipped a garrote over Derek's head and pulled it tight around his neck before he had time to react.

"Hold him still." Elliott moved forward with his unsheathed Ka-bar knife and grabbed Derek's left hand. With one move, he sliced through the bottom half of the pinky finger with the serrated blade. Blood spurted, and Derek wrenched away. The pilot loosened the wire, and Derek slumped to the ground, wincing in pain. "Wrap up his finger, and let's get out of here."

Besides the pain, Derek recoiled with the stern realization that his time was limited. Elliott was a maniac, and there was no way to rationalize with him. He staggered to his feet.

Elliott put the knife away but pulled his Beretta from his pants and shot twice, the bullets kicking up sand close to Derek's feet. "When, and if, I decide to kill you, you'll see it coming. I will slice different parts from your pathetic body and send them Express Mail to your sister. You never have been worth shit. Don't make the same mistake again. Understood?"

Reprieve,...you sick son of a bitch. Quick to thank whatever god he believed in, Derek climbed back into the Jeep, putting pressure on his finger. Elliott sat in the front seat and cleaned his knife. Derek had to change the conversation and decided to show an interest in Elliott's new enterprise. "What kind of income will we get from selling women? Have you thought that through?" He peered out the window as the night grew dark and the unpaved roads to the hideout gave way to massive chuckholes in the dirt trail. Rocky and treacherous, the road was used mainly by the bison to travel at night. Other than the headlights, the only light came from the suggestion of a rising moon.

Elliott scoffed, "You think this is just a folly? Any beautiful, full-bodied, white female, age eighteen through twenty-six, will bring five hundred grand easy. Our dark-skinned friends love the white, luscious bodies, and they have bundles of money to spend on any perverted idea that suits them."

"Why not sixteen-year-olds? They should really be tender stuff." The thought nauseated him.

"Too many inquisitive parents looking for their brats. Emancipated is what we need. Heady, healthy, self-centered women looking to break into the movies. There should be scores of them in Orange County ready to throw themselves at us. Narcissistic bitches."

"Yeah, well, say we only sell twenty a month. That's peanuts to what we've been doing with those body parts." His finger was throbbing. "You should rethink the price. Five hundred large is nothing to their sort. And what about the start-up costs? Marisa should look at the numbers."

Elliott's scowled again. "Since when do you tell me how to run my business? Remarks like that don't bode well with me. Don't push your luck."

At least he's off the subject of Amanda and Grace. "All of your other escapades haven't involved direct contact with the personnel. Think about it. We'll be on board with the victims. What if something goes wrong? Money laundering, body parts, illegals…You never got close to the action. You were just the boss, the overseer. But this? It's too risky."

"Careful, Derek. Don't overstep your position. Your last transgression is still pretty raw."

Derek decided not to respond. He raised his arm above the level of his heart to relieve the throbbing finger and glanced toward the horizon. Lights were beginning to twinkle from the boats moored off shore. As night fell, an uninvited, ominous dark spread through his thoughts, making him oblivious to the beauty and peace that surrounded him.

Tension was thick. The household was fragmented. Luke and Grace spent forty minutes on the boat dock discussing Meg's outburst. Inside the house, Amanda and Rachael packed and tiptoed around Meg's high drama. Meg, flipping back and forth between feeling betrayed, pissed off, and hurt, decided to phone her new brother.

"Yes, hello. Is this Carl?"

"It is. Who's calling?"

Meg waited. What to say? Exactly who am I? "Well, my name is Meg Pennington, and, well, I guess I'm your half sister."

Silence. "I've been waiting for this phone call for a long time. How are you, sis?"

Meg, expecting questions, was surprised by the response, momentarily losing her focus. She anticipated explaining a bunch of history she didn't know anything about, but here was this open, friendly man—her brother—who had been waiting for the call. "I'm, well, I'm not sure how I am. Apparently you know about me?"

"Dad told me the whole story about five years ago, after my mom died. Made me promise to keep the secret until, gosh, until now, I guess. I can't wait to meet you."

"Me too," she stammered. This new relationship was like instant oatmeal. "Wow, that was easy." Now what to say? "I guess we should meet?"

"I live in San Diego. Your mom's house is in Yorba Linda? How about I come up there and take you out to dinner? Work for you?"

"Dinner?" This was going too fast. "Sure. What about your sister?"

"She's a little fragile. Lives in Seattle. I'll give her a call, but honestly, I know she won't want to meet you right away. I'll talk to her. Sorry."

Meg felt the first pangs of sibling rivalry but quickly dismissed it. "No problem. It's her right. Well, my mom and your dad—our dad—just came in. Guess I'd better go talk to them. I don't have a clue where to begin. I'm really pissed off at Mom for not telling me sooner. Feel like I've been cheated out of a relationship with your dad. Any suggestions on where to start?"

"Your call. Just know that he's loved you and your mom all of your life. No doubt on that."

"Weird way of showing it. You know I'm twenty-three, don't you? They've had years to do this, so why now? My sisters are only half, you're half, and I'm a bastard kid. Proverbial gal without a country."

"Dad said that Grace didn't want to tell you until you'd had some life experience so that understanding would come easier. Sounds logical. What do you think?"

"What do I think?" Meg leaned into the chest of drawers and drew a deep breath. Her reflection in the mirror startled her. The pursed lips, the sad eyes— not the Meg she was used to seeing. "Shit. My life just tumbled into a trash can."

Carl waited, searching for an appropriate word to say. He remained silent.

"Guess I'm beyond thinking right now. One thing for sure: it seems like they both cheated on their spouses."

"Water under the bridge. Have you ever been in love?"

Such a poignant question; she paused to find a truthful answer. "Probably not. Not real love but heavy infatuations. Why?"

"Their relationship has lasted two decades, so I'm thinking they're the lucky ones. I figure, who am I to question that? Or throw the first stone? I'm okay with it, but I've known about it for years. Probably hard for you to get."

"I have so many questions. Don't know where to start. What's he like?"

"Smart, genuine, compassionate. Can be hardheaded and definitely strong as a mule. He's a great guy. He did a bitchin' job in raising us. God, I look back on it and wonder how he got through it…I mean, loving your mom like he has. Well, go easy on him, if you can."

"Hmm. Strange. As of an hour ago, I now have the perfect father, a new brother, and a sister who doesn't want to meet me. A brother…something I always wanted, but I didn't expect the stork to deliver you full grown." She felt Carl was being sincere in his portrayal of Luke. She sighed and collected her thoughts. "There's something you should know about me. I'm a pistol, and going easy isn't my style."

"So I hear." Carl laughed and continued. "I also hear you are a loving, forgiving person. Might want to concentrate on that."

"Advice already?" She bristled a little.

"Oops, looks like a stepped over the line. Sorry 'bout that."

"No problem." And she meant it.

"Sorry to say this, but I have to go. Staff meeting. 'Bye for now, sis. Glad you called. I'll be in touch tomorrow, and we can make plans. If you need to talk, call."

"Be careful what you offer, bro. Might take you up on it."

Carl could hear the conflict in Meg's voice and understood her struggle. "'Bye. Tell Dad hi for me."

Meg was still unnerved when she walked into the living room. All conversation stopped. Grace crossed her arms, a move not missed by all three sisters. She was ready to take on Meg if necessary.

Well, I guess I could be the pouty Meg and make everyone uncomfortable, or I could throw a fit and belittle Mom and "Dad" about all the secrets, or I could do what my heart tells me to do. She padded across the wood flooring in her bathing suit and stopped in front of Luke. Looking into his eyes was like looking in the mirror. Same blue. "Welcome to the family, Dad." The same blue eyes filled with mist.

Luke folded his arms around her and pulled her close. Meg felt the caring. Grace looked at her other two daughters, tipped her head, and the three left the room.

***

Grace, Amanda, and Rachael took their drinks and settled in the rattan furniture on the balcony overlooking the river. No one knew where to start.

"You okay, Mom?" Amanda began. Her heart was twisted like a fraying rope between happiness for her mom and sadness for Meg.

"Sending Luke away before Meg was born was the most difficult thing I've ever done. My heart was shattered, but I knew it was the right thing to do for everyone except the two of us. So many of our young years had been spent apart, and yet our love never diminished with time. I often think of Meg as being my beautiful shoe I left behind at Cinderella's ball. Now my Prince Charming has found the shoe, and we will live happily ever after. Stupid, huh?" She fought back the tears.

Both Amanda and Rachael put their hands on their mother's knees and softly patted them. "Meg will be fine, Mom. Just give her some time. She'll see how much you two love each other and recognize the sacrifice. Just be patient with her," said Rachael.

"How much more drama does this family have to endure? You know this Elliott thing is not over yet," said Grace. She slowly shook her head and felt her age.

"Mom. You concentrate on Luke and get your future set up with him. We'll take care of Elliott. I promise to destroy his little red wagon. He won't survive our next encounter. Count on it," said Amanda.

"Ditto," chimed in Rachael.

An hour later, the sliding door opened, and Meg yelled. "Hey, it's okay to come back in the AC. You guys must be sweltering out there." Luke had his arm around her shoulder, and everyone breathed a sigh of relief as they headed inside.

It was time to get on with life, so the family spent the evening eating, drinking, probing, and laughing. The girls tried to wrangle some CIA stories out of Grace and Luke, but they would simply reply with, "No comment."

Sleeping arrangements were a little awkward at first, but Meg insisted, "Luke has to shack up with Mom for the night." When she handed out earplugs to her sisters, Grace threw a pillow at her.

The next morning Rachael took off in her Camaro for Yorba Linda. "Mom, is it okay if I leave my car at your house? I'll take the shuttle to Balboa and catch the *Flyer* to Catalina. I need to find Josh."

"Oh, of course. Make sure the neighbors are taking good care of the dog. Isn't Josh answering his cell phone?"

"No, and the sheriff's department hasn't heard from him. That bitch has him hidden."

"That story is pretty bizarre, Rachael. Have you tried his partner, Greg?"

"No answer there either. That was my first call. Greg knows everything that goes on around Avalon. He must be busy, 'cause he hasn't called back yet."

"Well, do what you have to. The department's put you on leave?"

"Six months. Then we'll see. Depends on what happens. Love you guys. I'm out of here." She grabbed her suitcase handle and started down the hall, stopping only to blow a kiss to the portrait of Grandma Pauline, a ritual with the family. Meg walked Rachael out through the garage into the searing heat, opened the trunk, and tossed the suitcase in. "Here's a water for you. Drive carefully."

"You okay, brat? Seems like you're taking this too casually for the Meg I know. I expected a tantrum, throwing shit, cussing, and crying. What gives?"

Meg smiled. "It is what it is. Talking to Carl helped a lot. I'm not the only kid that was involved in their transgressions."

"Hey, cool it with the 'transgressions' shit. You know better than to chastise anything Mom does."

"Sorry. Didn't really mean to say that. I know Mom has sacrificed the only love of her life for me. How cool is that? And Luke? Well, I think he's growing on me already."

"Well, well. Baby Meg is growing up. Love ya, sis. Gotta go." She backed her Camaro out of the driveway and cranked up the air-conditioning. Inserting the *Mamma Mia!* CD into the slot, she took off on her four-hour trip to Yorba Linda, hoping the fun music would drown out the worry over Josh and the ever-present Elliott.

Amanda was next. "Got a taxi out front waiting to take me to the Oasis. Gonna meet with Matt. His assignment is over now, so we'll head back to LA for debriefing on Elliott and work out details on my new job."

"Are they going to pursue Elliott?" Grace's voice had an edge to it.

Amanda had the same concerns. "I'll let you know what I can. You know my primary role in life is to keep Meg safe. I screwed up twice now but never again."

Grace looked at her oldest daughter, understood the urgency in her voice, and decided to lighten the parting subject. Her daughters were everything to her, and she was in awe of the loving, capable women they had become. "Anything going on between the two of you? You and Matt looked friendly at Christmas."

"Oh, Mom, ever the matchmaker. Time will tell. He's a great guy, but romance and guns aren't always the best combination for a long-term commitment. The FBI kind of frowns on it, too."

Grace laughed. "Well, the Penningtons aren't known for always following the rules, you know. Have you...well,...done it yet?"

"God, Mom, give it up." She threw an arm around Grace and laughed. Amanda glanced over as Luke entered the kitchen. "Not as lucky as you. I'm so happy for the two of you, I could cry. You're a good fit." She gave Grace another squeeze. "Hey, Luke, how about a little help with my bags? Taxi's waiting."

"No problem." He was delighted that the girls seemed to accept him. "FBI, huh? Let me know when you decide to join a real agency." He grinned at her scowl.

Meg rushed back into the house and grabbed her luggage. "Hey, wait. I need a ride."

"You the next to leave, honey?" asked Grace as Meg reappeared.

Meg could tell by her mother's expression that she wanted her to stay for a while longer. "Yeah. I'm packed and ready to go. I'll pick up my car from the casino and then zip over to get Jessie at the hospital. Her brother's been organizing the funeral in Norco. That'll be tomorrow, and then we'll go to your house for a week or so before heading to Catalina."

"Funeral. That's going to be really tough on her. Are you ready for that?"

"It's about time I start taking care of grown-up problems. I'll be fine, and I know she can use the support."

"Then what?"

"There's a casting call for 'bikini' girls at Balboa. Some movie they'll be making at the beach. Jess really wants to audition for it, so I said I'd go with her, but I won't run around in a bikini looking for work. That's not my style."

"Hey, it might be fun. Looks like you've got a cute little body like your mom." Luke grinned at Grace, who blushed.

125

Meg had to laugh at that. "Never seen you blush before, Mom. Cool. So, what are the plans for you two?" She was still a little cautious with the situation but decided to put her happy Meg into play.

"We'll clean up here, and then I have to get back home. My agent's pushing me for more chapters of my new book."

"How about you…Dad?"

"Agency has a new job for me in LA. Down the street from Amanda."

"Pushing a pencil? No more fieldwork?"

"Something like that."

Meg caught the sideward smile Grace threw his way. Sly fox. Mom's already told me about your promotion to CIA assistant director, running the LA office. Wow. A bigwig.

"You've got your dad's numbers. If anything or anyone looks suspicious, call us. Elliott is still out there. CIA seems to get answers faster than the FBI these days. Be careful. You're our baby."

"Oh, please. Baby?" She tossed her long blond hair back and crawled into the backseat of the taxi with her sister. "Well, here we go."

Luke took Grace's hand as the taxi pulled out of the driveway. Growing concern made her tense, and the charge coursed through his body.

"Don't worry. I've got it covered. Let's go fix a drink and fool around."

Grace threw a swift punch to his shoulder. "Beat you to the bedroom."

31

Stella continued lying to Josh. "The hospital's full. No beds for three days, so I found a rental close to the hospital for your outpatient care." She stopped the cart in front of a neglected wooden-frame structure surrounded by dead landscape. The street was dotted with summer rentals, and no pride of ownership was present.

He experienced a slight recall about the house as she steered him up the steps, unlocked the door, and entered the dingy living room. The house, a small one-bedroom rental with living room, kitchen, and bath, stood partially isolated from any caring neighbors. A nasty, brown, dilapidated couch slouched in the living room corner. A painted and chipped table and lamp; a fake Oriental rug, distressed from time; and grimy nicotine-stained shades decorated the room. Sparse, at best. A decorator's nightmare. Stella didn't want any local news to be flashed, fearing Josh might hear something about his disappearance, so she hid the vintage 1990 TV. There was nothing to worry about if he got noisy. No neighbors. Only passing deer might lift their ears.

"Isn't this the tear-down house I've been patrolling for the last three years? Druggies hang out here?" He felt dizzy as he stepped into the grimy living room. His toe caught on the frayed carpeting, and he grabbed the doorjamb to avoid falling. "Can't figure out why I can't go home, Stella. I think I'd be more comfortable. This is a rat hole."

"Oh, I forgot to tell you with all the other stuff going on. Your sister found termites in the kitchen and family room. She's having it fumigated. Tent goes on tomorrow, and we can't go in for four days." She smiled at another impromptu lie.

"Hmm. Weird. Seems like I should have noticed. God, Stella, I really don't feel good. Shouldn't I feel better by now?" A musty, dead odor permeated the room, which added to Josh's nausea.

He slumped onto the crusty couch and tried to focus on the room, hoping the whirling sensation would pass. Stella went to the kitchen, let the tap water change from rusty brown to clear, and poured a glass for Josh. The bipolar meds she'd bought from a dealer at the airport were kicking in, so clear thinking had returned. She had forty-eight hours to get pregnant. No time to waste.

"Here, honey. It's time for your medication."

"No, Stella. No more. They make me—"

"Don't argue. Doctor's orders. They'll make you feel better."

He swallowed his "antibiotic" medication, which was really Viagra. She knew he would remain groggy and easy to manipulate from the light dose of Versed he had taken earlier.

Stella plopped a pillow behind Josh's head and gently pushed him into the arm of the couch for balance. After he fell asleep, she put on a long brown wig and dark glasses, started up the cart, and dashed over to the hospital. She slipped past the nursing team and attempted to break into the med closet, but an intern stopped her.

"Hey, are you authorized for meds?" The intern was new but not dumb.

"What are you talking about? You're new here, aren't you?" She closed the med door and turned to walk away. "It's my day off. Someone left the unit open, so I locked it. Saved 'em from getting a good ass kicking, as I see it." She finished turning and left. Before going outside to regroup from the encounter, she checked the surgery schedule and watched as a patient was pushed down the hall to recovery. As the scrub nurse and surgeon left the OR, Stella sat at a nearby computer and waited. She slipped into the operating room and stole the Versed off the anesthesiologist's tray. On the way home, she made contact with her dealer, and she got a new batch of GHB, both liquid and powder.

When she returned to the house, Josh was stirring. "Just a few more days, darling. Everything's going to be fine." Stella pulled him off the couch, and with a heavy arm over her shoulder, they managed to reach the bed. "See, I've turned down the sheets. She leaned down and took off his shoes and socks. "Come on and lie down. You must be tired from the flight. I'll make some dinner while you rest."

"Yeah, okay." He collapsed onto the bed, still wrestling with the fact that he had no strength or energy. "Leave your cell phone with me. I need to call the captain." His foggy mind ached to see through the disorder that surrounded him.

"Oh, I guess you didn't hear my phone call after we landed. I told him the situation, and he knows that you won't be in for four days. Promised not to let the guys come around and bother you."

Josh struggled to sit up and eyed Stella. "They're no bother. I need to keep up with what's going on in town." His eyes were getting heavy again, but he forced a direct look at her. "Are you keeping something from me?"

"Silly. No secrets. Just doing my job. Can you think of anyone better qualified? I am a nurse, you know."

Next came his shirt, which she quickly removed. "Lie down, and I'll pull off your pants." She unsnapped the top button of his wranglers and tugged on them, finally accomplishing the task. "Lift your hips again, and I'll pull off your shorts."

"I'd rather keep them on for now." Besides being tired, Josh displayed an annoyed attitude.

"What? Bashful after all the lovemaking we've done? You know I've practically memorized every inch of your body." She tried to coax him to strip all the way, but he resisted. I can take care of your shyness after you pass out. Two more hours, and you'll be mine, my love.

After a light meal, Stella returned with a syringe filled with Versed. "Time for your next shot, sweetheart." When the drugs finally took effect, Josh fell into a nirvana state. His euphoria was complete, and he floated through reality. Stella quickly cuffed his wrists to the iron headboard, removed his shorts, and stripped off her clothes. "Now, darling, we are going to make a baby. When you realize I'm pregnant, then you'll propose. I know you will."

Tired of the make-believe with her favorite vibrator, Stella drew in a deep breath as she stared down at Josh's naked body. She ran her hands over her bare skin. Finally, you have returned to me. Her nipples grew hard at the touch, and a carnal longing was rising between her legs. She mounted him.

Josh sensed her hands run across his body. He wanted to resist the initial instinct of pleasure, but confusion surrounded him. He tried to open his eyes and focus, but his strength faded. Stella kissed his mouth and stomach, then moved farther down his body.

He moaned. "Rachael." He felt a strong, urgent drive as his erection grew harder.

If it's Rachael you want right now, so be it. "Yes, darling. It's Rachael. And our storybook love affair has come full circle. Let's make love. Let's make a baby, like we've always talked about."

Josh tried to move his hands. He wanted to hold Rachael, love her. The cuffs startled him for a minute, but Stella whispered it was part of their fantasy lovemaking. Josh's body conceded, and the fantasy raced through him.

"Yes, yes, darling. Love me, take me." Stella moaned. She was fully engaged, but all too soon, the moment passed. She felt triumphant as she collapsed onto his chest. She had her guarantee. His semen swam within her fertile body, and she was spent.

32

Meg picked up her car at the Oasis and dashed over to the hospital. She found Jessie sitting in a wheelchair, ready to leave. When they got to the parking lot, Jessie was impressed. "Wow, a convertible. An orange Mini Cooper. Good taste, Meg." The girls settled in for the three-hour trip to Norco.

"This Mini has an awesome reputation. I'll put the top down so we can wave good-bye to all the peasants as we leave town." As they drove down 95, past the Safeway Store, El Palacio, and Hastings, numerous cars honked, and everyone waved at the girls.

"Do you know everyone in town?"

"Just about. In summer most of us meet up at my house on weekends. Lots of boats, so we ski or go wakeboarding, or we go through the gorge, play naked volleyball, or whatever."

"Naked volleyball?"

"Oh, kind of kidding on that one. Topless for some of the girls, but while I'm definitely not a prude, I usually abstain. Hi, Jerry," she waved at her buddy from the dam.

"Who's Jerry?"

"A close friend. Used to work with him at the dam." Meg reflected on their relationship for a minute. "He really helped me through my healing after...well...after."

"I don't know the real story of what happened. Do you want to talk about it?"

The flashback wanted to start, but Meg stopped it. Too painful, and she wasn't one to share intimate details with new friends. "Not now. Maybe later."

Meg glanced over at Jessie. The bruises and cuts on her face were starting to heal, but the bright desert sunlight exacerbated their presence. She remembered her own shock upon seeing her image in the mirror. She immediately touched her face, then rubbed the inside of her wrist where the cigarette burns had left a nasty scar. Meg sighed.

Jordan watched her, sensing this was a very traumatic story. "Sorry I asked. Not my business."

"No. It's okay. Counselor says it's good to get it out and face it. Well, Rachael and Amanda saved me from that sadist, but he got away. Hence, the second attempt where you got hurt." And your sister got killed. "So, back to Jerry. Just one of my fave friends."

"Boyfriend?"

"No, I like him too much to put him through that agony."

"That's funny. So, how about your sex life?"

"Nada. Still have some hang-ups, I guess." Meg drove on in silence for a few miles. And Derek is one of them.

Jordan got the message that the conversation about Elliott was over.

The rest of the trip was filled with music and girl talk. Jordan was practicing her new Jessie lifestyle on Meg, with only a few blunders.

***

Payden Kraemer was an enigma. Everyone in Norco knew his cowboy side. He was always driving his John Deere tractor, dragging the arena, assisting in delivering the new foals, setting up veterinarian days, and especially hosting the bar at the new saloon he'd built at the ranch. Horses and family were his happy life; selling off his billion-dollar computer company was the other side of his gold coin. His sisters were unaware of the clandestine business dealings and would have been surprised at his acumen.

"Why do you have to go to LA again?" Jessie would ask on occasion.

Never good at lying, Payden would hem and haw, eventually coming up with some excuse that would be applicable to the stables. "Got a lead on some new John Deere machinery that's available and thought I'd check it out." Boom. Discussion closed. On those days, which were many, he escaped to his corporate world of computer programs, the last one of which he'd sold to Apple for an obscene amount of money. He'd purchased a corporate jet, one of his new toys.

The rodeo was an integral part of his family life. His two younger sisters were well skilled and highly competitive in barrel racing and would practice daily at the open field or Ingalls Park center. Payden, a winner in his own right, scored high in the circuit rodeos each year. But now all the happy times had imploded. Jordan was dead.

Payden's concern over Jessie's coping was well founded. Accepting Meg's invitation to turn her back on the ranch and room with Meg in Catalina was a shock. Typically, Jessie would stay around and clean up all of Jordan's messes. But leaving? She's hiding her real feelings. Hasn't mourned yet.

Meg and Jordan pulled into the short driveway at the ranch, and Payden and his two labs, Jennie and Forrest, immediately greeted them. "Put a move on it, girls. The funeral's starting in half an hour."

The girls quickly changed and piled into the pickup with Payden. Parking had been reserved for the family, next to the hitching post where forty horses were tied. Meg gave Jordan a squeeze as they separated at the church. There was standing room only. Everyone in Norco loved the twins and was overwhelmed with grief at the death of Jordan. No one whispered in the room. No one could cry. Total disbelief filled the room. Payden and Jordan sat behind the partially blocked area reserved for relatives and stared at the photographic memorial built on Jordan's behalf.

"So young, so full of life," the minister was saying.

So full of death, Jordan was thinking. Her eyes focused on the pictures of her own life. So now I'm Jessie, accepting the love from all of our friends—love always given to her, not me. I like that. But I do miss you, sis. Jessie, my Jessie, my other half. How will I make it without you? We shared everything except our toothbrushes.

She glanced around at the packed room filled with friends she had known all twenty-three years of her life, and then her eyes found Meg. She knew Meg had empathy for her loss, as she should. If it weren't for Meg, none of this would have happened, so now…what? Go to Catalina and play like it never happened? You take the place of my sister? Oh, I think not. I'll play the part of best friends, and then I'll kill you. Jordan jerked upright at that thought.

Payden reached over and touched her hand. "You okay?"

"Yeah, think so. It's nothing." But it wasn't "nothing." It was something big, earth shattering.

After the service, Meg joined "Jess" and Payden, and they drove back to the ranch. Friends had gathered at Rock-n-C's Saloon earlier in the day and had tied one hundred balloons around the riding arena, with felt-tipped markers tied to their strings.

"You all grab a shot glass of tequila and find a spot around the arena," yelled Payden.

As the people filled in all open spaces, they started writing good-bye notes on the balloons to Jordan. Payden and the new Jessie led Jordan's riderless horse to the center of the arena and wrote their notes.

Payden raised his shot glass. "We love you, honey, and will miss you like crazy. To Jordan."

Everyone joined in the salute, raised their glasses with a "Hear, hear," and released the love messages to the heavens.

***

From sheer exhaustion, everyone went to bed early and didn't move until the rooster crowed around 5:00 a.m. When Meg climbed out of bed, she wandered to the back of the ranch and found Payden mucking stalls.

"You have an early day."

"How'd you sleep?" He looked at her. Tangled hair, no makeup, nothing pretentious about her, and he liked what he saw. His corporate life had been inundated with calculating, silicone women, and he'd felt he had to be on his game at all times. This relaxing sensation he felt with Meg proved to be extremely refreshing.

"Must have been wonderful, 'cause I didn't wake up till the rooster said hello." She smiled at him. My goodness. Never seen jeans fit so tight. "How are you doing? Must be tough to keep going like nothing happened."

"Well, Jessie needs my strength right now, and I won't let her down." He pitched some road apples into the manure bin.

"I've never known identical twins before. Was it hard to keep them straight?" She stepped out of the way in case his aim was off.

"No, not to me, unless they planned on fooling me. There are little things they do, like Jessie always licks the corners of her mouth after the first sip of Starbucks, and Jordan used to twitch her nose funny when she didn't like the smell of something. Little things. When you get to know them, there are personality quirks too."

"Like what?"

"Jessie has more empathy; Jordan has...had...a quicker fuse. Just little things."

"Hmm. This is really messed up. I'll do the best I can to keep her busy. Think that should help."

"I really appreciate it." Payden started walking toward the barn and ditched the apple picker. "Let's get back to the house and see how's she's doing. She's a tumbleweed."

Meg punched him on the arm. "You're funny."

"Careful, little girl, or I'll put you over my knee and spank you." He looked at her. "Don't take kindly to women abusing me."

She hit him again. "You're a real character."

Payden cooked a hearty breakfast for the girls and started quizzing them on their plans. Jordan was calculatingly obtuse about sharing with him. She was still formulating her plan of surviving. "We're going to a casting call in Balboa in a few days. I don't have any gigs with the studio for now, so I'm basically out of work."

Meg finished her last bite of biscuits and gravy and pushed back from the table. "I talked with the previous owner of the horse stables in Catalina, and he thinks there's enough interest in town to open again. She could work there, and me—well, I'll see if Jack's needs a waitress when I get there."

A small look of disapproval appeared on Chef Payden's face. "Must be nice, living by the seat of your pants." Payden was pissed at Meg and his sister for living life so frivolously. Shouldn't they be cautious and nervous about life after what they've just been through? "Mind if I tag along to Balboa with you?

It's been a while since I've been there. Maybe ride the Ferris wheel and grab a frozen banana."

"What are you—ten?" The girls laughed at him. "Don't be ridiculous, Payden. All you want to do is babysit us," Meg said.

He knew it was a lost cause, but he did make them promise to call him each day for a while.

The threesome, bags in hand, walked to Meg's car. Payden smirked. "What's the matter? Couldn't afford a real car? Had to settle for half of one?"

"Don't be bad-mouthing my orange bomb. She can outrun any of those four-legged things you have in the stables." She turned and punched him on the arm again.

"Hey, watch it." He laughed. "You hit like a girl."

"You're lucky I pulled my punch. Guess you didn't hear that I'm one of less than a hundred women who hold the brown belt in Krav Maga."

"Wow, impressive." He rubbed his arm and smiled.

Before piling into Meg's car, Payden hugged Jessie, and to her surprise, he pulled Meg in close and gave her a long hug.

"Hey, Payden, I think you made her blush." The demonstration amused Jessie. My God, I've never seen Payden hug a stranger. Interesting.

They shouted a loud good-bye and jumped on the 15 freeway, then eased onto the 91 to Yorba Linda. Jessie looked at Meg. "He's got it bad for you."

"You jest." Those were the words, but Jessie saw the glimmer of a smile pass across Meg's face.

***

The next few days, Meg showed Jessie around Yorba Linda, met some of her friends, and went shopping at the Brea Mall. They shared lunch at Kelly's Korner bar, followed by a quick drink at the Canyon Inn to laugh with friends. The mail had stacked up, and much to Meg's dismay, there was a letter from the superior court, inviting her to jury duty. "Oh, good grief. This letter's been here for three weeks. Well, I'll call them and say I'm relocating to Catalina, and they'll let me off. They couldn't expect me to take the ferry every day."

Unfortunately, when Meg made the call, they were delighted to tell her she could report for jury duty in three weeks in Catalina. A branch of the superior court was there, all staffed and ready for trials, both criminal and civil.

Day two, they took off for Balboa, bikinis under shorts and T-shirts, to battle it out with the scores of Orange County beauties who were also responding to the casting call. As usual, the freeway was a parking lot, and Balboa was a logjam, but eventually, after following a couple who were leaving, they squeezed into a partially blocked spot.

"Traffic is wicked here," said Jessie. "Grab your purse and makeup bag. We'll have to fill out some forms and do our own makeup for the photo shoots. I'll bring my portfolio along in case they need some professional head shots."

"Hmm. That's a problem for me. No head shots."

"No worry. Most of these girls won't have any either." Jessie was excited about the possibility of a movie job, but Meg seemed noncommittal to her.

As they hastened across the asphalt parking lot to the beach, a man recognized the girls and quickly headed for the travel trailer hired for the day. "Oh, thank you, God," Elliott whispered.

33

Marisa had joined Derek in Newport to finalize plans for the casting call. "He cut off your finger? Bastard." She took her brother's bandaged hand and brought it to her cheek. "I am so, so sorry, Derek, and so frightened. What's next?" Her face couldn't hide the anguish.

"We need to be careful and not cross him, sis. He's really lost it." He wasn't ready to share the deeper threat Elliott posed or his changing loyalties with her yet. "Look, he'll be here soon. Let's get started."

They had a million details to manage before Elliott's plan of trafficking could be put into play. First, they leased the super yacht, *Nannette*, at $200,000 a week and made arrangements for it to be repositioned from San Diego to a point off Balboa. The 230-foot, German-built yacht could comfortably accommodate twelve guests; it had a massive Jacuzzi, a sports bar, a theater, and a gym with a staff to ensure the pleasure of the passengers. Elliott's suite had its own Jacuzzi and all the amenities of a five-star hotel.

Next, ten international billionaire playboys were invited to a Texas Hold'em card game aboard the vessel. They supplied their own transportation to Orange County but would be hosted aboard after that. The final plan was to gather some college students from Saddleback College's film department and hire them for a day to photograph the girls at Balboa. An ad ran for four days, announcing the call date, where to go, when, and what to bring. The ad inferred that ten girls would be selected, with another ten as potential callbacks. It was to be a two-day shoot on the beach and yacht, with an overnight stay. Hopefully, any parent or friend would be misguided if the kidnapped girls didn't show up for a day or two, giving Elliott enough time to relocate.

Now that the day had arrived, last-minute arrangements were thrust upon Derek. "Did you pick up the questionnaires from the printer? Do we have all the supplies needed to hold the girls on board for three days? Food…"

Marisa was coming unglued. "Yes and yes and yes. Why the nerves? This is one of our more simple plans. Everyone is coming to us, and the onboard staff will manage it all."

"We said there would be a hair stylist and makeup artists for the girls. They pay. Are they here? Are the tables ready for sign-up? Do we have their numbers? Pins?" Derek rummaged around the trailer, messing up Marisa's desk.

"You're driving me nuts, Derek. We're ready. Go outside and enjoy the ocean air." Marisa pushed him toward the trailer door with an attitude as the door flew open and Elliott stomped in.

"Oh, thank you, sweet Jesus. You have delivered the essence of life into my master plan. Guess who just drove up?"

They knew without asking. Only one person could bring such sadistic pleasure to him.

"Are you sure it's her? Elliott, she can identify all of us. Shit." Derek glanced at Marisa and headed for the trailer windows. "God, I see her. Who's the other girl?"

"Some bitch she met in the hospital. Oh, the gods are smiling down on me. Maybe I should stop the show and take her now." He froze and anticipated the move. "Yes. Let's do that."

"Are you crazy?" Derek asked. "We have a shitload of people out there. Meg has to wait."

Elliott dropped back into reality. "Yes, of course." He twitched.

Derek and Marisa passed furtive glances.

"We shall do nothing. Have one of the college kids run the show for us. We'll watch from the trailer."

"Wait. Are you sure she didn't see you?"

"I'm sure. The cops would be surrounding us if she had. Eliminate Meg on the second round. Take her address and tell her we'll let her know when the next casting call comes. Get the other girl's name, too. I don't have time for Meg right now; you're right." His arms were flying around, his lips stretched over his teeth, and he grimaced. "Yes, yes." His hand reached into his pants pocket and found himself, and then he smiled.

Both Derek and Marisa reeled from his antics. His driving force for the last two years had been Meg. It was all he could focus on. Derek said, "Let's think about this—"

"You know better than to think, brother; in fact, next time you bother to try, just look at your finger. Oh, that's right. It's not there. This is perfect. We'll have an opportunity to run the trafficking scam one time, work out the kinks. Meg is planning on going to Catalina next week. I overheard her conversation in the hospital. We'll pick up my little princess when we drop anchor in Catalina and run our second contest. Just think about it. I'll have time to arrange all of her pleasurable torture." His lascivious madness had taken over.

Derek had seen with his own eyes the results of the damage Elliott had inflicted on Meg last year. When she'd finally begun to socialize with her famous rat pack at the river again, her flesh wounds had healed, but Derek had seen the leftover fear and humiliation. She had endured his torture but hadn't forgotten it. I can't let him wound her like that again. "Yeah, that's a better plan."

Marisa looked at Derek with a questioning expression.

"Derek, call the captain. See what time the yacht will anchor today. Get the film director in here for last-minute changes." He looked out the window at the collection of girls, who were primping and posing for their big chance, and searched for the one rare beauty he called his own.

Seagulls were picking through the washed-up seaweed, and kids on surfboards waited for the perfect set. A large group of people gathered on the Balboa pier, enjoying the bright sunshine and modest breeze, curious about the hubbub below. It was a normal summer day at the beach, with the exception of two hundred stunning bathing beauties huddled around a man with a megaphone.

Inside the well-positioned trailer, another three onlookers watched the scene unfold. Despite the crowd, Elliott noticed only one girl. "Oh, this is indeed going to be fun." Elliott massaged away.

34

The twenty-four-mile trip from Balboa to Avalon on the *Catalina Flyer* was uneventful, allowing Rachael time to enjoy a momentary escape from her trying week. She climbed the steps to the upper level and settled into a spot away from the masses. Usually on the voyage over to Catalina, she would sit below, toss down a Bloody Mary or two, and watch the excitement of kids as they spotted their first dolphins breaking through the water, but today she needed some solitude to formulate a plan. When the boat nestled next to the dock, she joined the vacationers spilling off the boat and sauntered down the long wooden wharf, stopping only to pick up a corn dog.

Instead of returning to the summerhouse, where the family had always stayed, Rachael picked up a rental cart and headed directly to Josh's house. She whipped around Claressa and Beacon Street and pulled up in front of his ranch-style home on Eucalyptus. Deferred maintenance? That's not like Josh. She raced up the steps, stopped to look in the window, and then banged on the door. When no one answered, she located the hidden key under the potted geraniums and entered. No sign of life. She could tell no one had been in the house for a while because of the mail on the living room floor and the feathery cobwebs draped across the doorjambs. So if he and Stella left Bullhead by plane three days ago, it's obvious she didn't bring him here.

***

"Captain. This is Rachael Pennington, calling about Josh." Rachael was multitasking by canvasing the corrals and checking the horses while talking to the sheriff's department.

"Rachael. How are you? I've been a little concerned about Josh myself. Is he with you?"

"No. You heard he was shot, didn't you?"

"Yeah and taken to the hospital for surgery. Then nothing."

"Well, three days ago, this weird redheaded woman came to the hospital and took him."

"Took him? What do you mean? Like, in kidnapped?"

"I'd like to call it that, but apparently he knew her. Called her Stella. Do you know who that is?"

"Stella?" The captain groaned. "Oh, hell yes. The whole department knows her. They had a thing going last year, before you came back to the island. She's a fruitcake, and Josh broke up with her. Had to get a restraining order. Real piece of work."

"My God." Rachael's mind was whirling, trying to recall everything Meg had told her about Stella. "Well, I checked the airport at Bullhead before I left. Apparently a small private plane took off with a pilot and two passengers, heading to Catalina. One man fit Josh's description. Landed at Airport in the Sky three days ago. He hasn't called in yet?"

"Haven't heard a word from him. I'll have Greg drive by his house and check it out. They're partners, ya know."

"Don't bother. I'm here right now. Lots of mail on the floor." She headed back into the house. "Looks like the horses are being fed and watered okay. Probably a neighbor. Can you give me an address on this bitch, Stella?"

"You got a cart?"

"Yeah, I rented one."

"I'll have Greg meet you at her house. Stella must be off her meds. Guess she was diagnosed as bipolar. You don't want to take her on by yourself. Crazy as hell. You packin'?"

"Yeah, my Glock. Look, I'm fine on my own. Greg doesn't need to meet me."

"My city, my rules. I'll text you the address on Whittley. Will take about ten minutes to get there. Wait for Greg. And, oh, you need to come in and register your gun."

"Right." Rachael locked the house, put the key in her purse, and jumped in the cart. Whittley Avenue was only a few blocks away, and Rachael had no intention of waiting for Greg. She covered the distance in minutes. Once she pulled the cart to a stop, she stared at the house, looking for any sign of life. The lady next door was watering nine square feet of dirt she must have considered her lawn. So Rachael decided to move with caution and get as much background information as possible. "Hi, I'm looking for Stella. Have you seen her today?"

"No, honey. She's been gone for about four days now. Must be over town." Rachael ducked the spray of water intended for the planter.

"Over town?"

"That's what we locals call the mainland."

"Oh, I see. Well, I'm worried about her. She usually tells me when she's leaving. Think I'll take a look around." Rachael went behind the small house and peered into the living room. Looked deserted. She jimmied the door lock and entered. After searching through the two bedrooms, she was about to leave when Greg stomped in.

"Well, Rachael, guess I have the goods on you now. B and E? Really?"

"How goes it, Greg? Just trying to find my boyfriend."

"Has crazy Stella got something to do with it? That's bad news." He started searching the rooms as he talked.

"Looks like it. The airport says a small Cessna landed a couple of days ago. Two passengers. I'm trying to track down the pilot."

"Oh, I know who that'll be. Has to be Fred. He flies all the commuters. Let me check on it for you. I know what Stella's cart looks like, so I'll have the department keep an eye out. Why don't you try the market. She'll need food, and they all know her."

"Good idea. I'll stop by headquarters and get one of the department walkie-talkies so we can communicate."

"Cap said okay to that? Wow. He must like you."

"He does. Practically raised me each summer."

Greg completed his room search. "Nothing seems to be out of place, and I don't see anything that belongs to Josh. You sure she's involved?"

"Sure as shit. I'm taking off. Check around and lock up when you leave. By the way, she's built quite a shrine to Josh in the bedroom." Rachael led him into the room and took some pictures on her cell phone. "Take a look. Scary."

Pictures of Josh and Stella where thumbtacked to the walls. Boating, fishing, swimming—all the fun summer days were recounted, along with some naked shots of Josh sleeping.

"That? Oh, hell, that was from last year. But scary? That doesn't begin to describe her. I hate to think what she's putting Josh through right now."

Rachael stopped in her tracks. "Are you saying she'd hurt him? What does she want from him?"

"Babies."

35

Registration for the anxious wannabe movie stars was complete. The bikini-clad girls rummaged through the props stashed on the beach. Surfboards, beach balls, squatty chairs, and umbrellas were all available to them for their photo shoot. Some swimsuits were so skimpy that pinning a number on them was impossible, so tape was used.

Meg was more interested in the beautiful day. She waded along the shore as the sunlight danced across the blue Pacific, daydreaming about a promising future and putting the past behind her. Resiliency was a great part of her makeup. Jessie yelled at her when their numbers were called, and she ran through the hot sand, heading for a large piece of driftwood that had floated up on shore.

"I'm going to use this for my picture," she yelled. "Okay?" She leaned against the arty log, put one hand back to steady herself, flipped her wavy blond hair so it partially covered her face, and said, "How's this? Do I look like Marilyn Monroe?" The photographer was clicking away. "How about a pouty face?"

The photographer had been given instructions to take a lot of pictures of Meg, so he positioned her five or six times before finishing. Jessie only had two shots taken.

"Well, guess the camera likes you better." She tried not to show her irritation, but Meg noticed it.

"Think I kept moving at the wrong time."

145

"Feeble excuse," Jessie mumbled under her breath. "Yeah, that's probably it."

Jessie had never been to Balboa, so they wandered through the amusement zone while the rest of the girls posed for the cameras. "Wanna ride the Ferris wheel?" Meg grabbed Jessie's hand and pulled her over to the ticket booth. "My treat." They rocked the hanging chair when they reached the top and threw their hands overhead, laughing like kids.

"My God, it's beautiful up here. You can see for miles." Jessie was enthralled.

"See that house at the point? Third inlet down the coast. That belongs to the Duke's heirs."

"John Wayne? The original? It's huge. What kind of pesos would it take to buy that?"

"Last time I heard, it was around twenty million, but that was a while back."

Traditional chocolate-covered frozen bananas conquered part of their hunger, and after some kettle corn, they bummed around in the arcade, took a quick swim, and headed back to the pier for the elimination.

Elliott sat in the shade of his cabana, using his binoculars to watch Meg. He was surprised when she didn't seem disappointed by the elimination; in fact, it looked like she was relieved. She laughed with the other contestants and started to leave, stopping only to listen to the next announcement.

"The following girls are backups and will be called within a week." Meg and Jessie's numbers were called, and they reported to the registration table to get further instructions.

"We'll give you ladies a call within the week. You made the second cut. We've set aside your applications. Look them over. Make sure your e-mails and phone numbers are correct. If the first ten girls don't cut the acting part, we'll let you know when the competition continues. It will take place on Catalina."

Neither Meg nor Jessie was crushed by the information since the audition had been just a lark. "Hey, let's go. We have to be back here at seven in the morning to catch the *Flyer* to Catalina." They headed for the car, laughing and flirting with life, as Elliott watched.

Ten beautiful young women stood on the beach, eagerly waiting to hear what their roles were going to be. Elliott strolled down with Derek and Marisa once they saw Meg pull out of the parking lot.

"Girls, my name is Lance, and I am the director of the movie. You beautiful girls will be showcased in my production. As a little reward for making the cut, we'll be having cocktails and dinner on my yacht anchored offshore." He pointed to the sleek super yacht, which had split the horizon within the last few minutes. "Here comes the dingy now to take you to the boat. Be sure to bring your personal items with you. It'll be late when we get back. You'll need to call and break your dates for tonight."

Some of the girls were hesitant because of prior commitments for the evening. Elliott gave them a minute to discuss the alternatives. "If you can't commit to this, then I'm sorry, but we'll have to eliminate you now. Time to decide. More photos will be taken on board when you arrive. So, what'll it be?"

All of the girls eagerly agreed to board, without the slightest clue of what awaited them.

36

The one and only market on Catalina was crowded when Rachael arrived, but she located the assistant manager and asked about Stella. "Have you seen her within the last few days?"

"Can't say that I have, but I'll check with the clerks. What's the nutcase been up to?"

Rachael was getting used to all the nicknames for Stella. "Police business. Sorry." She gave him a pleasant smile.

"You with the department, now, Rach? Didn't know they were hiring."

Rachael wasn't surprised by the question. Since the island was so small, all the locals knew each other—and each other's business. "No, just helping out for a few weeks. Got my application in at the Conservancy for ranger."

"Well, it's high season, so there shouldn't be a problem."

"Hope not, but back to Stella. Does she have a girlfriend, or anyone, who might know her whereabouts?"

"You mean, besides her brother? There is a girl she hangs out with, think her name is Trish. Works at the hospital. Cindie Lou can let you know where to find her. You know, small-town stuff. Gotta go."

"Thanks for your help." Since she was so close, Rachael headed for the hospital on Falls Creek Road, where Stella used to work. She bypassed the clinic on the bottom floor and went directly to the hospital wing. A receptionist told her that Stella had abruptly quit a week ago and disappeared off the radar. Her friend, Trish, was still around but not working that day.

"Could you give me her address? I'm really concerned about Stella." *Liar, liar.*

"Can't do, but try HR. Since you're a cop, they can probably help you. Down the hall and to the right. Can't miss it."

The fragile old lady in HR was suspicious and hesitant to give out too much information: privacy and all. "Hmm. You say Stella is missing? Are you sure? She's a dingbat. Sometimes she'll go to the back side of the island for a week and just live on bugs."

"Yeah, no one has seen her for a few days, and Trish is the best chance to find her. Just this once? Please? You know I'm a cop. Don't want to go to the courthouse to get a subpoena to search your records. Come on, please?"

You can never spread on too much honey. Out the door she flew with a verified address in hand. First, Trish, then what? Dead end? Rachael and her sisters always listened to their instincts, and hers was wrapped with fear. What's she doing to him?

37

Two of Elliott's henchmen, who were dressed as crew, helped the contestants on board the yacht. Elliott had changed out of his beach attire and donned a tuxedo, impressing the contestants with his grand mannerisms. His new Grecian face, which had cost a pretty penny in Mexico, glowed in the afternoon sun. Taking the microphone, he stepped forward and informed them of the room assignments. "Ladies. Welcome to your floating paradise. Please feel free to wander around this magnificent yacht after you change. There are evening gowns awaiting your approval in designated staterooms. Derek, please." He pointed to the upstairs balcony, where Derek appeared, holding two Armani gowns, replicated from the last Oscar party in Hollywood.

Tittering giggles rose from the lower level to where Derek was standing.

"Please dress in the one of your choice, redo your makeup and hair, and join us on deck for happy hour. Our financial backers, directors, and producers are all here and breathless to meet you. Look your best, and it's okay to be a little flirty. This could be the chance of a lifetime for you. The next Angelina Jolie."

The girls noticed the men staring at them from the upper level of the boat, whispering back and forth, smiling, and occasionally waving. "Ah, Lance," asked a tall blonde, "are those guys the backers you're talking about? Not a Brad Pitt in the group." The girls laughed at that, and after Elliott told them that the men were millionaires, the contestants smiled and waved to the moneymen.

The international playboys, or their seconds, had spent the day engaged in a game of Texas Hold'em, competing for a position to select a model to take home. Each could afford to buy any woman, but the challenge was to win the card game. This unique approach, which Elliott initiated, had piqued their interest, and they rose to the contest. Bragging rights. A new game for the idle rich. A gourmet meal with accompanying wine followed the game as the men awaited the first appearance of the girls. As the ladies stepped on board, each man conversed with his second about their potential. Living trophies.

When the girls reappeared, resplendent in their expensive gowns, they gathered at the stern of the yacht. Each was handed a glass of champagne and told to start mingling with the men. "And where are you from?"

"France, my dear. You certainly are very beautiful. Tell me about your interests, your desires."

The second glass of champagne had a special ingredient, a closely measured amount of scopolamine. The drug didn't alter the taste of the alcohol, so the contestants didn't notice it.

Derek watched as Elliott monitored the dosage. "You're using Devil's Breath? My God, Elliott, why? Roofies would be enough. You're walking a tightrope with that shit."

"We need the girls to be cooperative without passing out on us. They'll be very receptive to any and all suggestions the men have, and they will go quietly. I know what I'm doing. Stand down."

Most of the girls were unsophisticated, and finding casual conversation with the millionaires was difficult. One man from Italy made a suggestive comment to a lovely brunette; Elliott noticed it. He pulled the man aside. "Curb your appetite. We don't want to spook the girls. Give the drugs time to work, and then you can do what you please. Let's have a smooth transition."

Twenty minutes later, the drugs kicked in, and the girls, one by one, headed for a chair or chaise lounge. They all seemed very relaxed. Elliott browsed among them, testing their sense of cooperativeness. This perfect substance had trapped their memory and stolen their souls. "Would you like to go kill some monkeys on a safari with me?" he asked a petite blonde.

"Of course. When would you like to leave?" She smiled sweetly and was ready to go anyplace, anytime.

Elliott climbed the stairs to the second level, overlooking the party area, and made an announcement. "The selection will now begin."

"I want to see a little more of the package I'm purchasing," a man from Argentina said. "A million is a bit much, for what...ninety-five pounds of flesh?" The men all agreed and pushed the point.

Elliott didn't want to lose control of the bidders, so he immediately addressed the man who had won at Texas Hold'em. "We'll have no discussion within the group. If the first bidder picks a lady that you desire, you may challenge him. Negotiations will be entirely between the two of you, and I'm assuming it will be in the form of money. I am not a part of that. If Mr. Dahl, who is number one, is challenged and agrees to take the money, he will go to the back of the line. Those are the rules. With that in mind, who is your first pick, Mr. Dahl?"

"The brunette with the blue strapless dress." She was sitting at the small cocktail table, hands neatly crossed, smiling at the man's acknowledgement of her. All the men gathered around to take a look and decide whether they wanted to go for the challenge or await their turn to pick. "Unzip her dress. What's between the legs will do, but I want to see her breasts. Implants? I'll take a feel." He moved toward her.

The girl stood. "Am I supposed to unzip my dress?" She smiled, looking a little bewildered.

"Sorry." Elliott's dislike for this man was beginning to show. "No feelies. Look only." He motioned for a crewman to assist the girl, but she was already lowering the top half of her gown.

The boat rocked a little, and she lost her balance. The investor caught her and felt her breast in the process. The Italian carefully examined her breasts: the curvature, the nipples, and all around, looking for incisions. "Wiggle for me? I can tell by the way they move."

The crewman wiggled the brunette a little to the left as the man watched intently. "Nice, round, tender melons. These will do. Get her bag and bring her to my boat." Decision made.

The brunette smiled and pulled up the top portion of her dress. "Are we going on another boat? This is a lot of fun." Her sense of right and wrong had disappeared, and only the desire to comply and satisfy was present.

The next selections went by quickly. All playboys left the yacht with their purchases, except number ten. There was only one girl left when the representative from Spain moved forward to assess his purchase. She hadn't moved in the last ten minutes, and everyone assumed she had passed out. "Well, let's see what this tiny blonde has to offer." He motioned for his assistant to help her sit up; but when the man tried to awaken her, he backed off, shock registering on his face.

"She's dead."

Elliott rushed over to aid the man, but he could see she was dead, apparently allergic to the poisonous addition to the champagne. Fortunately, the other bidders had left the boat with their women, so only the captain, crew, Derek, and Marisa were on board, meaning few witnesses. "Okay, everyone, the show's over. Go back to your stations. Senor Nadal, come with me, and we'll discuss some options. Derek, take the body to my stateroom for now."

Elliott took Nadal's arm and directed him to the bow of the yacht. "Sorry for the inconvenience, senor, but I'm sure we can find a quick solution to this untimely problem." He waved to a waiter, signaling a request for drinks. "I'm so sorry for the mishap."

"Mishap? I don't want to be a part of murder, you imbecile." The Spaniard was livid.

The man's remarks immediately annoyed Elliott. "I understand and will deal with this myself. However, in the interim, we will have a fresh batch of girls within the week, and, of course, you will have first pick. During that time, please remain as my guest on the yacht, and I will furnish you daily with new ladies for your pleasure and the best of gourmet meals. Will that satisfy your immediate needs?"

Senor Nadal disliked Elliott and didn't trust him, but the terms were satisfactory. "Fund my stake in the next poker game, and we have a deal. I am to be first for selecting the beauties, even if I don't win at poker."

"Done." Elliott was thrilled with the results of his new enterprise. So much better, and more profitable, than handling those nasty body parts. "I'll go attend to your dinner, say, black tie at eight?"

"I'll need a woman tonight. Make those arrangements also." He decided to challenge Elliott.

This was a problem for Elliott since all of the girls had been sold, except, of course, for the dead one. Necrophilia? Probably not. "Sorry, sir, but all of the women have left the yacht."

"Perhaps your sister is available."

He didn't take the time to pause or think. "Yes, of course." As he walked away from Nadal, he noticed his siblings were deep in conversation.

***

Derek and Marisa had met at the upper deck to enjoy the night air after all the foreigners had departed. Eager to discuss the evening's events, Derek needed to share his surprise of his own feelings with the one person he could trust. "That's appalling. The men act like they're in an outdoor market, buying something at a fruit stand."

"More like a meat market." Marisa grabbed his arm. "Careful, little brother. Sounds like you're finding some kind of humanity. That doesn't work in our family. Don't talk that way in front of Elliott."

"For God's sake, Marisa, these girls have families waiting for them. The next time they hear about or see them, it will be from the cops or Interpol. They'll either be dead or so strung out on drugs and sex that they'll be unrecognizable."

"Stop. Don't go there." She pulled him closer to the rail and squeezed his healthy hand.

"Who's going to dispose of the body? I had to carry her to his cabin. You know what he'll be doing for the next few hours. Poor girl. If it's anything like what he did to Meg, the girl's lucky to be dead. Necrophilia? I wouldn't put it past him. I guess the sharks will do the rest." Derek turned from his sister and watched the rise and fall of the other boats in the harbor. Turning back, he concentrated on Marisa's face, watched her long hair move in the ocean breeze, and he realized that she didn't have much of a life either. Money was never their problem; Elliott was. "What went wrong, sis? How did we end up here? Our family is so fucked up."

She shot him a meaningless smile. Shrugged. "Same old war stories told to the psychiatrists by the perverted people. Wimpy mother, mad father, no money. Throw in a little incest and a lot of physical abuse, and you've got it. Just a victim of our times, so they say."

"But Elliott was the oldest. Didn't he have an obligation to protect us? They always do in the movies."

"Oh, how soon we forget. Elliott took your beatings and protected me from Dad when he found out why he was coming into my bedroom. He was still a kid. He couldn't protect you from mom's sexual advances. Probably why you're gay. No, he did his part, but the scars that riddled his body took him down a depraved path, deep into the rabbit hole, and he took us with him." She faced the sea and took a deep breath, hiding any emotion from him.

"I went along with him when I was told to befriend Meg. You know, she's really a good person. I reported to him daily when I talked to her: where she went, with whom. I knew she was going to be his next victim, but I felt I owed him the information. When I found out what he had done to her, it disgusted me. No one deserves that. He's a monster." His gaze dropped to the plank flooring, and he fell against the railing as the boat dipped. The ocean spit a spray of salt water across his face, and he left it there. *I wish it could cleanse me.*

Marisa didn't know how to address his pain because her pain was identical, and she had no answers for herself. She wiped the water from his face, looked into his eyes, slowly shook her head, and walked toward the stern to be alone.

Derek headed for the galley. "I'm going to get a drink. This makes me sick. Maybe alcohol will help." He thought about how the last man had boarded his skiff. His assistant had been leading the girl, but the man had already been unzipping her gown. *Seeing something this degrading happen to a woman shouldn't bother me. But…God, what will the next twenty-four hours bring for those girls…and their families?* This was the second time within days that Derek was questioning his lifestyle. So much empathy for those women. *Maybe I can help. Maybe…*Concerned that Elliott had him so entrenched and controlled, he feared he would never have a chance to explore that possibility.

***

"Ah, I was looking for you." Elliott found Marisa relaxing with a cocktail, enjoying her silent moment.

She wasn't ready to talk to him but knew she had no choice in the matter. "Well, everything went quite well, with the exception of the dead girl. Is that going to be a problem?"

"No, after I'm through with her, I'll have one of the crew wrap her in plastic, except for an arm, and attach an anchor. Take the dinghy out a few miles offshore and dump her. Probably have to slice her up a little to attract the sharks. That's not a problem. However, we do have one with the Spaniard." He waited and then forged ahead. "Do you have plans for the evening?"

"Yeah, sleep." Extremely intuitive, she knew where he was headed. She elected to remain silent.

When Elliott tired of the silent game, he walked over to her chaise lounge and grabbed her arm. "You know what has to be done. Go to his cabin at ten and take care of the problem."

"No."

"I'm not losing a million dollars just because you won't spread your legs one night. You've had worse than him, I'm sure. You've never carried your weight in this partnership. You will do this. Don't disappoint me." He squeezed her arm, and when she winced, he strolled away, whistling, "Let It Be."

Beyond crying, Marisa turned to gaze at the undulating waves, craving a better life. She raised her hands to eye level, moving her fingers like she was playing a piano, and thought about Derek.

Pounding on Trish's door brought no results, so Rachael moved to the back of the small house. The wooden-frame building needed repair, and the sparse landscape was struggling to live; the overall picture was one of neglect. Probably a rental. She pushed aside a dead oleander bush and spotted a young woman lying on a blanket, topless. Rachael cleared her throat, hoping not to startle the girl.

"Err, excuse me, are you Trish?"

The girl quickly sat up and pulled a towel over her breasts, wide eyed with apprehension. "What? Who are you? What do you want?" She frantically searched around the yard to see if there were other Peeping Toms.

Rachael was dressed in comfortable island clothes: shorts and a blouse that concealed her Glock. "My name is Rachael, and I need a minute of your time. Sorry I startled you."

Trish recovered quickly, feeling no threat from the woman. "Okay, so what's up? Am I late on my electric bill or something?" She tucked the towel under her chin, slid her bikini top underneath, and slipped it on.

"No, silly." Rachael took on a girlie attitude. "I work at the hospital, in administration. I'm trying to find Stella. You know she quit a few days ago, and I've got her final paycheck. Told payroll I'd drop it off at her house on my way home, but she's not there, and the mail's piling up. Have you seen her? She can probably use the money." Slow down. You're talking too fast.

"I don't recognize you. Are you new?" Trish was still uncomfortable with the situation.

"No, but always behind a desk or in the copy room. I hang around with Rosie from the Conservancy. You know her?" Come on, I'm dropping enough names.

"Oh, yeah. Great gal. But how'd you get my address?"

"Well, duh. Friends with HR."

"Hmm, okay. Stella's been acting weird for the last week. Think she's still pining away over Josh. But, anyway, she called me from who knows where and asked me to get the lights turned on for a rental house on Camino Del Monte. She's so screwy sometimes. I asked why, 'cause she already has a house. But she just tuned me out. That's all I know."

"Hey, thanks. Remember the house numbers?" Rachael quickly pulled her notepad out and wrote down the information. "I'll drop by there, and if she's not around, I'll take the check back to the hospital when I go to work tomorrow. Not going to spend my day off tracking her down. If I miss her and you see her, let her know about the check."

Trish turned over onto her stomach, returning to her sunbathing ritual. "No problem. Good luck with that weird one."

"Gotcha. Thanks."

Rachael jumped back into the golf cart and called Greg, relaying her updated information and the new address for Stella. She drove the distance in minutes and waited for him. When he arrived, Rachael was ready for action. "I see some motion in the house. You know her; how should we play it?"

"What a dump. This is a house that gets rented to druggies. Josh and I have busted it a lot of times, so I know the floor plan. The only bedroom is in the back, on the left corner of the house. I'll go to the front door to distract her, and you look in the bedroom window. If he's there, call me on my shoulder mic and say to report back to the office. I'll work my way into the house."

"Good. If there's an open window, I'll go in."

"Are you packin'?"

"Always."

Greg hesitated. "Don't use your gun, Rach. She's probably off her meds. Talk her down. Don't shoot her."

"Jeez. I'm not going to shoot her unless she comes at me with a knife." Rachael picked her way through the straggly vegetation and headed for the bedroom.

Chipped paint, cobwebs, and dirt rested on the wooden-frame house. As she neared the bare window, she heard someone, or something, making noises from inside.

"Rachael, you're hurting me. Slow down."

Josh?

The first glance through the dirty window incited shock and then panic. It wasn't easy to make out the figures, but then she recognized Josh through the glass. What the hell was going on? She backed out of sight so the other person wouldn't see her. Another quick look verified what she thought she had seen. He was cuffed to the headboard, and some wild woman with red hair was riding him like a bareback rider hanging on for the full eight seconds. Her hair was flying around, her back arched, and she was moaning his name. Rachael froze. Finally the woman began to slow down, finishing her illicit gyrations on Josh's body. Her face relaxed from the tortured, maniacal visage, and she dropped onto his chest, hair straggling over his face. She resembled an over-painted puppet, awkward and lifeless as the puppeteer lowered the strings.

Rachael continued watching as the woman whispered something to Josh and crawled off him. Though muffled, she got sketches of Stella's words: *cleanup, baby, love.* Josh just lay there, eyes rolling around, not fighting the cuffs, just wasted.

Rachael returned to the front of the house. Greg was gone. She moved away and called him on the walkie-talkie. "Where the hell are you? They're in there. Stella must have Josh drugged, 'cause he's just lying on the bed, and she... well,...she's screwing him."

"God, Rach, sorry. Got a call and had to leave. But...what? That doesn't make any sense. He's out but still having sex?"

"Yeah, damn it. I'm going in. If the door's locked, I'll kick it in. Need to help Josh. He's handcuffed to the bed, so he won't be any help. I'm sure I can handle the redhead." She stopped and wondered if that was true. "She looks tough."

"Not too many in town would take her on."

"I've got my persuader."

"Don't shoot her. I'll call for backup. Might be a while; we're short staffed. You'd better wait."

"No way." Rachael pulled out her Glock and started for the front door.

39

When the alarm went off, Meg rolled over and pulled the covers over her head. *When will I ever get some rest?* The last year, with the kidnapping, rescue, and second kidnapping, was taking its toll on her, and she knew it. *How much longer will I be able to hide this from my family...Or are they playing along with me and know what's going on? How much longer will it take to open up to strangers and not jump when a man puts a hand on me?* She sat up and stared through the miniblinds, her toes nestling in the plush carpeting. It was nice to be home, away from the desert. Lush green grass lay like a carpet beneath the flowering evergreen pear trees that cast cool shadows over the lawn. Fragrant jasmine wafted through the open window, and Meg inhaled deeply, enjoying the calm of the moment. At times like this she understood why Mom didn't want to leave Yorba Linda, the Land of Gracious Living, and join her in Bullhead, the land of heat and sin.

Her mom and "new" dad had stayed behind to clean up the Bullhead house. Amanda had driven to the Port of Los Angeles and set sail aboard Carnival Cruise Lines, joining the FBI team bound for Mexico. Rachael was headed for Catalina, and now she and her new best friend, Jessie, were going to follow. The smell of freshly brewed coffee drifted into the room, and she dragged her tired body down the hall to the kitchen.

"Morning, sleepyhead." Jessie was browsing through the *Orange County Register*, munching away on some sourdough toast and washing it down with coffee.

Meg shuffled around the island, spotted her favorite "I Love New York" mug, and poured the steaming brew into her cup. "Hmm. Smells good." She looked in the refrigerator. "Crap. No cranberry juice. Mom always stocks that for me. How long you been up?"

"I heard the neighbor's truck take off about five thirty, so I rolled out. Nice town you have here. I read the sheriff's blotter for the week, and you had two burglaries, one DUI, and a cat stranded in a tree. Not exactly like Bullhead."

"Was just thinking the same thing. That's why Mom will never move. So, are you ready to set out on our new adventure?" She added some Bailey's to her coffee and plopped down on the kitchen chair.

"Well, I've been thinking about that."

Meg grimaced and wondered whether she was going to have to convince Jessie again or, for that matter, if she wanted to put any more effort into this new relationship. She took a sip of coffee and waited. She knew she was barely functioning on her own, and she questioned her ability to take on another wounded duck. "Do as you please. Just make up your mind and stick with it for a while. If you're not going for at least six months, I need to know. I don't want to get stuck with a rental that I have to pay for by myself." She tried but didn't manage to repress the antagonism she was feeling.

Jessie contemplated Meg's ultimatum. What's waiting for me at the ranch? Old friends who will overwhelm me with sorrow because of my sister's death? I'd have to wear Jessie's clothes and act sweet like her. Her horse would buck me to hell and gone. Don't know if I could pull that off now. Maybe later. I don't want their pity, damn it. I want…What do I want? Somewhere deep inside came that evil thought again. Retribution? With a faked heartfelt burst of words, Jessie jumped up and said, "Enough of this shit. Yes, yes. I'm committed to Catalina and you. Let's get ready and kick some ass."

Meg returned the enthusiastic entreaty, but she wondered what was really going on with this girl. Jessie's language surprised her. She wasn't offended, but Payden had described her as anything but potty mouthed.

***

A SuperShuttle picked up the girls, and forty minutes later, they were in line for the *Catalina Flyer*, along with 150 other vacationers. The large boat pulled away from the dock, passed the fun zone, went by the zero-lot-line million-dollar homes, and finally left the bay and jetty for the open sea. Since this was the first time Jessie had been to the island, Meg filled her in on the trip. "You've heard the song 'Twenty-Six Miles across the Sea'? Well, that's how far it is from Balboa. Sometimes we see flying fish, but that's pretty rare. The island is only twenty-one miles long and eight miles wide, and it was a huge hot spot for movie stars in the forties, like Clark Gable. Oh, and Marilyn Monroe." Meg wanted to continue, to share all the wonderful history of the island, but Jessie wasn't paying attention.

Silence. Then Jessie feigned interest, but it was obvious she was just biding her time.

"Well, so much for the history lesson. What's with you, girl? Something must interest you."

When Jessie shrugged, Meg changed the subject and focused on the approaching shore. She had e-mailed some of her island friends about her plans, so she wasn't surprised to see a swarm of fifteen friends with signs and banners that read, "Welcome back home, Meg." Acting surprised and excited, she introduced Jessie to her friends, hugging and kissing as she moved from one to another. "So what's the plan, party animals?"

"We borrowed a cart for you two. Don't have to pay for it for two weeks. Best deal we could do. Your rental is ready, and here are the keys." Rosie, from the Conservancy, was in charge. "Party at El Galleon tonight. And then, who knows? You're home, and we're happy."

Jessie was pushed around and hugged like an old friend. While she tried to act cool with the closeness, Meg noticed she was trying to pull away. "Okay, thanks, let's get this show on the road." Meg grabbed Jessie's hand and pulled her away from the crowd. Walking along the wood pier, she stopped at Eric's. "Want some fish and chips before we go to the house? There won't be any food there."

Jessie looked at the signage. "Maybe a burger and beer."

"You got it." Orders were placed, and the girls sat at the outside tables, watching the town fill up as a Carnival Cruise ship spewed passengers onto the shore. "The tourists are almost frantic when they land. Too many things to do."

"Like what?"

"Oh, tour buses, snorkeling, fishing, kayaking, submarine rides. You name it."

"How does the town survive in winter? No tourists."

"They're close knit. Support each other's stores. It's kind of folksy and cool." She swallowed her last swig of beer and hopped off the stool. "Okay, let's hit the road."

After grabbing her suitcase, she yelled to Jessie to get in the cart, wondering how she would acclimate to island life. What would help her heal? Make her happy? As they started toward their new home, both Jessie and Meg were quiet, sharing the same thought. Was this a mistake?

40

Before heading back to Yorba Linda, Grace and Luke enjoyed their private time, something they had seldom shared before in their twenty-five-year history. As the years had slipped by, they'd had had little opportunity to keep in touch and had communicated only when there was a happy moment to share in Meg's life or some immediate danger that was lurking. All the girls had departed for their various venues, which had left the lifetime lovers alone.

Luke poured two glasses of wine and wandered out to the balcony, recoiling at the extreme heat but enjoying the beautiful river as it flowed past. Grace walked down the hall, watched him close the sliding glass door, and admired his physique. She smiled to herself. Wow. This is really happening. She grinned as she joined him on the balcony, stepping over his crossed ankles to sit next to him. She tucked her feet under her on the chaise. She didn't know where to begin or whether this was the time to begin. Are we really going to have time to talk about…what…a future? She picked up her glass of chardonnay, took a sip, and slipped into a simple reverie, tipping her head to the side, allowing her lavender eyes to scan the horizon. How special are these moments?

Luke turned toward her, amazed at her still-glowing beauty. "What a rare creature you are, Grace Pennington. How many years have we been surreptitious lovers? Dear God, what a waste."

She leaned back and reached for his hand.

"If I were a casual observer, I would never believe you were a former CIA agent, capable of huge mayhem. You look…well…almost reserved, pensive."

"How about *wary* for a word?" she said.

"How's that?"

"Not sure what we do now, for one thing. Let's see, for twenty-five years we have communicated with calls, notes, e-mails, and texts. Heavy-duty relationship, huh? You've saved my butt and helped my kids, and we've never spent more than two nights at a time together, ever. And here we are, with an open calendar, and I don't know what to do. Were we kidding ourselves all these years?"

Luke sprang to his feet, surprising Grace out of her melancholy. "Don't you dare give me any of that shit. Woman, I am your man." Before she could finish her smile or begin to speak, he reached down and pulled her to his chest. "Look, I may have a few more gray hairs and put on a couple of pounds, but I have words that need to be whispered in your ear, love to spread over your heart, and—damn it—sex to pour on. So let's get with it."

Grace threw her arms around his neck and kissed him. "Come on, Sir Galahad, carry your woman to the boudoir. Always wanted you to sweep me off my feet." Happy beyond happy.

Luke threw her over his shoulder instead. "Sir Galahad, my ass. I'm Caveman Charlie, and we're doin' it my way."

41

The exchange of money, via wire transfer, was complete, and the first human trafficking transaction proved to be a great financial success for Elliott. With the small problem of the dead girl resolved, he turned to Derek for the final profit and loss numbers.

"Did all of the playboys end up happy?" The brothers sat and sipped martinis as the lights along the coastline blinked over the bow of the boat. Elliott was getting his sea legs now, and he considered buying, instead of leasing, a mega yacht for future business.

Derek keyed in a few shortcuts on his laptop and found the file. "All except the Spaniard, who will be included in round two. Looks like there were three men and one woman left over from the first list. They might still be waiting to hear from us."

"A woman? Hmm. What country?"

"France."

"Interesting. Well, we'll have to accommodate them quickly. If they're still interested, that means we only need to recruit five more millionaires. Let's set up the casting call for next week in Catalina."

"That's too quick. Why rush it?" Derek took a conservative stance.

"Besides the fact that someone might be calling the cops over a missing daughter, with the five investors on the hook already, it would be wasted effort not to proceed quickly. Catalina may be too close, but it's still convenient, especially since we have prepaid for the yacht. It will have to be next week; then we'll head up north."

"We'd better move the yacht this evening."

"Tell the captain to head to the back side of Catalina." Elliott couldn't be bothered with minutia.

"I thought you'd probably want to head to Miami, but north? Any city in particular?" Derek probed for answers.

"Probably San Francisco. Needs to be a large and interesting area for our paying friends. And in San Francisco you could visit some of your gay friends."

Derek chose to ignore the sarcasm.

The sun had set two hours earlier, and while the weather was still hot for August, a cool breeze had picked up, and small swells pushed the yacht around, tugging against the mooring. Elliott yelled to the captain, "Let's lift anchor. Take her around to Two Harbors. We'll tie up to a vacant mooring and head to China Cove at sunup."

"I thought I'd be going back to San Clemente to handle the coyote business with Marisa. It can't run itself." Derek was pushing to get off the boat and away from Elliott.

"You told me it was functioning okay. I'm considering ending that business, but now you're telling me something different? A specific problem?"

"Someone needs to be there for the day-to-day operation. Besides, I can't afford to be seen on Catalina. Everyone knows by now that I'm your brother."

Elliott thought about that. His mood darkened as the dusky night turned to black, drawing his mind into his own private abyss. He sensed Derek had other reasons for wanting to leave, but he wasn't ready to cut him loose. "Marisa can go back to San Clemente for now. She has something to take care of tonight, but she can leave when it's over."

"What's that?" Derek looked at his brother with gnawing fear.

"Not your business. You'll stay on the yacht until we get the next load of lovelies ready for sale. A week from now." He watched for some adverse expression to cross Derek's face, but nothing materialized. "Maybe this time I'll get a girl for you. A fresh one. Maybe you'll change your mind about being gay."

Derek stared at his brother, slowly blinked, stared, blinked again, and then finally turned and left the upper deck. Hatred was again nibbling away at any brotherly fondness he had ever felt for Elliott.

At midnight a dinghy tied up to the stern of the yacht as Marisa packed her bag for her trip to Balboa. Derek sat on her bed and watched.

"How come you're the lucky one?"

"Lucky?" Marisa stopped packing and leaned against the bed. The last two hours with the smelly Spaniard had crushed her spirit.

"What's wrong? You're acting weird." Derek grabbed her arm as she walked to the closet. She winced. He released his grip and saw the beginning of a huge bruise. "How did you get that bruise?" Looking closer, he saw whisker burns on her face and a swollen lip. "Did Elliott rough you up? Talk to me."

"No, it's not that. It's…" She slumped onto the bed, hid her face in her trembling hands, and started to cry. "Elliott drugged me with some of that Devil's Breath and took me to the Spaniard. I was his consolation prize for the dead girl."

"That sick bastard. Oh, sis, I'm so sorry." Derek held her and rocked her back and forth. His emotions vacillated between sorrow and hatred. "What kind of an animal would do that to his own sister? That's it. I'll take care of this problem. We deserve a life, and I'll…well,…I'll take care of it."

"What do you mean?"

"I'm smarter than he is. I'll figure it out."

Marisa straightened up. "Do it. Just do it. I'll help in any way I can." With shaking hands, she finished packing and leaned heavily on the suitcase. "Who knows what evil he has planned? He's been so obsessed with Meg. I can't imagine him allowing anyone to touch her, and yet he wants to have her win the contest. But…Christ, who knows? Weird that I only saw Meg that one time in Yorba Linda. I don't really know her, yet I feel sorry for her." The physical pain from her recent encounter could not be denied. She winced as she lifted the suitcase off the bed.

Derek reached to help her. "You are on board with this coup, aren't you? I need to know that you won't change your mind. You know he'll kill me if I'm caught."

"Is the plan to disappear, or are you planning something stupid like turning him in and testifying for immunity?"

"Just running—at least that's the plan for now. Elliott's tentacles are too long to try to snitch on him. I just want a life, sis, for both of us."

Elliott yelled through the intercom for Marisa to get her butt on board the dinghy. The two left the cabin and snaked their way to the aft deck. As Marisa hugged Derek, she whispered to him, "I'll go with you. I'll set up transferring funds but won't transfer them until you tell me. Be careful. Don't raise any suspicion. Buy a separate cell phone and call me."

42

Becoming more and more concerned over Jessie's mental health, Payden finally gave in to his common sense and picked up the phone to call the Island Company. After a continuum of transfers and holding, he was connected to the vice president in charge of planning. "My interests would be to reestablish the stables on Catalina, rent stalls and horses, set up camps for barrel racers, bull riders, and bareback riders, and eventually entice the rodeo to include Catalina in their circuit with full benefits to the PRC."

"That's a tall order, mister. We'd have to get the EPA involved and have an environmental impact study done. Well, let's put it this way: probably won't happen."

"I know it wouldn't happen overnight, but I would appreciate an opportunity to present the plan."

"That's going to involve a lot of money. Do you have the means for this type of production?" He knew that was a very personal question but felt it was necessary to ask. Why get started with a pipe dream?

"Money is not an issue." Payden had checked with his accountant earlier in the day and had found that all the money from the sale of his business had been transferred. "If the interest is there after a year, I'll build an outstanding covered arena that will be a tribute to your majestic island. Free of charge to the city of Avalon."

The vice president salivated. New business to Catalina? What a feather in his cap. "Well, you could present a proposal to the city council, and if they approve, we would be excited to have your business in Catalina."

"Good. I've done my homework but would like you to verify some facts."

"Like what?"

"I'm interested in the area off Avalon Canyon Road. Any skeletons or bones under the main street, or ghosts that might be irritated by my work?" Payden had done some research on the notorious ghost of Catalina.

"That area is okay—just don't touch the city stockyard or cemetery. All hell would break loose, including a visit or two from our resident ghosts."

"Okay. I need to make another visit to the island, which I plan on doing in the morning. I have access to a private plane and will take off around nine. Can you meet me at Airport in the Sky around nine thirty?"

"Glad to. I'll be driving the company's EV, and we'll take a tour. Thanks for the call."

"I'll bring a rough sketch of my plans and have my accountant push the pencil a little for a tentative cost analysis. See you tomorrow. Nice talking to you."

Payden leaned back in his office chair and glanced out the back window at the ranch activities. Two horses were tied to the hot walker, little Emilie was taking her riding lesson in the arena, and a few of Jessie's girlfriends were grooming their horses. *I'll need someone to run the ranch while I'm gone.* He was usually a calm person, but Jessie had him rattled. The rushed friendship with Meg wasn't normal, not her style. Usually cautious, here she was running away from home to an island, turning her back on her career and what was left of her family. He realized that his decision to follow and watch was a good one.

"Abel? Payden here. Fuel up a small plane or use the corporate helicopter. Whichever you prefer."

"Where to, boss?"

"Catalina for a few days. Oh, we need to take the corporate logo off the plane. Can you handle that?"

"No problem. Going incognito?"

"Something like that."

43

The door to the tattered house was unlocked, and Rachael, gun in hand, silently turned the knob and slipped into the front room. She heard water running in the bathroom and Stella humming an unknown tune. Rachael entered the bedroom and quickly went to Josh's side. He moved around, pulling against the handcuffs, but his eyes remained closed.

"Josh, it's Rachael," she whispered. "Be quiet, I'm going to take off the cuffs and get you out of here."

His eyes opened and a half smile appeared on his face. "Not sure what's happening. Rach, is that really you? I like having sex with you, but you don't need to be so rough." He was totally oblivious to his role in Stella's gyrating game.

She winced. "We can talk later. No more talking now," she whispered. She lowered his arm down to the bed and tiptoed around to the other side. Stella's off-key singing and the sound of water splashing around in the tub gave Rachael confidence that she was still unnoticed. She laid her gun on the bed and reached up for the second handcuff. With a quick twist, the cuff gave way, and she lowered Josh's arm in the process.

Stella burst into the room. "What the hell do you think you're doing, bitch?" She was naked and dripping wet.

Rachael grabbed her gun and pointed it at the redhead. "Back off. I'm taking Josh with me, you maniac. How could you do this to him?"

"He loved it, and guess what?" She raised her hand at Rachael, a single digit protruding. "He'll really be happy when he learns I'm pregnant. He still loves me, you know." A sadistic smile crossed her face.

Rachael was horrified. "You liar."

"Afraid not. And if I know my man, he'll stick by me. We'll be married and raise our baby together." She brushed her tangled hair away from her face and walked toward the bed smiling an evil, yet pathetic, grin. Running her hands down her wet breasts and then down to her stomach, she strutted like a peacock. "Soon there'll be a baby bump."

Beyond frustration, Rachael steadied the gun at Stella, shaking Josh with her free hand, trying to get him to focus. "Come on, Josh. Wake up. Let's get out of here."

Rachael didn't notice a creak in the floorboard behind her and the change in direction of Stella's eyes. Before a muscular, hairy arm encircled her throat and choked the breath from her, she noticed a faint fragrance of men's after-shave tickle her nostrils. She struggled, but the armlock pressed harder until she passed out and slumped into the man's arms.

Greg held on to the unconscious Rachael, and then he gently lowered her to the floor. "Shit, sis. Now look and see what you made me do. These are my friends. He's my partner. Now what?"

"Get rid of her. She annoys me"

"Kill her? Are you crazy?"

"I have what I want. I know it's just a matter of time before Josh remembers everything." She started back for the bathroom and then stopped, totally blasé regarding her nakedness. "I'm going back to Orange County, where I'll wait for the birth of our wonderful child."

Greg's frustration was mounting. "Get some clothes on." He averted his eyes. "Are you off your meds again? Shit, now I've got to hide Rachael and Josh until you get out of town. This is it." He checked Rachael's pulse.

Stella looked wrung out, and her wild red hair, tangled and wet, underscored her crazy behavior. She sat on the edge of the bed and started to pull down the sheet; the desire to mount Josh again was building.

Josh pulled up the sheet and tried to focus on Greg. "What's going on, partner?"

Greg ducked out of the line of vision and whispered to Stella. "Look, sis, this is the last time I can be part of your schemes. Josh is my friend, my partner. I owe him. He's saved me more than once." He stood inside the bathroom, hiding from view. "I'll take care of these two, but you need to get out of here now." He checked his watch. "The *Flyer* will be heading back to the mainland in two hours. That's enough time for you to pack and make some calls to Newport for housing arrangements. Have you spent all of your allowance for this month?"

Josh was struggling to sit up. He tossed the sheet back and swung his legs over the side of the bed. Momentary slices of awareness were plaguing him. "Greg? Is that you?" He checked out the room, but Greg was nowhere to be seen. "Did you just clock Rachael?" He concentrated on the inert body on the floor. "What's going on?"

Red faced, Greg stepped back into the room. "Hey, good buddy. Rachael? Oh, no, she started to faint, so I caught her." He turned his attention to Stella. "Josh needs another shot. For God's sake, something to relax him."

Stella was coherent enough to get the message. "Oh, yeah." She reached for the syringe on the nightstand. "Josh, time for your antibiotics," she said in a singsong voice.

Josh pulled away as she grabbed for his arm. "For Christ's sake, Stella, put on some clothes." He tried to push her away. "Greg, pull her off me. I've got to help Rachael."

"Sorry. It's for your own good." Greg pushed Josh back on the bed, snagged his arm, and stabilized it as Stella inserted the needle. It took a minute for the medication to act, and Josh finally relaxed again. The Versed would make him compliant for now.

Stella puckered her lips and twitched her nose, like she had to sneeze. She tried to concentrate on Greg's instructions but with little comprehension. "What did you say? Money? Yeah, I guess I have money." She walked to the bureau, groped around in her purse, and finally emptied it on the bed.

That obtuse answer didn't comfort Greg. He quickly took inventory of the purse contents and found some money. "Fifty-five bucks—is that all you have? Nothing stashed away in the teapot?" He tore a check from her checkbook and stuck it in his pocket, pulled out his wallet, and added another hundred to her cash. "This is the deal. Get dressed. Pack your clothes; be sure to take your phone charger. Catch the *Flyer*, and when you get to Balboa, call me. I'll rent a place in Costa Mesa for you until we can contact Mom and see if she wants to help. Take a taxi. I'll put some money in your account." His words rattled through the progression as his mind raced around the unacceptable consequences of his actions.

Stella twisted strands of her unruly hair into knots and wiggled toward the bed. "I think I'd like to make love to Josh one more time. You wanna watch?"

Her insane intentions almost tipped Greg over the edge. He knew she wasn't capable of traveling alone, and yet calling a friend to help her would mean involving a stranger in their conspiracy. "Shit, no!" yelled Greg. "Go to the bathroom, put on some fuckin' clothes, and pack while I figure out where to hide my best friends. You really did it this time, Stella."

He looked around the room and located some jeans for Josh. Dressing him was no easy task, but the meds Stella had given him helped with the chore. Josh didn't know what was going on, but he was capable of following Greg's directions.

"Stella, you'll have to give Rachael a shot of that stuff you've been injecting Josh with. I'll need her cooperation for at least two hours. That shit isn't lethal, is it?"

Stella yelled from the bathroom. "No, it's just zombie shit."

He checked his watch again. Knowing that he might need an alibi for this time frame, he shouted further instructions. "Hurry up. I'll take you to town in the Jeep and drop you off on Whittley. You'll have to pull your suitcase to the pier. Can't be seen together." He knew he couldn't leave Stella with Josh and Rachael. She'd probably kill one and screw the other to death. God, what a mess.

44

Derek called the rental offices in town, and with the excuse of being an old friend of Rachael's, he obtained her address. He felt Meg would live with Rachael temporarily until she found another rental with her new friend. When he located the house, he noted the security camera on the front porch and a heavy metal screen door. He made notes and reported back to Elliott.

**

Elliott took a day off to drive his cart around Catalina, deciding on locations for the photo shoot, hiring a computer kid to set up the fliers, notifying the local paper about the casting call, and acquainting himself with the various neighborhoods. He was sitting on a stool at Eric's, enjoying lunch, when Meg and Jessie walked by. *What a nice dessert for me.* He swiveled around on the stool, used his napkin to hide his face as they passed, and then discreetly followed them to their rental. *Oh, darling, you look wonderful.* His erection was in full bloom, and images of sexual encounters raced through his mind. Several mothers on the dock noticed the bulge in his shorts and reached for their children.

"Derek," Elliott said through his cell phone. "I saw Meg. Drop what you're doing and head back to the boat. Now."

"Got it. I've done everything except invite the mayor to the contest. Can you do that?"

"Yes. Get his information for me, and I'll take care of it." Elliott smiled, thinking of his future plans for Meg.

***

Derek still had one huge job to handle. He decided that using his cell phone to make the most important call of the day was stupid since Elliott could easily demand his phone and access any number or text. Instead, Derek located an old-fashioned phone booth on Claressa Avenue and looked around to make sure neither Elliott nor Meg was in sight. He called information. "The number for the FBI in Los Angeles, California." It took a minute to have the operator find the number and connect him for a nominal fee.

"You have reached the Los Angeles office of the Federal Bureau of Investigation. All incoming calls will be recorded."

Derek waited, listening intently to the recorded message, and decided to ask the operator for assistance in finding his targeted person, Amanda Pennington.

"Sir, is this Ms. Pennington a secretary, perhaps a clerk, or an agent?"

"I don't have time for any runaround." He knew the conversation was being recorded. "Tell her that Derek Turner wants to cooperate. I'm on a pay phone in Catalina. Don't come, or Elliott will disappear. I will contact her tomorrow at this same number. She needs to be available." Derek's hands were sweating as he replaced the receiver and quickly ducked out of the phone booth. He glanced both ways, felt a sense of relief, and headed back to the cart.

***

When the two met up on the yacht that evening, Derek could tell Elliott was anxious to get the plans completed. "Did you hear back from our investors? How many?"

Derek ran a print of his laptop screen and then closed it. He crossed the room with the paper and handed it to his brother. "We have eight confirmations, but Turkey and Scotland have not checked in yet. The rest are available and will arrive in two days." He headed for the Scotch. The thought of selling another set of women, like common cattle, depressed him.

"You're hitting the bottle a little hard, aren't you? What's wrong? No stomach for human trafficking?" Elliott laughed at his brother, regarding him as a pitiful excuse for a man. "Maybe we should have a casting call for men in bikinis. More to your liking?"

Derek hid his look of disgust and left the cabin without comment. He walked to the bow of the boat and gazed at the campfire lights that were beginning to appear in Shark Harbor. A plan was beginning to form, a plan that would extricate him from his brother's grip and save his sister as well. He knew his brother was evil and understood Elliott's innate cunning. Derek believed there was no other way to solve the problem. With a strong mental resolve, he headed toward his room.

Elliott, disturbed by Derek's departure, mumbled out loud. "That shit. Who does he think he is? Would he go against me? Ha. And yet..." Elliott spent the next hour pondering Derek's actions and then switched over to his project. Let's see. I cleared eight million on the last delivery of girls, and if this grouping goes as well, that will be another eight or nine. Will probably have to lie low for a month and then go to...where? I told Derek San Francisco, but maybe Florida would be better.

A goal, a certain amount of money, was never his motivation. Whatever evil pursuit gave him the most pleasure was his driving force; the money was secondary. Derek, however, was always counting the cash and talking about another life. Fool. What other life could there possibly be for any of them, and why? Elliott left the cabin, felt the rush of ocean air, and crossed to the stern of the boat. Leaning back in his deck chair, folding his arms above his head, he gazed at the stars; his thoughts of the young Meg and their first sexual encounter a year ago excited him. Knowing she was on the island, only a few miles away, stimulated him again, and he unzipped his pants, pulled out his friend, and stroked away.

45

Greg realized that dumping Stella off on Whittley Avenue would be a mistake because of her incoherent condition and the distance that needed to be covered before she boarded the ferry. He hid the Jeep in the rental garage and changed out of his uniform into Josh's clothes. He drove her cart the long way up Country Club Drive, then took Tremont Street to Clemente Avenue and ended at the intersection of Beacon and Claressa. He pulled his baseball cap down to his eyebrows and shut off the electric cart. "Get out here, sis. It's just a short walk to the *Flyer*." He pulled up the handle on her luggage.

"Are you going to take good care of Josh for me? He's going to be a daddy, you know." She kept blinking her eyes and rubbing her mouth. Her pale, drug-ridden body shrieked against the blazing-red, unruly hair. With a height of five feet nine inches and only ninety-eight pounds of flesh and bones to hold her up, her age of twenty-eight seemed more like forty. She needed help getting out of the cart.

"Put on your sunglasses. Your eyes are totally dilated. Yeah, yeah. I'll watch Josh. A baby? I know, I know. God, how I know." There are so many things that can go wrong. "I printed a ticket for you off your computer, so you don't have to wait. Stand over there like we always do when we go to the mainland. Don't stop by the Conservancy to talk to Rosie. Go directly to the pier." He wondered whether she comprehended any part of this. "Aunt Sharon will be in Balboa to pick you up. She volunteered to help until we find Mom—*if* we find Mom."

179

Stella smiled weakly at her brother, her lip catching on her yellowed teeth. "I want to stay here and care for Josh."

"No. Damn it. No. Get going. Don't stop and talk to anyone. Don't buy coffee at Eric's. Keep looking down and get straight in line. Got it?" He pulled off his baseball cap and shoved it on her head.

His words were pretty jumbled, but she forgave him for drinking. Then she wondered whether she'd been drinking. Drugs...drugs, she thought. Need a normal baby, no more drugs.

Greg drove around to Pebbly Beach Road and found a spot where he could watch Stella board the *Flyer*. Done. Now for an alibi. He retraced his steps back to the rental house, checked to make sure Rachael and Josh were still knocked out, and cuffed Josh again in case he got rowdy while he was gone. Then he changed back into his uniform, drove his Jeep to Sumner, parked in front of a vacant house, and walked around the corner to the main street. He was short of breath.

"What's the disturbance?" he yelled at the El Galleon bartender. The bar was packed with tourists, and the noise level was way past tolerable decibels.

"I didn't call. Noisy but under control," said the bartender.

"Hmm. Well, I'd better take a look around anyway. Someone called the station." He pushed past the karaoke stage and small tables to the back booths and then to the restrooms. On the way out, he yelled to the bartender again. "Everything checks out. Bum call, I guess. Sorry to bother you. Say, have you seen Meg and her friends? Rachael said they're arriving this week."

"Yeah, they were in here earlier. Wild bunch looking for fun."

"That's her. I'm outta here. An hour to go, and then I'm off duty. Have a good one."

Now that his alibi was concrete, he headed back to the rental house, just as the sun was beginning to set. He had a plan so that no one would get hurt, and yet enough time would elapse so that he would be in the clear. Before anything else, though, he needed to dump Stella's cart somewhere in the bushes off Hiawatha and sprint back.

Josh was still handcuffed to the bed when Greg arrived, but he was awake and pulling against his restraints. Stella had told Greg about the compound she'd been dosing Josh with, so locating the drug and administering the right amount were imperative. Jeez, what am I doing? He's my best friend. Guilt riddled him, but he pushed forward out of sheer desperation to protect his sister and his own ass. Here it is. He swished the compound around in a small amount of beer and handed it to Josh. "Here, buddy. Drink it down, and then we'll head out to the patrol car and get you home." Per Stella, his memory would be blocked, but he would still be able to function on demand. "Okay, man. Help me get Rachael to the car." The key popped the cuffs open.

Josh wasn't much help, but between the two of them, Rachael was strapped into the backseat of the patrol car, and Josh settled into the passenger seat.

"I'll just be a minute. Gotta hit the john." Greg rushed back into the house and expertly wiped down all fingerprints, not knowing whether the step was necessary but taking no chances. Neither Josh nor Rachael should remember anything about the event, but they were both smart, and bits and pieces of their combined memory might paint the full picture. That couldn't be helped, and when they awakened from their forced sleep, well, time would tell what would happen then.

Greg drove the back roads again, up County Club Drive and then up Avalon Canyon Road, to the Wrigley Memorial Garden. The area was deserted, so parking at the dead end would go unobserved. The fifteen-by-twenty room adjoining the custodian's workshop was padlocked, barring anyone from entering, especially the inquisitive island teenagers experimenting with drugs and sex. Greg and Josh helped Rachael to the door, and the three looked like drunken sailors on leave as they stumbled along. Greg pulled out his gun and hit the padlock with the butt end of his Beretta. The dusty room reeked of fertilizer, age, and decay, and the only light poured in from the open door. Greg located two dusty chairs in the corner and plopped Rachael down on one. Her body was limp; sitting wasn't going to work, so Greg laid her on the dirty floor. "Josh, I need to go get some help for Rachael. Will you stay with her and protect her?"

"What's wrong with her?" he mumbled. "Has she been drinking? Have I been drinking? I feel weird." He gazed down at Rachael's body but didn't feel like helping her.

"Yeah, you guys were partying, and I found you here, but I think she needs some attention. I'll call for help. Be right back. Don't leave her." He left the room and wired the door shut from the outside. *God, help me.*

Josh sat in the chair next to the inert Rachael, fighting the urge to sleep. "Rach, you okay?" He leaned over and brushed the hair away from her face. "You sleeping?" He sat on the floor next to her and then gave in to his weariness and finally lay down. "Greg's gone for help. We'll rest till he gets back." He relaxed onto the floor next to Rachael and immediately fell into a deep sleep. His dreams were filled with erotic lovemaking with Rachael…Or was it someone else?

46

Following the successful meeting with the Catalina Planning Committee, Payden bypassed all small requirements, posted a bond, and moved ahead with his plans. It was obvious that Grace liked to be involved with Meg's life, so he used the crisscross directory and called her Yorba Linda number. After a few pleasantries, he began, "Grace, I wanted to let you know that I'm shipping six horses over to Catalina tomorrow morning so that Jessie and Meg can get started on setting up the ranch."

"I hadn't heard about any of this. That bratty little Meg is so secretive. What's the plan?" She turned to Luke and shook her head, putting the phone on speaker.

"I know my sister. Jessie needs a project to keep her distracted while recovering from Jordan's death, so I came up with this plan about resurrecting the old stables on Catalina and making it available for the rodeo circuit."

"That's a huge project. I know the area. Needs lots of work. Do you have time to help the girls?" And expensive too. An insurance salesman? What's with that? Grace's CIA mentality was taking over.

"Full-time, much to the chagrin of Jessie, I'm afraid. She hates to be manipulated, but so what? What are brothers for, if not to micromanage their spoiled kid sisters?"

"Been accused of the same thing myself." They both laughed. "I was thinking of spending a few days on Catalina and bringing a friend. I'm not as horsey as my kids, but how about we hitch a ride on your barge? That sounds like fun. What time do you leave?"

The bizarre group left from the Balboa Fun Zone at 2:00 p.m. with six horses, twenty bales of hay, grain, and tack. The last two people to join the happy entourage were Dick, the groomer, and Brian, the trainer.

Luke, the consummate CIA agent, was always careful when meeting new people, and since Dick presented himself as a good ol' cowboy, he directed his attention to Brian. "So have you been working at Rock-n-C Ranch for a long time?"

"Actually, only a week. The last guy started drinking too much, so Rocky had to let him go."

"Who's Rocky?"

"Oh, he's Payden's foreman."

"How did you hook up with Rocky?"

"Craigslist."

Brian wasn't much of a talker, so Luke decided to make a phone call and have him checked out. Any guy working with my daughter needs to meet my specs. The phone call was made, and he nudged Grace. "New trainer. You get a read on him yet?"

Grace flashed one of her most charming smiles. "You rascal. I was ready to ask Rachael to handle a background check through the PD." She waded through the water and attempted to climb onto the barge.

Luke reached for her hand, pulled her up, and then conveniently pulled her closer and kissed her. The satellite station picked up the whole scene: a flat-boat with six worried horses pushing against their makeshift pipe corrals, two cowboys smoking their cigarettes, one outsider, and two "older" people neck-ing as the pontoon boat crashed through the swells, heading toward Catalina. Luke glanced at his watch and looked up at where the passing satellite would be. "Wave hello. My friends back in the office will get a kick out of this."

47

Jessie set her alarm so she could get to the kitchen before Meg stumbled in for coffee. She broke open the box of rat poison and with gloved hands took out ten pieces of the green granules. Taking a mug from the cupboard, she ground the pieces into dust, added them to the cranberry juice, gave the bottle a good shake, and returned it to the refrigerator. She quickly took the poison back to her bedroom and hid it on a high shelf. With a satisfied sigh, she looked in the mirror and contemplated her image, superimposing a faux figure of her dead sibling in her stead. Well, sis, we just took the first step at getting even with Meg for killing you. Everyone says it was some guy named Elliott who was stalking Meg. But me—I know she's responsible for your death. She lured him there to the casino. Her fault entirely, and she will pay.

Jessie strolled back to the kitchen, poured a little cranberry juice into a glass, and quickly emptied it down the sink, leaving only a trace of juice in the bottom. Their tiny house on Whittley Avenue was well situated so that the sparkling ocean would greet them each morning and get them started. She walked out on the front porch, pried her mind away from her sister, and focused on her immediate mission. Payden had said he would be on the island by three thirty with the horses. She needed to hustle and complete the work before he arrived. Heading down the hall with a cheerful ring in her voice, she yelled, "Hey, Meg, time to get up and have some breakfast." Giving a couple of raps on the door, she entered and found Meg all twisted up in her blankets. "Time's a wastin', girlfriend. Get a move on." Her Norco jargon was taking over.

"Yeah, okay." Meg rolled over and caught a glimpse of the gorgeous day awaiting her. She tugged on her tan shorts, leaving on her pajama top, and ambled out to the kitchen, hair all askew. "So what's on the agenda today?" As she poured a large glass of cranberry juice, she sorted through the mail on the table.

Jessie was overcome with happiness at the amount of cranberry juice she poured and proceeded to relay the adventure that awaited them. "Horses are arriving, so go change. You'll need jeans and boots. We'll pick up some food on the way and start bossing those high school girls around to clean up the stables."

"Girls? Why not guys?"

"The girls' club was associated with the stables a long time ago. I found that out on the Internet and called them. They want to help. Free. Won't cost us a dime." She stood there, tapping her foot, waiting for Meg to move. "Come on."

"Jeez, you're worse than my mother. I've got to touch base with Rachael before we get started."

"What for?"

"See if there's any word on Josh or Elliott." Her voice projected a slightly annoyed attitude toward Jessie. What? Life just rotates around you and your stupid horses now?

She dialed Rachael's phone number and was immediately transferred to voice mail. "Weird, she always answers when I call. Must be busy trackin' down that crazy redhead." Meg stood and was starting toward the bedroom when a wave of nausea rushed over her. Grabbing her mouth and running full blast, she barely made it to the toilet in time to vomit up the juice. She yelled to Jessie, "Check the expiration date on that cranberry juice and throw the rest away. It's bad!"

Jordan was annoyed to think she might have to come up with another way to poison Meg but resigned herself to checking out the Internet. Maybe I'll start with a smaller dose. You're the one who's going to be expired.

On the way to the stables, the girls stopped off at Rachael's house. Her cart, the one Greg had returned the previous night, was parked out front. When Rachael didn't answer the door, Meg went inside and disarmed the alarm system. "Strange." The alarm was set to AWAY, and yet the cart was outside. She checked for the three hidden guns, and all were accounted for. "Guess she walked to town for breakfast. Oh, well, we'll catch up with her later."

"What's with all the guns? Does Catalina have a problem I haven't heard about?"

Meg didn't realize Jessie had followed her into the house. "Oh, when you live with two sisters, one FBI and the other a local cop, you get used to the firearms. Ever fired a gun?"

"Payden used to take us to the shooting range, but I never tried to shoot a person." Time will tell on that.

"Me neither. But…if Elliott ever shows up in my sights again, I won't have a problem." Meg covered the .38 with the bathroom towels and set the alarm, and they headed for the stables.

The girls drove to the Catalina Coffee and Cookie Company and ordered coffee. Meg watched Jessie as she took her first sip of latte and placed it on the small table. Hmm. Payden said Jessie always licks the corners of her mouth after her first sip of latte. She didn't. That's curious. Stop. You're getting like your detective sister. Leave it alone.

They met up with the volunteer girls at the corner of Sumner and Tremont and caravanned to the old stables past Avalon Canyon Road. Jessie immediately set out organizing the jobs. Meg and Jessie started the tractor and dragged the whole five acres, while the girls mucked the stalls. It was getting hot, so Meg demanded a break. "Hey, take it easy on the staff. Let's take the cart for a ride and cool off, maybe find a gallon of cold water up the hill."

"Okay, how about showing me the Hermit Gulch Campground? We might be able to do something there. Love the name."

"Sure, it's right up the road, and then we'll swing by the Wrigley Memorial."

"Is that the botanical garden area?"

"The same. Come on, let's go. The girls can handle most of the rest, and then we have to meet Payden and the horses."

Jordan was less than impressed with the campground but saw potential. "Let's make the gardens a quick trip; we really need to get to Descanso Beach. We'll have to take the girls with us. Someone's got to ride the horses back to the stables, and we'll drive the cart back." She was beginning to worry about the encounter at Descanso. Riding Jessie's horse wasn't an option. He'd throw her.

"Okay, no problemo." They took a quick trip to the garden area, talked the clerk out of charging them admission, walked half the distance to the memorial, and then turned back because of time restraints. As they neared the museum, Meg stopped abruptly. "Did you hear that?"

"What?"

"That cell phone."

"Nope." Jessie turned around, canvassing the area. "And no one's up here. No carts, no people, no cell phone. You're hearing things."

The ringing had stopped. "That's weird, 'cause that was Rachael's ring... the USC fight song." She pulled her phone out of her pocket and started dialing.

"What are you doing? Your sister's not the only one with that ring. Absurd."

Meg tried not to show her irritation. "Calling her. I know you think I'm creepy, but if there's anything I've learned living with a cop...well, it's follow your instincts." The ringing started again. "See, the sound is coming from behind that building. Rach, is that you?" No answer, so Meg waited a minute. The sound stopped. She dialed again. The ringing commenced in concert with her phone. "See? Shit. What's going on?"

They followed the sound to an old structure attached to the service building. Meg looked at the ground. Signs of struggle were apparent. "Someone's been dragged here. Look. Be careful—this doesn't look good." She held her arm out to stop Jessie from walking through the prints.

"Who are you—Nancy Drew or something?" Jessie couldn't believe how much Meg was overreacting.

Meg untangled the wire from the lock, opened the door, and peered into the dark, musty room.

"Hello. Is anyone in there? Rachael?"

48

After purchasing two throwaway phones, Derek walked up Sumner and ducked into the first alley.

"FBI."

"Derek Turner for Amanda Pennington, please."

"Just a moment, Mr. Turner. She'll be right with you."

"Agent Pennington. To whom am I speaking?" Amanda pulled the cushioned chair forward and started the small tape recorder attached to the phone. She had closed the cruise ship's library, awaiting Derek's call. As an undercover dancer on the cruise line, she had to perform certain duties, other than dancing, so she had elected to work in the library to keep an open line to the FBI. She pushed the RECORD button and sent a hookup to her immediate supervisor in Los Angeles.

"Amanda, it's Derek. I need your help. I don't have much time." He leaned against the wooden building, seeking some shade in which to hide.

"Help? Depends, Derek. Last time I saw you, you left me in the Mohave Desert to die."

"Amanda, you'll have to get past that. Elliott is going to grab Meg again, and I can't let that happen."

Huge red flags surrounded the conversation. "Since when have you been so caring? You've helped Elliott all along."

"She changed me." He glanced around the corner to see if he was still alone.

Amanda knew if anyone could change Derek, it would be Meg with her honest, caring nature. "I'm more than suspicious of anything you have to offer involving that psycho brother of yours, but okay, fill me in." The two names, Elliott and Meg, in the same sentence flipped a mental switch, and she focused.

Derek told her about their last operation in Balboa—the human trafficking, the success, and how Elliott was planning to do it again on Catalina in two days. "Marisa and I both want out."

"How involved is Marisa?"

"She almost leads a normal life, but she does all the accounting and handled the business for Elliott when he was involved in money laundering for the casinos. Elliott won't hesitate to kill us if he finds out what I'm doing. Can you help?"

"Perhaps. I'm not authorized to make any deals, but I can make arrangements to stop Elliott. Tell me his plan."

Derek hesitated. He knew this was the pivotal point. "I need some kind of reassurance from you that Marisa won't be prosecuted."

"I can't give that, but I will help, if you're telling the truth."

Realizing she was holding all of the cards, Derek knew he had nothing to negotiate. Time was short, so he continued. He quickly explained to Amanda that a rigged casting call would be held on Descanso Beach. Afterward, a tender would take the girls to the yacht anchored off shore, and then they would travel to the back of the island to Shark Harbor. "There are going to be ten international playboys waiting to meet the girls."

"How are they arriving, and how are they leaving with the girls?" She wanted to climb through the phone and choke the information out of him.

The bony skeleton of Elliott's plan was laid out. "They take care of their own transportation to Newport. Each millionaire has his own day cruiser waiting with two hired assassins on board. The men will arrive the night before the auction. After the women arrive and the auction is complete, the hired men will assist with putting the drugged women in the day cruisers and then head back to Balboa. The playboys are on their own once they leave the yacht." Derek felt the time slipping away. "God, last time one girl died from the drugs she was given, so the man from Spain is a holdover. Is this enough for you to help me?"

"What happened to the body?"

190

"Elliott sliced her up a little and bagged her, and a guy took her away in the skiff. They were supposed to dump her for the sharks. Sorry."

"Tell me more about the day cruisers. Where are the buyers renting the boats?"

"Somewhere out of Balboa. Don't know. I didn't handle that part."

"Crew and weapons?"

"Besides Elliott, there are four well-armed and trained mercenaries. AR-15 assault rifles, and I saw some Glocks. They're part of Elliott's crew. The yacht crew isn't involved."

"Shit, there's not much time. Hold on." Amanda checked with her supervisor on the other line and came back. "We'll have to get the Coast Guard involved to take over the boat." Don't tell him too much. May be part of Elliott's plan. "Can you protect Meg and the other girls when this goes down?"

"Timing is everything. Once the girls are on board, they'll change into evening gowns, and then they'll be drugged with some Devil's Breath shit. The men select their girls, and transport off the yacht begins. Timing wise, it would be too messy to come on board when the girls are changing, so the best bet would be to take over the individual boats after they leave. Out of sight, of course."

"We can time that. Not so many innocents to be accounted for that way. Why not stop Elliott before he gets started?"

"Your choice. You won't have anything on the foreign lechers that way."

"True."

"Gotta go before Elliott sees me. Damn it, Amanda. You have to do something." He stepped out into the sunlight and looked around. "I'll try to call tomorrow."

"Thanks, Derek, and I mean that. We can't let anything else happen to Meg."

"I know." The line went dead.

Derek headed back to Crescent and was assimilated into the street swarming with vacationers. He stopped and watched some young girls crowding around a flier stapled to a palm tree on the beach. The flier said, "Casting Call Saturday. Show up in your best bikini and be discovered." Derek winced.

49

As the barge slid onto shore at the freight line on Pebbly Beach Road, Payden yelled instructions to his small crew. "We'll saddle the horses on board so we don't have to carry the tack around. Brian, go over and tie a tether line between those two palm trees. Grace, have you located Meg or Rachael yet?"

Grace liked the way Payden took control. "Sorry. That's not like either of them. Guess I'll try the sheriff's department. Maybe they've found Josh, or maybe his partner might be able to help."

"Good idea. Luke, can you help saddle up Jessie's mare?"

Luke shrugged and started on the task. "No training classes like that at Langley, but I used to ride as a kid." He enjoyed the challenge, and Grace grinned at his agility. He smiled back. "God, we're like two teenagers. Come here, wench, and give me a kiss. I've got to corral the horses." He hooked his thumbs in his Levi pockets, tipped his cowboy hat, and strutted toward Grace like John Wayne in action.

Once she was finally connected to the sheriff's dispatch, Grace asked for either Josh or Greg. After a brief interrogation, the deputy supplied little information. "Greg called in yesterday, said he had talked to Rachael, and was going to meet her, but she didn't show up at Stella's house. Stella is missing, along with Josh and Rachael. The whole department's out looking for them."

Grave concern crossed Grace's face as she joined Luke, cinched up the saddle, and continued talking. She conveyed her anxieties to him, and he immediately opened his cell phone. "Give me both Rachael's and Meg's phone numbers. I can have them tracked in minutes."

"Is Jessie missing too? Did you ask about her?" Payden had overheard the conversation, and he jumped right in.

"Sorry, Payden, no one knows Jessie, so they wouldn't have any info. I'm sure the girls are together. Meg is tough. She can protect Jess."

"That won't be necessary. Jess keeps up with her karate because of her movie stunt work. She'll be taking care of Meg, probably. But here, take her cell number too." Payden continued on with saddling the horses but with rising concern. "Is this the way your life goes, Grace? Huge drama all the time?"

"There was a time a year ago when life was wonderfully boring. If anyone would have told me what we would be facing,…well, I would have taken my girls to an unknown island and waited it out."

When all the horses were led off the barge, the tack and hay were loaded onto a waiting truck. Payden paid the barge tender and turned to the group. "Any word yet?" When Luke responded in the negative, Payden continued. "Looks like we'll have to ride the horses up to the stables without the girls. Saddle up."

Grace mumbled, "Oh, dear."

Luke gave her a leg up and pinched her butt. "Oops, sorry." He smiled.

"Sorry, my ass."

"And that, too."

***

"Rachael?" Meg repeated the question as she slowly sidled toward the figure lying prone on the floor. The only light in the room crept in from the open door. "Josh, is that you?" she asked as she strained to adjust her eyes. "Open the double doors, Jessie. Quick. It's Rachael. She needs help." She dropped to Rachael's side and felt for a pulse. "Call nine one one. No wait; that won't help here on the island; call…Rosie…yes, Rosie. Tell her to bring some blankets and water and call the cops and paramedics. Hurry. Here's my phone."

Jessie quickly pulled out her phone and dialed Rosie's number. "Meg, I don't know where we are. What shall I say?"

"The building behind the custodian's garage at the Memorial Gardens. She'll know."

Rachael was coming around, so Meg crossed over to Josh. "What's going on, Josh? Why are you guys here? Are you okay?"

Josh looked at Meg, and she could tell he wasn't with the program. "I'm supposed to take care of Rachael, I think. Who told me that?" He looked around the room. "Is that her? Is she okay?"

"Oh, brother. You're not much help." Meg pulled Rachael to a sitting position and straightened her clothes. "Come on, sis. Talk to me."

"Meg? What are you...?" She didn't finish her sentence because she saw Josh in the dim light. "How'd we get here? Is he okay?" She tried to stand, but her legs gave out, and she fell against Meg. "Meg, I'm a mess. Help me."

"I've got you." Josh left the chair and went to Rachael's side. "Come on, Rach, hold onto me." He pulled her up from the floor and wrapped his arms around her. "Don't know what's been going on, but we're okay now. The rest we'll figure out later."

She tried to return his embrace but was met with weak muscles. Is he back?

Within ten minutes, Rosie arrived with short supplies, and then came the troops. Meg's GPS system revealed her position, so instead of going to the stables, Payden's posse rode directly to the gardens, while the paramedics, an ambulance, Greg, and the PD arrived next. Josh and Rachael were strapped onto gurneys, IV drips were started, and the two were pushed toward the ambulance, complaining all the time that they were fine.

All the activity surprised Meg. "Jeez, Mom. What are you doing here? And Dad? Where the hell'd you all come from? And Payden with a posse? Shit, it's a three-ring circus."

Grace got off her horse and embraced Meg. "You okay? God, we couldn't find Rachael or Josh, and then we find you in this abandoned shack. What the hell's going on?" She stood back and checked out Meg.

Luke tried to question Rachael and Josh before the ambulance swept them away, but he gave up since neither could recall the last eight hours. In fact, Josh could remember only bits and pieces of the last three days.

Greg insisted that Luke get out of the ambulance as he climbed in and took over the questioning. "Everyone step back. Give 'em some air. That's all you can remember, Rachael?"

"Yeah, I was trying to call you for backup, but you were responding to a call, and then everything went black. But wait. I do remember…" Rachael's words trailed off as the scent of a man's aftershave lotion tickled her nose. She paused, trying to focus.

"What?"

"Nothing solid, just something."

Greg nodded, jumped out of the ambulance, slammed the door, and gave the driver a signal to leave. Thank God she doesn't remember. Or does she? A nose twitch? I'll change my aftershave tomorrow.

**

Luke broke away from the rest of the family and walked the perimeter of the abduction scene. He checked for footprints around the exterior and was more than interested in the extra tire marks outside. His curiosity focused on Greg. Doesn't seem like he's doing a good job preserving evidence.

Luke introduced himself to Greg, saying he had some law enforcement experience and would like to examine the room where Josh and Rachael had been held hostage.

"Sorry, old man, can't do. The sheriff's department will be handling this."

He didn't like the rebuff, but Grace pulled him back from the group. "It's fine, old man. Let them do their job. Rachael will call us before she talks to him. Pennington women know what to do. Didn't look like any physical harm was applied. Just drugs. All very strange."

When Meg joined them, Grace looked concerned. "You sick?"

"No, I was working pretty hard at the stables this morning. Probably a little dehydrated."

"I don't think so." She put her wrist on Meg's forehead. "No fever. No symptoms of any kind?"

"Well, the cranberry juice didn't agree with me this morning. I barfed."

"Pregnant?"

"Not hardly, unless you want to rename me Mary."

"Oh, you impertinent little scruff." Grace pulled Meg to her and gave her a hug. "Come on, girls, mount up. Let's ride these horses back to the stables and find some carts. Luggage is still at the beach, so everyone needs to lend a hand. Looks like a family reunion again."

Payden had been talking to Jessie. "I thought you would like the idea of an arena and all the improvements I have in mind. What's with you?"

"Nothing…nothing. Fine, everything is fine." She tried to walk away.

"Boy, Jess, you're getting more like Jordan every day. Crusty. I brought your horse, so saddle up and let's get started."

"I'll take the cart. I'm too tired to ride. Let someone else ride Charlotte." She shied away from Jessie's mare.

"Hey, Mom," Meg said. "Speaking of reunions. How come you're here? Thought you and…Dad…would be off honeymooning by now. Oh, that's right, you're not married."

"Not my fault," Luke quickly exclaimed. "She won't say yes."

"Typical Pennington woman. Rachael ran away from Josh till he gave up, and now she's running toward him. Amanda ran away from her cop lover, and me, well, I don't even have a guy to run from anymore. Yup, Pennington women are tough to figure out."

"Maybe so, but don't be surprised if you get a phone call one of these days from your mom saying she's married. I don't give up easily. Might have to get her drunk."

"Go for it," Meg said, not revealing her mixed thoughts. She wasn't sure she wanted a dad after twenty-three years.

***

By the time the horses were stabled and the luggage collected, Meg and Jessie said their good-byes and left for their house. Darkness surrounded the cottage when they finally got home, and Jessie headed for her room, not interested in dinner. She wanted to sneak another dose of rat poison into Meg's food, but the opportunity didn't present itself.

***

Grace and Luke stumbled around, laughing, as they tried to fit the key in the cottage lock. Once they unlocked the door, bypassed the security system, and turned on the lights, everything settled down. Grace showed Luke around the house, and they put their luggage in the guest bedroom since Rachael had settled in the master.

"Merlot okay?" Luke rummaged around in the kitchen pantry.

"Perfect. Good luck finding a corkscrew," Grace answered. "Bring it out to the patio."

Luke laughed as he opened one drawer after another. "You women certainly like your gadgets." He grabbed two glasses and joined Grace on the patio.

"Couldn't ask for a more beautiful night." Grace snuggled in his arms. The twinkling lights of Catalina provided the entertainment.

"Oh, and peaceful and serene. Now we'll have some real time together." Luke smiled and pulled her in closer, tipping her chin upward to meet his gaze.

The phone rang. It was Amanda.

50

When Stella stepped off the *Catalina Flyer*, Aunt Sharon was waiting for her, car keys in hand, appointment pending. "Here, over here, Stella." Watching her niece descend the ramp—with a ridiculous baseball cap trying to hide unmanageable hair, ragged cutoff jeans, and a faded T-shirt covering braless boobs—made her depressed. As a girl, Stella had such potential—until she didn't.

Old bitch. I was hoping she wouldn't show up. "Hi, Auntie." Her suitcase got stuck on the bottom of the ramp, and she tugged it loose. Expletives poured through her mind. "Did you find a place for me to stay? I know it was really short notice."

Sharon had anticipated that that would be the first question and was prepared for it. "Nope, we'll have to look tomorrow. Have an appointment with a real estate lady in the morning. You'll get to bunk with me tonight. Lucky you."

Her smug smile irritated Stella, and she moaned inside. Should have known. "Okay, but I don't want to be a burden." *Bitch.*

"No such thing." Sharon started to throw the luggage in her trunk.

"Wait. I need the small thermal bag. Hand it to me."

"What? Did you bring some abalone from Catalina?"

"No, just a precious gift from Josh." She had saved some sperm from her last tryst will Josh, stored it in a condom, and packed it on ice. Her backup plan.

Sharon shrugged off the comment, and they climbed into the front seat and buckled up. Never known for her subtlety, she jumped right into the pending problem. "Greg says you might be pregnant. That so?"

Thrilled to talk about it, Stella started in. "Yes, Josh and I are having a baby. I haven't told Mom; we just found out." She circled her stomach with both hands. "No baby bump yet."

"You peed on a stick?"

"Not yet, but I know. For sure, I know." She rolled her head around and forced a bashful smile.

Sharon needed Stella's cooperation, but how to get it would be tricky. "You know, your mom had a lot of trouble with her first pregnancy, so Greg and I thought it might be a good idea for you to get a checkup right away." She waited for the signal and turned left, heading for the Pacific Coast Highway.

"I didn't know that. What kind of trouble?" Paranoia was creeping in.

"Oh, she had to stay in bed the first month or lose the baby."

"I can't lose the baby...can't lose the baby." Paranoia gave way to full-fledged manic takeover. "Gotta see a doctor. Now. Gotta see a doctor." She started pulling at her seat belt frantically, eyes searching around the car for a quick exit. "Drive faster. Hurry, drive."

"Calm down, dear. We knew you'd be concerned, so I made an appointment for you."

"Now, okay, now. Let's do it now. Okay, now." She leaned forward, pressing her hands on the dashboard, willing all signals to turn green.

Sharon's words seemed to pacify Stella for the moment, and they drove in silence. She knew Stella needed help. The mood swings during Stella's childhood had been few, but with her recent behavior, the desperate need to be pregnant and the kidnapping of Josh, it was obvious she needed twenty-four-hour care. No time to think about it.

They drove to Hoag Hospital in Newport, parked, and entered the facility. It was late in the day, and the waiting room was nearly empty, so they were escorted to the doctor's office immediately. Stella pulled at her clothing, raised and dropped her shoulders, and mumbled about the health of the baby. She was totally unleashed when the doctor entered.

Earlier in the day, after Greg's call, Sharon had set up the appointment, informing Dr. Schmidt about Stella's history, her bipolar condition, and her recent activities on Catalina with Josh. Preparations had been made to admit her, but without power of attorney, Sharon and Dr. Schmidt had to convince her to do voluntary commitment.

Stella found Dr. Schmidt easy to talk to, and she shared all her enthusiastic plans for her future with Josh and the baby.

"How wonderful for you, Stella. Well, the first thing we need to do is a quick exam to make sure that everything is where it's supposed to be. Okay?"

Stella frantically looked at Sharon, but Sharon patted her hand and said, "It's all right, dear. We need to make sure the baby's fine. Remember what I told you about your mom."

"Oh, right. Sure." Stella was led to a changing room and then to the exam room while Sharon and the doctor talked.

"I can see that she needs help, and I feel confident that I can talk her into staying for a while. How long is beyond my control. At least we'll know if she's really pregnant. People who struggle with bipolar disorder can also experience psychosomatic false pregnancies."

"It's only been a day or so since, err, exposure, and I don't know how frequent it was. She said she hasn't peed on a stick, but she did tell Greg she was pregnant. Is it too early to tell?"

"Maybe. That's another reason I can convince her to stay…until we get confirmation from the lab work."

"Don't tell her she's not pregnant. She'll go ballistic on you, and that's not a pretty scene."

"No worries. I handle this type of situation all the time."

A rush was put on Stella's blood work while the doctor performed the pelvic exam. Snapping off her gloves, Dr. Schmidt rolled the stool over to Stella's side as she sat up. The exam paper crumpled under her body. "Well, for starters, there's a fair possibility that you're pregnant, but we'll have to wait on the lab results. There is some inflammation of the pelvic region but nothing significant. The only problem I see is that your mom had six miscarriages, all within the first trimester. The one time she held on to you was a result of bed rest at the beginning of her pregnancy."

Stella began to panic. "Are you saying I could lose the baby? Josh will be crushed. What should I do?"

"Let me make a call to admitting. If there's a bed available, I think you should stay overnight. We'll have the test results by morning. We need to be careful right now. How does that sound?"

"Yes, yes, of course." Stella stood up and started walking around the room, mumbling to herself. "I'm fine, the baby's fine. Josh loves us." Then the tears came, accompanied by moaning. "Bed, get in bed. I'm fine. The baby's fine...Where's my bed?"

An attendant appeared and waited to escort Stella to a semiprivate room. "Sharon, would you call Josh and Greg? Tell 'em I'm okay. Be home in a week or so. Tell Josh I love him, and I'm doing the right thing for our baby." She took a swing at the male attendant when he tried to help her down the hall.

Dr. Schmidt didn't want to use restraints, so she gently took Stella's hand. "Come, now, Stella. Let's go find a nice place for you to rest."

Sharon said good-bye to Stella and then turned to Dr. Schmidt. "Thanks, doc. I'll contact an attorney in the morning," she whispered. She felt relieved. She watched as her niece was escorted out of the room and then grabbed her cell phone and dialed Greg. When voice mail came on, she left a message. "Mission accomplished...at least for today. Looks like she might be pregnant. Oh God, I hope not."

Never had a task force been organized so quickly. Amanda had reviewed Derek's proposal and presented it to the FBI. Since Elliott was on the Ten Most Wanted list, they allocated immediate attention to the matter, assigning Special Agent Jeff Jakes to the case with Amanda. She was granted permission to include Rachael, Josh, Grace, Luke, and Meg as consultants on the task force, which was scheduled to assemble Friday at 9:00 a.m., PST, by satellite.

The Carnival ship wasn't scheduled to anchor off Catalina until Saturday, so the FBI had to get creative regarding Amanda's transportation off the cruise ship. Amanda informed the ship's captain of her imminent departure. The FBI chopper landed on the twelfth deck of the ship on Thursday night. Jeff greeted Amanda as she boarded, and they subsequently flew to the Edison facility at the south end of Catalina.

Friday arrived, and everyone was present at Rachael's cottage, with the exception of Meg. Rachael and Josh were also absent; they were still recovering from their recent trauma. Agent Jakes, the only unknown, was introduced, satellite hookup with FBI headquarters was complete, and the plan was discussed for the final tweaking. Meg had no clue about the forthcoming venture, but when summoned by her mom, she showed up.

When Amanda opened the door, Meg knew there was a problem. "What gives?" She walked into the living room, and her family greeted her, all wearing long faces. "Oh, shit. What now?" She was dressed in a waitress uniform, with her hair gathered in a ponytail. "I'm starting my new job this morning. What's up?"

Somber faced, Amanda took charge, moved toward Meg, and said, "He's back and with a plan that includes you again." Nothing else needed to be said. Grace walked over to Meg's side and gently placed a wary arm around her shoulder.

Meg wanted to scream. Her life was just beginning to show signs of normalcy, and now this? "Oh, come on." She pushed away from her mother and walked over to the window, hostility seeping through her pores. Turning, she said, "What gives? That son of a bitch. Rachael should have shot him when she had the chance."

Amanda began speaking quickly. She didn't want Meg to start asking questions. "True, but she didn't. The FBI is ready to take him down. A plan's in place, but it involves your cooperation. We don't have much time to get this together, so listen up. Remember last week when you and Jessie went to Balboa for the casting call?"

"Yeah, so? What's that got to do with this?" Meg looked around the room and realized she was the only one not in the loop. "Jeez. Spit it out. You all look like you're attending a funeral."

"Take it easy, Meg." Amanda quickly described Elliott's involvement with the missing girls. Meg listened and began to piece together what the meeting was all about.

"What do you mean? The girls were used for the night?"

"No, they were bought, like cattle. It's called human trafficking. The men paid huge amounts of money for the girls and then took them back to their respective countries."

"Kidnapped? No ransom? Never returned?" Meg was horrified. The reality of the situation was becoming apparent to her. She zeroed in on Amanda's words.

"Right. When the men get tired of them, they turn them into drug addicts and put them out on the street until they die."

Meg turned her head so no one could see her reactions. How like Elliott. Is this what he had planned for me? She glanced down at the inside of her left wrist. The scars from his cigarette burn had almost disappeared. She stiffened at the thought of his foul breath panting over her body. "Are you saying that he was in Balboa for the last casting call? He was watching me?"

"Yes, as far as we know." She wanted to move forward, but Meg interrupted again.

"Why did he go to all the trouble of a contest if he only wanted me? And how did he know I'd be there?"

"We believe it was just a nasty trick of fate. He planned the human trafficking scenario as a new enterprise, but you showed up, and he didn't have time to alter his plans. With that in mind, he decided on Catalina to snare you." Amanda waited.

Ever determined to console, Grace walked over and again put her arm around Meg, pulling her close. "I know how this hurts, honey. I'm so sorry you have to be involved again."

"What do you mean, *involved*?" Her eyes grew wide as she looked at her mother, and then her eyes rested on Luke.

Grace took her hand, and they started down the hall. "Give us a minute." She led Meg down the hall to the guest bedroom and closed the door behind them. "Sit down, honey."

Meg shook her head and walked to the window. "Mom." She bit back the tears. "I don't think I can do this again. And what about Jessie and Rosie? They're going to try out tomorrow." She looked for answers. "You know how strong I can be, but Mom, I can't go another round with him. He's too evil." She couldn't look at her mother and wanted to run.

"Amanda is handling this, and we have to trust her. She wouldn't let you do this if there was any way you'd get hurt. Ask her. Come on. Let's go back and listen." Grace took Meg's arm and turned her around. She was surprised at her countenance. Was it fear? Resentment? Hatred?

"Wait. I can't put my friends in harm's way. I won't do it." She pulled back from Grace's grip.

"Amanda has that handled too. Please, time is running out. We need to finish this."

"Give me another minute." Meg leaned against the doorjamb, chewed on her upper lip, and tried to focus on one of those happy moments in her life before the joy of youth had faded. The river, of course. The cleansing, cold water filled her thoughts and renewed her spirit. Grace knew exactly where Meg had mentally drifted and remained silent. Meg took a deep breath and turned to her mom. "Okay, let's do this." Grace flashed an outward smile, but fear stangled her heart as they rejoined the rest of the family.

All professional, Amanda began. "Derek reported in again this morning on his throwaway cell. The casting call is advertised for Saturday, from noon to three at Descanso Beach. We have located Elliott's yacht anchored on the back side of the island, near Shark Harbor. It's been under surveillance for twenty-four hours. Nine buyers are aboard and will remain there until the girls are delivered. Once the girls have been drugged, selected, and transported to the small jet boats, Elliott is no longer responsible for the transaction."

"There will be ten of us?"

"Yes."

Jeff took over from Amanda. "There are five mercenaries on board, along with the captain. He will cooperate and isn't part of Elliott's plan. No physical threat from him but no assistance either. We'll substitute the small-craft drivers with armed FBI agents and Coast Guard personnel. When the signal comes for the girls to be picked up, the FBI-manned boats will drive to the yacht, assist in moving the drugged girls onto the small boats, and take off. A medic will be onboard. Each buyer will have one assistant, so overpowering them when out of sight should be easy. The girls will be out of danger at that point. When nine of the girls have been transferred, our last boat will approach with six armed agents and Navy SEALs, who will overtake the yacht and capture Elliott. Meg should be the only girl on board, and Derek will be guarding her. That's the plan. Any questions?"

Meg was quick to ask, "Derek is going to help me? What fool would believe that? He's so afraid of Elliott that he'll crumble. He's no help."

Amanda said, "We *do* trust him. He's turned on his brother. He's with us on this and will take care of you. Besides, one-on-one, I feel you could take Elliott by yourself."

Meg rolled her eyes, feeling like the sacrificial lamb, and looked around the room. "And you are all willing to take this chance?" She made eye contact with each member of her family and smirked. No one could hold her stare.

"Every possible scenario has been studied. We feel you will be safe, along with all the other girls. Just be sure to toss all the champagne," said Agent Jakes.

"Last on board with Elliott, a known evil wacko, Derek, a wimpy turn-coat, and a bunch of mercenaries? Yeah, what's to worry about?" She walked around the room, filled with all the people she loved, and sensed the confidence in them. "Okay, then go on from there. What about me? How soon will the FBI arrive? Do you think Elliott will sell me, or will he try to hurt me again if your plan fails?" All those in the room checked their involuntary moans.

"Derek says Elliott still wants you. He expects him to take you to his bedroom and tie you up while the auction goes on. You're not up for grabs," Amanda said.

Meg stood and stared at her family in disgust. She had listened to the "perfect" plan, one that could go so very wrong. "Shit. How much do you expect of me?" She shook her head and paced. "I won't do it again." Meg glared at her father. "And some of you should at least be trying to keep me from putting myself in danger again." She started for the front door. There has to be some other way.

Grace stopped her and gave her a stern look. "Stop. He won't hurt you. Derek is going to hide a gun in Elliott's room and stay there with you until the FBI and Coast Guard arrive."

"Derek! For God's sake, he's Elliott's brother. He kidnapped you and Amanda. He spied on me. He shot that cop in Bullhead. What kind of fools are you to believe him? And besides, like I said, Derek is no match for Elliott." She shoved past her mother.

Amanda had anticipated Meg's objection. "I believe that Derek has repented. He's sorry for everything that's happened to you, and the reason for his turning on Elliott is because of you. He can't stand the thought of anyone harming you again."

"Hmm. And you swallowed that?" Meg turned and displayed an amazed look on her face. She shook her head in disbelief and slumped onto the couch. She recalled the good times she had spent with Derek: the boat ride through the gorge, the night of the monsoon, his marvelous physique when standing naked on the balcony, his thoughtfulness, and finally, his deceit. Had he been following orders from Elliott that whole time? How much of that was the real Derek, and how much was the Derek completing a mission for his psycho brother?

"I did. Listen, Meg, you don't have to do this. Maybe you shouldn't, especially when you feel so strongly about Derek. We can pull this off without you."

"Good. I'm leaving." She pried herself off the couch and started for the door again.

"Don't tell Jessie or Rosie about any of this. You have to swear to that, or else we can't let you leave this room." Amanda stared her sister down.

"You're threatening me? My own sister? How dare you." Meg moved to stand toe-to-toe with Amanda, returning her glare.

"Not threatening. But if Jessie talks to any of the other girls on board, the cover will be blown, and Elliott will just move on to another city. We're too close to let that happen."

"Why not just arrest him now? You know where he is. Have the Coast Guard sink his boat."

"We need to catch the buyers too. Not your call, Meg. Do I have your word? If so, then go."

Meg backed off and looked around the room. Locating Luke, she walked over and sat next to him. "Seems like you should have an opinion. What do you think, hotshot Dad? Looks like this might be the first chance you've had to protect me after twenty-three years of failing to show up. I really can't let Jessie and Rosie walk into this. They're tough, but so am I, and look what happened to me."

Luke accepted the jab. "I'll be on the last boat and will head directly to Elliott's cabin. Derek will furnish a floor plan, and I'll take care of you. I promise." He took her hand but found it unreceptive.

Before Derek headed back to the yacht, he dropped by the post office annex and used the disposable phone to call Marisa, to apprise her of his recent association with Amanda and the FBI.

"What were you thinking? If Elliott finds out, he'll kill you without a second thought."

"I know, sis, but I can't do this anymore. The ten girls from Balboa are probably dead or wishing they were by now. I can't be responsible for any part of this. I'm done." He was fidgety, glancing around to see if he'd been followed, and yet determined to stay the course.

Marisa was quiet. Derek could imagine her staring out the window at the blue Pacific and trying to rationalize his words. There she was, only a few miles away on the mainland, thinking about a lonely island with their killer brother.

"I'm proud of you, Derek. You've done what I've only dreamed of doing. We're not anything like Elliot. He's manipulated us since birth. Fear, wow. What a force. I'm scared shitless, but what's your plan?" She sighed and leaned back into her swivel chair, glancing around the room at her small collection of personal favorite things. She and Derek had never lived in one location for more than a year, so collecting wasn't a part of their lives. A shelf of classical books, a clock from Solvang, and a coffee cup from New York. Pitiful, she thought.

He gave her a brief synopsis of the FBI proposal, and once she understood, he moved to the next subject. "You need to transfer money from Elliott's account to two new accounts he can't follow. Clean them out. We'll need the cash to get started over. Transfer funds to the Caymans for the long term and to the Bank of Mexico for you to use right away.

"I can do a triple transfer of banks. No one can trace it that way, not even Elliott."

"Good. Pack a bag, take all of your computer stuff, shred anything that can implicate us, and head to Mexico today. Leave some evidence compromising Elliott. If he gets wind of any of this, he'll think you'll head to Rosarito Beach, so don't go there. Go to La Paz. Stay at the Hotel Miramar in the center of town the first night and then move to the Casa Verde Inn. I've been there before, but Elliott hasn't."

Transferring the phone to speaker, Marisa scrambled around the room, searching for her passport.

"Set it up to receive messages at the hotel for a few days so I can find you. It's close enough to drive to, and when I get free, I'll join you. Rent a small hacienda outside of town after the first week."

"When's this going down?"

"Saturday. Don't contact me. Dump your phone, 'cause for all we know, Elliott's been tracking you all along. Bastard."

"Should I take my own car? Maybe lease a car or fly to Mexico? I have two passports."

"He knows about your various passports, so, no, don't fly. Drive your car to San Diego and leave it in the monthly parking lot at the airport. Then take a taxi across the border and rent another car to go to La Paz. Change your identity. Be careful."

"Derek, I'm afraid for you. Is Meg going to go along with this? She won't trust you, you know, after all you've done to her. She might decide to get even with you somehow."

"That's crossed my mind, but we can only hope for the best on that. She wants to catch Elliott as much as I do, and I'll be there to protect her this time. You know, I really like her, probably could have loved her." Probably do. Derek felt the pressure of time and started up the alleyway. "If things don't go as planned, find some happiness, sis, and live your life for both of us. Gotta go. Get started right now and be in Mexico by dark. Love ya. Hurry."

***

"Love you too," Marisa said to a dead line. She slumped down into the chair and visually followed the ocean as it drifted to infinity. God, can this really happen? Can we break away and have a real life? As if a lightning bolt had hit her, she recoiled to an erect position. My God, we're talking about crossing Elliott. Maybe I should tell him what Derek is planning. Maybe I'd live a little longer.

She ran the numbers on Elliott's accounts and found an excess of $6 million available. I wonder what he has in his personal accounts. She went online and opened two new accounts and transferred funds. "Oh what a tangled web we weave, when first we practice to deceive" kept running though her mind.

Twelve hours under careful supervision by the nursing staff at the Catalina Island Medical Center found Rachael and Josh responding to the IVs flushing the drugs from their system. Now they were awake, alert, but completely without any memory. Rachael had lost eight hours, and Josh had lost four days. No matter how hard they tried to fill in the story line, nothing came forth.

Rachael rotated between blinking and shutting her eyes, hoping that her inner eye would remember what had happened right before her memory went blank. She remembered Greg's phone call. Stella was in the room, and who? Someone else had to be there, but who? She glanced over at Josh and momentarily gave up on the analysis.

Josh had been watching her. "Headache?"

"Slight but nothing to worry about. Just trying for instant recall with no luck."

"Same here." He gave her his famous crooked smile and reached out to hold her hand. "It'll come. I know that crazy Stella is mixed up in this. Hope Greg isn't hiding something from me."

"Me too. I know how disappointed you'd be."

When Rachael moved to the side of his bed, taking his hand, he pulled her to him and quickly kissed her fingertips.

"What? You making a pass at me?" She could hardly contain herself. Thoughts of their recent troubles vanished as she slipped into the moment.

"Rach, I really don't remember much after the shooting, but I do remember parts of the summer." He threw the sheet back, dropped his legs over the side, and pulled her between them. "I do remember that we love each other, so that'll have to do for now."

She wrapped her arms around his neck and let him finish talking. "Anything else?"

"Yeah. I think a sexy Pennington kiss could go a far way in my recovery. Lay it on me."

He managed a partial smile before Rachael complied.

"God, I've needed that kiss."

Josh held her tight between his legs. "There's more where that came from."

"Man. You look like shit. What the hell happened to you?" Greg and Captain Kendry entered the hospital room, catching the two by surprise.

"Hey, you tell me." Josh moved the blushing Rachael aside and shook his partner's hand. "My brain's fuckin' screwed up on this. Rachael was just starting to fill me in."

"We'll be opening an investigation. Greg has point. FBI will be involved too. What's your take on it?"

Josh tried to recap the last few days, remembered the shooting on the boat dock, but after that nothing jelled. "Stella kind of hops in and out of the fuzzy picture. That's all I got. Oh, plus a lot of weird sex."

Rachael was scrutinizing Greg's composure. Her instinct, which was usually spot on, said he was involved. "Greg, what can you add for the captain?"

"I filled him in on the way to the hospital. You saw Josh through the window. I got called away, and when I came back, you two were missing."

"Well, it's obvious that Stella couldn't have moved the two of you. Josh, you're tapping, what, two hundred pounds now?" The captain mentally traced the scene, stopping again at how they had been moved. "She must have had some help. And why would she bother? Strange. Why didn't she leave you there? Josh, looks like you're in good hands...in more ways than one. Greg and I'll head over to the house. Forensics is there now. Maybe they've come up with something." They started for the door. "I'll have Greg call if we find anything. See ya later, buddy." He nodded in Rachael's direction.

Greg gave a high five to Josh but didn't make eye contact with Rachael.

"Now, back to us. Screwing Stella? Are you nuts? Why would I do that?" He pulled her close between his legs again while his hands moved around to hold her butt.

"You need to know what I saw through the bedroom window before we were moved. It's not pretty." She watched closely for his response. True surprise grew as she started at the beginning of his memory shutdown and the shooting on the boat dock, and then related everything else that followed. She ended with the events she had witnessed outside the window. "She was on top of you, screwing the hell out—"

He stopped her there. "You saw what? Hey, I remember the shooting, and then the next thing was waking up in that dark room with you yesterday. But screwing Stella? No way, not me. She's a crazy bitch."

"Hence the drugs. Yeah, now she probably thinks she's pregnant."

"Shit. Where is she?"

"Took off. Mainland, I guess."

"Why didn't you ask Greg? He should know her whereabouts. His sister and all."

"What? His sister?" Rachael pushed away and stared at him, complete disbelief registering on her face. "Greg's sister? Didn't know that. Why didn't you tell me?" Answers were flying her way.

"Thought you knew. Wasn't any kind of a secret. All the island knows it. They were raised apart but found each other two years ago."

"Those are the years when I didn't come back to the island." She started pacing around his room, analyzing Greg's movements from a totally different angle. She swiftly explained the scene at the house—how Greg had disappeared and failed to respond to her backup call. "Maybe that's why he didn't show up when I called him. Taking care of his sister before his partner? He'll have me to answer for that."

"I don't think Greg would go out of his way to protect Stella. They had a run-in about six months ago. He's really tired of her shit."

"They're still blood."

"Pregnant? Back to that. Please say you're kidding. There's no way I'd raise a kid with that wacko."

"She could be lying. It's too soon for a valid pregnancy test." Mental note. Have the department check out the last twenty-four hours of Greg's schedule.

"Greg and I've been partners for years. I'll handle this. I don't want his job jeopardized. You okay with that?"

"It's probably too late but okay." It had taken her years with the police department to understand the color gray. Nothing was ever black and white.

Before they had a chance to pursue the conversation further, Grace came into the hospital room. "How are the patients? Looking better, it seems, and friendly?"

"Well, Mom. Part of his memory's back. At least the important part. He remembers *us*." Rachael changed from her detective hat to a more social demeanor, moved back to Josh's bed, and messed with his hair.

Grace spent a few minutes with them, a short reprieve, breathing room from the disaster that was approaching. When she finished explaining Elliott's plan, they were both guarded but eager to participate in the operation.

"Not on your life," said Grace. "We've got it covered, and you two are so useless right now, you'd probably get in the way."

"Mom, I wasn't shot, just drugged. And that's worn off. I'm fine."

"Well, we'll see about that. It's all taking place tomorrow, so there's no time to integrate you anyway. Rachael, you can go to the sheriff's office in the morning and watch the operation, but I don't think they'll release you by then, Josh. Amanda is coordinating with Derek."

"The captain just left. Why didn't he mention this?"

"Why? For this very reason. Didn't want Josh to get involved."

"Blows my mind that anyone is willing to trust Derek after what he's done to Meg, Amanda, and you." Rachael grimaced, shook her head, and stared at her mother. "How are they going to communicate with the ship? They need eyes on board."

"Derek has agreed to wear a wire. That's all I know."

Rachael wasn't happy with any part of the plan. Too much exposure for Meg. If anything went wrong—and there were plenty of ways that could happen—then Meg would have to withstand Elliott's maniacal torture again. "Keep Josh company for a minute, Mom. I'm going to track down the doctor and get released."

"Take care of my release, too. There's no way this party is going down without my help." Josh tossed the rest of the bedding aside. "Watch out, Grace, don't want to flash you. These nightgowns are pretty short."

"Nothing I haven't seen before." She laughed and helped him stand. "Glad to have you on board. I know Amanda is being cautious because of Meg, but if anyone knows what she's gone through, it's you."

Josh remembered Meg's emotional breakdown in the golf cart last year and how long it had taken to get her back. "Don't worry, Grace. She's like my baby sister; I'll protect her. Now figure out how to take off this monitor and help me get the hell out of here."

54

"Where are you going so early? Everything is set for eleven, and it's only eight." Elliott entered Derek's stateroom, unannounced as usual, and found him moving far too quickly for the time of day. He spilled some coffee as he adjusted to the sway of the yacht.

Derek continued gathering his personal items and shoved his cell phone and wallet in his pocket. "I told the photographers and judges to meet me at nine to go over final details of the contest. Need to make sure that our spot is hidden from where the girls will be modeling. Just being careful." *I'm talking too fast. Slow down. Don't make him suspicious.*

Part of Elliott's cunning was his ability to read people, and while he could sense that something else was going on in Derek's mind, he decided not to challenge him. "Probably a good idea. Meg and her friend did sign up, didn't they?"

"Yeah, I checked on that yesterday. Their friend, Rosie, signed up too. She's quite a tart, probably one of the first to go."

"Knowing the guy from Spain, he'll take a liking to Jessie, Meg's new friend. I read her application. Not only pretty but robust—rides a horse and spars like a man. They like that sort."

Derek successfully hid his distaste for the whole subject. "Sounds right." He headed out of the cabin for the dinghy. "One of your henchmen can drop me off at the beach and bring the dingy back for you. See ya later." Derek hurried away before Elliott could quiz him any further.

"Right." Elliott followed Derek to the stern of the boat, pulled a napkin off the bar as he passed, and wrote a quick note. "Hey, Ramon, here's a shopping list. Some items for the men tonight. Buy the stuff after you drop off Derek." Elliott handed the note to Ramon before turning and going into the galley for breakfast.

The dinghy plowed through the water, and Derek turned to Ramon. "I have to go buy some stuff, too. What's on Elliott's list?"

Ramon continued steering the boat, but managed to pull the note from his jeans. He read, "Follow him. Don't let him know, and call me." Ramon didn't miss a beat. "Oh, he wants some special rum and more vodka. That's all. He said for me to get it, so I'm getting it. I follow his orders to the letter."

The conversation ended, but Derek knew there was more to it. Ramon steered the dinghy into a boat slip and tied up the bow as Derek jumped out and headed down to Crescent Avenue. Derek continued to glance over his shoulder and, not spotting Ramon, changed his direction, taking a left on Metropole. Another quick look convinced him that he wasn't being followed, so he ducked into the Atwater Hotel, rushed through the lobby, climbed the stairs, and knocked on room forty-two. The door quickly opened, and two FBI agents ushered him into the room.

"Take off your shoes."

Derek watched as the agent pulled out the lining of his tennis shoes and attached a GPS transmitter and voice-activated recorder. "Transmission is long on this unit. We'll be able to hear you from half a mile."

"I'll be wading in water part of the time. Might even have to take off my shoes. Will it still work if wet?"

"Yes, it's made for that. If you have to take off your shoes, then tie the stings together and wear them around your neck. A little nerdy, but necessary. Now, here's a set of baseball caps for the film crew. Your hat is fitted with camera and audio."

"Elliott will be suspicious of this. How should I handle it?" He picked up one of the hats and examined it.

"Give the box of hats to your director. Have him hand them out. Make sure you get the one in the bottom of the box. We'll leave a blue smudge on the right side. Look for it." The agent handed the designated hat to Derek for his inspection.

"Yeah, that'll probably work. Doubt that Elliott will wear one."

"Doesn't matter." They tried the sound, asking Derek to talk in a normal tone. It worked. "You should be all set. If one source fails, the other will pick it up. Any reason to take off both your hat and shoes?"

"Yeah. When we get back on the boat, I'll have to change into a tux."

"Cuff links?"

"Yeah."

The agent hurriedly looked through his briefcase. "Okay. Take these. This is the way to activate them." He handed them to Derek, who checked out their function. "You'll have to hide them during the day."

"Right." Derek was visibly shaking.

The agents knew they needed to diffuse his fright. "Agent Pennington wants a word with you. Here." They handed him a cell phone.

"Derek, you ready for this? If you can't relax and act normal, we can't proceed. Too many lives are depending on your part."

"I'm ready, Amanda. Just a little case of the nerves. Once I get out of here unnoticed, then I'll be fine. Have a lot of work to do. Is Meg okay with all of this?"

"It was a struggle to bring her around, but she gets the big picture. It's your responsibility to take care of her, understand?"

"Got it. Should have done it a long time ago."

Amanda had no reasonable comment for that. "Good luck."

Derek handed the phone back to the agent and took a minute to reflect. What a turn of events. On the side of the FBI and so ready to do my part. Watch out, big brother, you son of a bitch…Baby brother, the one you've been beating up all these years, is taking charge. "So how do I leave this place without being seen?"

"Stairs down the back. Lead to the alley. The cart you rented is there. Drive to Descanso Beach. If you see a problem, let us know. The abort word will be *leftovers*. Okay? Let's get a move on." The agent opened the door, cleared a space for Derek to exit, and closed it behind him. "I don't have a real good feeling about this. Let's give a heads-up to headquarters that he's on his way."

Derek slipped through the hotel door and followed the rest of his instructions. The cart was where it was supposed to be, and Ramon was nowhere in sight. From the alley, he turned right on Metropole and continued down to Crescent, stopping only to check for Ramon's dinghy.

***

Ramon had positioned himself on the first bar stool in the rear of the El Galleon bar and had ordered a beer. From his vantage point, he watched as Derek walked to Crescent and then take a right on Metropole. He hastened to follow him but lost him in the heavy pedestrian traffic. Later when Derek's cart was found again and turned left off Metropole, heading toward the beach, Ramon made a note of the time and direction on the scrap of paper Elliott had handed him. He knew the unexplained half hour would enrage Elliott.

***

Derek circled the block and parked around the corner from the market and watched for Ramon. He hadn't noticed Ramon's departure from the bar and had totally missed his entrance to Vons. Five minutes later, Ramon left the market with bags of groceries, so Derek made a U-turn, heading back to the beach. He felt safe. So far, so good. He took a deep breath and mentally ran through the plan. A few what-ifs were presenting themselves.

Descanso Beach was awash with the camera crews. Tables were set up for the judges, speaker systems were readied, and a small table with two chairs was tucked away in the foliage. Derek found the director and gave him the box of baseball caps along with instructions of how and when to hand them out. Next, he motioned to the main judge to follow him to the hideout.

"Three models have been selected by the producers." He pulled out the applications for Meg, Jessie, and Rosie. "We don't care about anyone else, but call Meg last. Got that?"

"No problem. We've got less than two hours to go. I need to get down there."

Derek didn't like the way he was being dismissed and wondered if the jerk was capable of following instructions. "Will you have a problem with the other judges about the preselection?"

"No. Most of these contests are rigged, you know." Without further comment, the judge grabbed the forms and proceeded down to the beach with the paperwork.

Derek had a little while to relax and take in the spectacular view in front of him. The Pacific was calm and clear, with no hint of fog or wind. Peaceful. I wonder if I'll ever be able to really enjoy a day like this. Or, for that matter, if I'll even be around to see another day like this. That depressing thought was amplified when he saw Elliott driving toward him.

55

Stepping out of the cart, Elliott paused when his cell phone rang. The beach, dotted with beautiful women, held his attention as he retrieved the phone and hit the answer button. "Marisa?"

"Yes."

"What?"

"I need..."

56

Derek watched Elliott walk along the path toward their hidden lair. He hated the way he walked, toes pointed out, pelvis jutting forward, cocksure. When Elliott put the cell phone in his pocket, Derek could see that he fondled himself and smiled. Disgusting. Then he realized Elliott had been smiling before he reached into his pants.

"And let the festivities begin." He dragged out the folding chair and sat next to his brother as the director walked up with the box of hats. "And what is this?" He pushed his designer sunglass up to his neatly coiffured hair.

The director opened the box and held one out to Elliott. "My treat. I always have my crew wear hats so they can be easily spotted during the day. Be my guest." He handed one off the top for Elliott and put one on himself. "How about you, Derek?" There were five left in the box.

Derek rummaged around in the box. "Are they all the same size?" Shit, no mark on this one. He tried on the hat, put it back, and grabbed another. He sorted through the box, finally finding the marked one, and put it on. "This seems to fit okay. Thanks. Nice touch."

Elliott scoffed. "Pussy hats. I won't be wearing one." He threw the hat back at the director as he walked away. "Are we ready? Are all the boats standing by to transfer the girls from the yacht?"

"Yes. Nine jet boats are anchored offshore, a driver and crewman on each, and the tenth is already tied to the yacht. Belongs to the Spanish guy spending

222

the night there. Everyone's on standby. Simple enough." He handed Elliott the binoculars. "You can see them from here."

Elliott took the binoculars, adjusted them to his taste, and commented, "Ah, the world is as it should be. Everything's in order." He handed the glasses back to Derek but held on a little longer during the transfer, pulling Derek's attention. "Everything's in order, right?"

Derek's heart skipped a beat, but he pushed forward. He hesitated to mention Meg but needed to know, before she got on board, if anything had changed. "What are your plans for Meg?"

"Plans had to be altered somewhat. You know how intuitive I am on occasions, and this is one. I feel we are being watched. That's all you need to know for now."

Panic. Derek jerked. "What do you mean, *watched*?" His head swiveled around, peering through the foliage and scanning the beach for obvious intruders. "If you think we're being watched, let's just scrap the whole damn job and refund the money to the buyers." Does he know?

"Meg and I will be leaving the party a little earlier than planned."

"What? You and Meg leave, and I'm stuck with whoever shows up? I'm not doing that." Oh, shit. I hope the FBI is picking up on this. He touched his hat. "Shit, if we're caught, then I'm stuck."

"You're an attorney. Weasel your way out of it." Elliott's exasperation was apparent. He had no time to suffer fool's talk.

"Did you rent another boat to take you away, or how do you propose to do that? The yacht's Zodiac is really slow, and so is the dinghy." Derek tried to keep his voice normal, but his tone sounded stressed, even to himself. The plan was already going awry. Can the FBI adjust their plans? "I don't know anything about the fine points of this operation. Tell me. If you leave, are you leaving some of your hired guns on board to help if I have to run for it?"

"There, there. Don't fret. It will all play out okay." End of discussion. Derek's nerves, coupled with the intel from his informer, cemented Elliott's suspicions. Something was going on with Derek.

The judges were settling into their appropriate spots behind the tables, and a stack of applications, pens, and water was placed at each spot, along with their name plaques. The MC tested the sound system, and forty girls listened intently for instructions. The balmy conditions, with a fresh offshore breeze kicking up, allowed the contestants some physical comfort, but the apprehension was thick as they waited for the competition to begin. The ten available spots were the topic of conversation. Meg was intrigued with the whole scenario, feeling that some of the girls were being overly seductive for the part. She nudged Rosie.

"Sure you want to be in a movie? Look at those two nuts over there. Too much silicone. They'll tip over if they lean forward."

Rosie glanced at Jessie's chest, at Meg's, then at her own. "Hmm, well, looks like I stack up with the best of them. And…silicone free."

Meg laughed aloud, too loudly for the serious audition, and the judges scowled at her. "You're hysterical, Rosie. Love your sense of humor. Stacked, huh? Well, it's our turn—let's go show 'em 'stacked.'"

The outrageous Meg strutted through the sand, tossed her striking blond hair over her face, threw it back, turned, and gave them a good look at her butt. After a pause she slithered around again and sent her very best, most seductive, smile floating their way. She had grown up with sand between her toes, so while some of the girls stumbled around in the uneven terrain, she stood out as stunning. She had a role to play, so she set aside the fact that Elliott was lurking in the bushes and fell into her fun-loving Meg character.

"Look at her, Derek. Perfection in motion. Oh, the plans I have for her this time. Our lovemaking was cut short last time, but I plan on making up for it within the next twenty-four hours."

Derek didn't have to look; he knew Elliott was rubbing himself under the table. Pervert.

When the last contestant had filed by, the MC walked over to the temporary podium and addressed the girls. "Good job, ladies. We have a minibus waiting for you at the entrance to the beach, over there to the left. You'll be taken to the casino theater, where there are refreshments for you. Thank you so much for your auditions. The winners will be announced within the hour."

Meg looked around at her competition, feeling that she might not have made it if it hadn't been a setup. Her preference would have been to jog on back to town and hang out with her other friends. A little more time, and then we'll catch the bastard. "Come on, you guys. Let's grab some seats on the bus."

She kicked some sand at Jessie and Rosie, then raced them toward the waiting vehicle.

Within the hour, after the girls had an opportunity to eat and settle into the historical theatre, the MC appeared on stage and announced the final cut. "Will the following girls report back to the minibus? One by one the names were read, and Meg had a moment of apprehension when her name wasn't called. Shit. Screwup already? How the hell am I supposed to get on the yacht if I'm not picked? She pushed to the front of the group and felt an instant rush of relief when her name was finally called.

The winners screeched with anticipation, crying and hugging, as they left the losers behind. "Sorry, girls, maybe next time. But I do want to thank you on behalf of Sunrise Pictures for your auditions. You're all beautiful."

On the minibus, the MC told the girls that a boat would take them to the yacht on the back side of the island, where more pictures would be taken and where they would have an opportunity to meet the producers, the men with the money. "Be on your best behavior, girls—attentive and seductive. These men have power and prestige and can slingshot your acting career. Best advice I can give you."

Meg watched him carefully, wondering whether he was part of Elliott's plan or just another lackey suckered in by the money. I wish I could have been fitted with a wire, but the bikini wouldn't have hid it. At least I have a tracking device in my purse. Hope they don't need to use it.

The launch was waiting for them at Descanso Beach, and the girls gathered up their bags and took the final ride to the yacht, where Elliott and Derek were waiting in the captain's quarters.

***

During the contest a minisub slipped under the yacht, unobserved by all, and surfaced in the hold.

57

Rachael and Josh were released from the hospital early Saturday morning and took Rachael's cart directly to his ranch house. Rachael beamed as they pulled up in front and ascended the stairs, recalling the romantic nights they had spent there last summer.

"You look like a Cheshire cat. What gives?" Josh was watching her.

"Memories."

Two weeks without any maintenance had left inches of dead leaves on the porch and chairs, and a few cobwebs brushed across Rachael's hair as she entered. "I've missed your place, Josh. Fits you. Comfortable, homey, and with a perfect view of the ocean." After unsnarling the cobwebs, she headed for the bedroom and unpacked her sparse belongings. "I'll have Mom ship more of my clothes over for me. She and Luke are going back to Yorba Linda once we catch Elliott," she yelled to Josh. Listen to me. Josh hasn't even asked me to move in. Pushy bitch. I'm not giving him a chance to change his mind.

Josh moved to the doorway and watched her, inwardly smiling at her strong, sure movements, the slight curl of her brown hair, the supple body. He, too, remembered those nights after riding the horses on the beach. The long talks, the sensuous lovemaking. All confusion lifted, and he was now back to his old reality. The only perplexing problem was Stella and the sex. He recalled the sex, but it seemed like it had been with Rachael with red hair. But now, a child? No way.

"What're you doing, Rachael?" Josh stepped into the room and slid his arms around her waist.

He startled her, and she almost took a swing. Her reverie was in full gear. "Wow, didn't hear you come in."

He turned her around and grinned. "Seems to me like we have some history in this room." He gave her a long, tender kiss. "I'm feeling wonderful right now. Let's make some more memories." The first button on her blouse cooperated with his touch.

Rachael kissed him back. "You remember? Oh, Josh, I was so afraid that you wouldn't find your way back to me. I really didn't want to start all over again."

He backed her to the edge of the bed. "Oh, I remember." He kissed her again and finished off the buttons, slipped his hand around to her back, and made short work of her bra. "If my memory serves me right, we have started at this very position before."

Rachael gently pushed him away. "Oh, sweetheart, I'd love to romp in the hay with you right now, but I have to catch the bad guy first."

Josh's hand came forward and unsnapped the waistband of her jeans.

Rachael stopped his hand. "There's a command post set up over at the sheriff's office. I'm not comfortable with the FBI plan. I have to get involved. It's Meg. Look, I won't be long."

"Shit, can't a guy catch a break? Maybe a quickie?"

Rachael smiled, and Josh knew a no answer when he saw one. He realized the time wasn't right to move forward on the romantic side, so he acquiesced to the moment. "Next time you have to ask me."

"Not a problem. Just be advised, if you say no, I can still whip your ass."

"That'll be the day."

Rachael quickly reached under her blouse, hooked the bra, and buttoned her jeans.

"But, hey, hotshot cop, I'm going with you. Don't forget who you're talking to. My badge is as shiny as yours, and this is my town. You can't cut me out of the action. May not be able to run the fifty yet, but my brain is coming around. Let's go."

"Hmm." Rachael locked her left arm around Josh's neck and slid her hand down the front of his pants. "That's not the only thing coming around. You will say yes, won't you?"

"Better not start something you can't finish, little girl. It's been a long time."

Rachael quickly removed her hand and slid out from under his embrace. "Come on, tough guy. Let's go kick some ass."

"I've got something to take care of first. I'll meet you in thirty."

Rachael wanted to question him but elected to pass on it.

When alone, he called Greg on his cell phone. "Need to talk. Where are you?" They met ten minutes later and sat in the department's Jeep on Chimes Tower Road, overlooking the Casino. The two had been with the sheriff's department for over ten years, the last five as partners. They were more than blue brothers. "Greg, you've gotta transfer out. Back to LA."

"What're you talking about? I love it here. This is my town."

"Don't give me that shit. I'm sure Rachael has figured it out and probably the captain too. They can charge you with all kinds of crap—aiding a criminal, kidnapping, drugging a witness, lying to the cops. Fuck, man. Put in your transfer, and we can work it out with the captain. Otherwise, well, your career's shot to hell."

Greg was devastated. "Josh, I'm so sorry. I didn't know what to do. Stella's been off her meds, and by the time I got involved, she'd gone too far. She's my kid sister."

"I know. But God, Greg, what if she's pregnant? That screws up everything for everyone. I won't marry her. And shit. A kid? What do I do about that?"

"I'll raise the kid for you. Least I can do if I can get out of this mess." Tough guys don't cry, but he was close to it.

There was nothing more to be said, so they parted with more questions to be answered than when they'd met.

Out front of the police department, Josh caught up with Rachael. Without asking she knew he had been with Greg. When they entered the office, which was abuzz with FBI agents and all twenty-five of the local department personnel, they located Amanda in the briefing room and immediately put on their cop hats. "Where are we?"

"Contest is over. Girls are being transported to the back of the island to the yacht, Derek is doing a great job transmitting, and Meg hasn't had to turn on her GPS yet. Must be okay with Derek."

They turned their attention to the incoming conversation between Derek and Elliott. "A change of plans? What the hell does he mean?" asked Grace.

No one had an answer.

Rachael was quick to jump into the conversation. "You're underestimating Elliott. He'll take any kind of device, cell phone, or watch away from Meg. That's no plan."

"Mom had a device implanted behind her ear that tracked us when we were dumped in the desert, but there was no time to do that. However..." She paused and smiled broadly. "The lab has come up with an alternate. The tracking only goes two miles, but that should be enough. It's a spray."

"You joke."

"Nope. And Meg is wearing a double dose. Apparently Luke gave her something also in case Elliott slips away from us."

"Like what?" Rachael was getting perturbed. Too many secrets.

"GPS with CIA satellite tracking."

"How long does it take to hook up with the satellite? The one thing we don't have is time," Josh said.

"This is something new. A pill. CIA shit. Like the endoscopy camera, only this is a GPS. Strong transmission. That's all I know. Ask him." She gave Rachael a nod to leave the room. "Look, sis. I know you're nervous about the plan, but you can't come in here and take over. This is an FBI operation now, so stand down."

"What plan? You've hung those women out to dry."

"Shape up or leave. Your choice."

Rachael realized she was helpless in the matter and acquiesced. They went back to the whiteboard, and Rachael found a spot next to Josh to sit and watch.

"You know it was probably Elliott who pulled this same caper off Balboa a week ago, don't you? The MO seems remarkably familiar. I read about that in the *Register*," Rachael said in a clear voice so Amanda would hear.

"We haven't found any of the girls involved in that yet, so we don't know for sure, but it looks that way. You know, I'm surprised he would try it again so soon and so near to the last job." Amanda was quick to take charge again.

"True. That's not like him. I still think we're missing something." When Amanda didn't stop her, Rachael walked over to the table and studied the map again. "You sure you've got the chase boats covered with agents?" The room was getting restless for the action to begin.

Josh stood behind Rachael and tapped her on the arm. "Slow down and listen."

"Covered," said Amanda.

"What about the yacht? Have you tracked ownership?"

"Yes, a fictitious person leased it for a week from a place in San Diego. Paid cash. The boat specs are there on the table. We know which cabin is his— and shit, Rachael, go look for yourself. I'm too busy to walk you through this."

Rachael examined the boat's layout. It was a luxury super yacht similar to the famous *Titania* she'd read about in the travel section of the *Register*. Exotic design, 219 feet long, with all the amenities. She ran a finger across the blueprints, tracing access to the entertainment area, galley, guest cabins, and crew quarters. Committing the schematics to memory, she stopped abruptly and started tapping the paper. "What's this large open area at sea level, next to the crew's quarters?"

Amanda joined her at the table. "Rec room, maybe? Swimming pool?"

"I think not. There's a huge Jacuzzi on the stern of the boat, and the Pacific is all around. No need for a pool. This area seems to be at or below the level of the hull. Maybe a cutout? Call the manufacturer—now. Maybe they can tell us. Have the girls reached the yacht yet?"

All eyes turned to the display board as it was updated. The girls had arrived.

58

Meg had also studied the layout of the boat during her briefing, and she immediately began analyzing the yacht's design as she stepped aboard. She waited for Rosie and Jessie to catch up with her.

"This boat is friggin' awesome," said Rosie. She got a glimpse of the spacious sitting area inside, highlighting a dance floor and bar that would seat twelve. "Wow." She admired the highly polished wood, the refined furniture, and the total ambience of the room.

"You got that right," said Jessie as she scanned the length of the boat. "Check out the bar and especially the bartender. Hot."

When all were aboard, the MC announced that the contestants were to go to the master suite, where refreshments awaited and evening dresses in all sizes were available. "There's a huge selection of designer gowns, so be sure to pick the one that will complement your salient points, if you know what I mean." The girls laughed. "Please look to the upper level of the boat and wave hello to the movie's producers and director. And one other thing—we'll be holding on to your purses and cell phones until we leave. Anonymity, you know, is what Hollywood is based on. Please place your cell phones, iPads, and whatever into the bag before proceeding to the boudoir."

Meg played the part and giggled to her friends. "Adventure time. Come on, you guys, drop your stuff in that bag and let's get there first. What fun. Evening gowns. Hurry." As they boarded the boat, she had time to snap three shots of the producers, crew, and girls and to text them to Amanda before tossing her cell in the bag. "It's this way. Come on."

The master suite was opulent. Beautiful evening gowns were displayed on temporary racks, and it was quickly apparent that little underwear could be worn. The three grabbed sequined gowns, helped with the zipping, and moved to the mirrors for makeup and hair.

"Maybe I should have taken the red Chanel dress instead. What'cha think?" asked Jessie as she turned from the mirror.

"No way. That turquoise turns your eyes into huge pools of sex," answered Rosie as she checked her own makeup. "How about my stuff? Showing enough cleavage?"

"Like you have a choice," replied Meg as the girls continued to primp. Pulling up the side zipper on her Armani gown, she mimicked a waltz around the room, and Rosie joined her.

The rest of the contestants entered the suite, and the decibels increased to an outrageous pitch. Now the room was bustling with excited young women, with dreams of stardom running through their heads. They popped grapes into their mouths and posed in front of the mirrors, showing pouty faces, sexy poses, and fluttering eyelids. Meg was totally distracted but tried to maintain a level of excitement to play her part in the game, relying solely on her sisters for the outcome.

Luke had given her the "pill" to swallow if plans went wrong, but now she had to find a place to hide it from Elliott's sharp eyes. She could feel his presence on the boat. She looked around the room and decided to hide the pill under the mattress.

"What are you doing, Meg? You don't have to straighten up the bed. I'm sure they have maids to do that. Look at this place," said Jessie as she walked into the mirrored bathroom. "Mirrors on the ceiling? Holy shit. Anyone ready for an orgy?"

Orgy. That word sent a spike through Meg's heart. She wanted to tell Jessie and Rosie what was going on, but the FBI had said absolutely no to that idea, fearing the girls would get nervous and mess up the sting. So she waited and watched and protected.

When everyone finished dressing, the girls went to the middle deck, where the foreign investors awaited their entrance. The contestants were impressed with the appearance of the dignitaries, resplendent in tuxedos. A quartet provided the music, and the buoyant craft seemed to roll in concert with the southern breeze gently blowing around Catalina.

A gold pin with a numeral etched in the center had been given to each buyer. The MC announced, "Please introduce yourselves to our producers and answer any questions they may have. If there's a language problem, we have an interpreter who will help. You will be presented with a gold pin to commemorate your evening on the boat. First, please join me in a glass of champagne to celebrate the evening. Hear, hear."

The girls took their champagne and smiled with each sip. Meg pretended to drink hers, but, turning her head, she spit it back in the glass. Following the MC's instructions, the girls separated and began to mingle. Meg tried to keep her friends close. "Hey, let's not split up. We really don't know these guys."

"Don't be such a wuss," Jessie said, irritated. "They're rich. Sounds like fun."

"Fun? They could be psychos."

Rosie looked around the boat. "Yeah. You're right, Meg. We don't know these dudes. If there's a problem, I don't want to have to swim back to shore."

The man from Spain had been eyeing Jessie since the tryouts on the beach. When he read her profile, he immediately knew she was his pick. "My dear," he said as he approached the girls and stood between Jessie and Meg. "Please join me over here. Have you been in other movies? You're so beautiful." He held a hand out to her.

Jessie was totally flattered and found him to be more than handsome. "I've been in a dozen or so, mostly as a stand-in or second for stunts. I'm also a barrel racer with the rodeo." She noticed he was a bit older than most men she had known but exotically handsome and polished.

"Enchanting. I have a large hacienda in Spain and the most striking horses and facility the world has to offer. Maybe when the movie is over, you will come and visit."

Jessie was smitten. "Well, I'd—"

Meg pushed in between them. In her brash way, she said, "Jessie, I think we're supposed to move around, like speed dating. Come with me and meet the man from Italy."

Jessie glared at Meg, letting her know to back off, and turned back to her Spanish hero. "I'm fine. You go ahead."

Meg rejoined Rosie but didn't change her focus.

"So, where were we?" he asked. "Oh, yes. If you don't mind my being too forward, I'd like you to wear this pin. That way the other men will leave you alone, and we can get to know each other better."

"Love it." She moved her long auburn hair away from her strapless dress, and the Spaniard attempted to place the pin in an appropriate spot. He stopped. "My name is Antonio, by the way. And you are?"

"Jessie." She smiled. Wow, pinned after five sentences or so. This has to be a record. She glanced around the boat. No one else was wearing a pin yet.

"Well, Jessie. I cannot put the pin on your dress without pricking your beautiful skin unless I slide my finger behind it. Will that be all right with you?" He proceeded without her answer, and when his fingers slid between the dress and her ample breast, she took a deep sigh. He was excited to see her passion and vulnerability show. "There. Now you are officially mine." He smiled down at her, and Jessie blushed.

Elliott, observing from the upper deck, sent a text to the other nine men stating that number one had been chosen, so number two would make his selection next. The man from Italy looked around and headed for the petite blonde. His interpreter conversed with the girl from Redlands, and finally she accepted the number-two gold brooch and pinned it on her dress.

Rosie pinched Meg. "Did you see that? The guy from Italy, with the beard, just put a pin on the blonde we met on the beach. What's going on?"

Meg knew but couldn't tell. "Don't know. Maybe that's the order for the final casting? We need to keep watching."

"If that's the case, I'm going to look for the guy with number three. This sounds fun."

"Rosie. No."

"Huh? What's wrong with you? I don't want to get cut out of this opportunity. You're on your own."

234

Rosie walked away and tried to break into two conversations, looking for the next spot to grab.

Elliott watched from the third deck as Antonio and Jessie joined hands and started walking toward the bow. Meg tried to stop her. He couldn't hear the conversation, but Jessie insisted on going. He witnessed Meg spilling her second glass of champagne overboard. His intel was right on. Meg definitely knew something, and that meant the FBI also knew. Time being a major factor, he decided to take care of her now before she had an opportunity to mess up his plans. He headed down the stairs.

Derek stopped him.

"She knows." Irritation oozed through his words.

"Knows what?" asked Derek.

"What have you done?" Elliott demanded. He grabbed Derek's shoulders and pushed him against the bulkhead.

"Nothing. What are you talking about? Shit." He rubbed the back of his head from the blow. "Maybe it's time to lock her up, though. You know Meg. She's always snoopy. I'll send a waiter to get her and take her to your suite."

"She won't go."

"He'll tell her that her friend, Jessie, is sick. She'll go. I need to go below to the Spaniard's room and give him the signaling device so he can send for his boat. We can't get behind on this." Derek rushed away before Elliott could ask any more questions.

Deception? Betrayal? So Derek has a set of balls after all?

When the waiter delivered the message to Meg, she searched for Derek and found him walking toward the steps leading to the staterooms. He turned, quickly gave her a heads-up, and disappeared. Meg grabbed the waiter's arm. "Looks like my boyfriend wants me," she slurred as she staggered down the stairs. "But you're kinda cute. Maybe I should go with you. How about it?" She pinched his butt and laughed. The waiter held both of her arms to protect himself from her advances.

Derek came out of his stateroom. "What's going on here? What's the ruckus all about?"

Meg threw her arms around Derek. "What'cha doin' here, old boyfriend o' mine?" She continued to slur her words, turned, and grabbed at the waiter's butt again.

Derek whispered in her ear, "Good, now I'll get rid of the waiter, and we'll go into Elliott's room." He untwined himself from Meg and turned to the attendant. "I've got this. Thanks. They need you upstairs now to help transport the women." He took Meg by the arm and pushed her into Elliott's stateroom.

Once the door was closed, Meg turned and slapped Derek across the face. "Bastard. How could you have done this to me? Rachael should have killed you along with your brother."

He rubbed his face and took a step back. "She may still have the chance if you don't settle down." He realized that getting Meg's cooperation wasn't going to be easy. "Okay, let me have it. I'm sure there are things that need to be said." He looked directly into her fiery blue eyes, which were shooting laser beams of hatred into his soul.

"I accepted you into my close circle of friends. You were part of the brat pack. We boated and danced and drank and kissed and saw each other naked. And all along, you were plotting with your evil brother to torture me...almost kill me...and leave me mentally disfigured? And now you ask that I trust you?" The tears of anger and hurt came spilling out.

Derek wanted to hold her, to cry with her, because he understood her pain. "Listen, please. Marisa and I were complicit in the money laundering and other illegal practices of Elliott. We helped because of fear. I had no idea what he had planned for you. The only thing I was supposed to do was let him know your schedule."

"He was a serial killer, for God's sake. Has been for years. And you say you didn't know?"

"I swear I didn't. We moved locations with him because he said the cops were getting close to our other businesses. We were gullible."

She said nothing. Just looked away.

"Meg, I'm so sorry. I never knew what he was going to do. I would have saved you from all of that then, and now, maybe now, I can make up for it." He finally admitted to himself that he loved Meg, always had. "For what it's worth, I've been working my way back to you. This is my only way of proving it."

She studied his handsome, pained face and felt he was telling the truth.

"Meg, we don't have time for any more of this. Know that I'm sorry, really sorry."

She knew he was right and, with great reluctance, switched. "Well, okay for now. But someday I'll get my ounce of revenge from you, guaranteed." Her normal instincts and good judgment took over.

"Fair enough. Now there's a new problem. Elliott's slipped in another twist to the abduction. I checked out the whole yacht when I boarded and found a weird setup in the lower level. Looks like he's got a holding area for a small sub."

"A sub? Small? Like a two seater or something?"

"I guess. But besides that, somehow he's been tipped off and knows the FBI is watching."

"Shit. Can you get a message to Amanda?"

"No. He took my cell too. He's changed his plans—that I know—but I'm not sure what they are."

"Does he know about your involvement?"

"Possibly. But I think he's planning an early getaway with you, using the sub. We've got to get you off the boat and away from him."

Meg considered. "Maybe I can leave on the first getaway boat. I'll go back on deck, and when they start to leave, I'll shove forward and get into the dinghy first."

"He'll stop you."

"Then I'll jump overboard and swim for it. There is no way he'll take me again."

"Wait. Let's think this through." He took her hand and pulled her back.

"My dad gave me a GPS tracking device that I have to swallow." She broke away from his hold. "CIA, satellite hookup, but I don't know if they've had enough time to coordinate it." She hurried to Elliott's bed, located the pill, and detached it from the small magnet. The pill was huge, and it took several attempts to get it down. She continued, "I have a tracking spray on too. Its range is short, but here's an extra transmitter." She handed it to Derek. "If he does get me into the sub, you need to stick it to the exterior. Inside would be better, but if you can't, then outside will have to do."

"Will it activate automatically?" He quickly examined the device.

"Yes. There's a Coast Guard boat hiding in the Cottonwood Canyon Harbor. Only job is to track this device." She hesitated, mentally challenging the overall scene. "How soon before he comes for me?"

Before Derek could answer, Elliott burst into the room.

Jessie was feeling the effects of the drugged champagne, and her normal poise was compromised. When she walked into the elaborate stateroom, she turned to the man. "What's your first name again? If we're going to be making a movie together, then I should know your first name." She smiled impishly and raised her empty champagne glass to him.

"Antonio." He took her hand and pulled her in close. "Would you like to call me Tony?"

His breath was sweet, and he smelled so masculine. "Oh, no, Antonio it will be. Too bad you're not starring in the movie. Then we could play a romantic role and ride horses across the plains of Spain together." She tugged away from him. "Oh, I think there's a song like that." She hummed a few unrecognizable bars.

"Why do you pull away, my beauty? Maybe we should seal the contract with a kiss?"

Jessie had never been introduced to a suave, foreign, handsome stranger before. What to do? I'm from Norco, for God's sake. She snuggled in a little closer and tilted her face up. "Of course. I'm game."

There was a light knock on the door. "Senor Nadal, your boat is waiting."

"Fine. We'll be right out. Come, my dear, we're going to take another boat ride to the island. You ready?"

Jessie was confused now. "Are all the girls going?" She followed Antonio's man from the stateroom and climbed the steps. "You know, maybe I should talk to Meg. Is she going?" As they reached the bow of the boat, she froze. "What's going on?" She went over to Rosie and started shaking her. "Rosie, wake up. Rosie." She quickly glanced around the deck and realized all the girls were in a stupor of sorts. The Arab playboy standing by Rosie pushed Jessie back. She panicked.

Antonio caught her before she fell and handed her over to his assistant. "Put her in the boat. Tie her up and gag her if she fights you. She's very strong." Antonio turned to the Arab. "Don't touch her again," he said.

Jessie broke away from the attendant, threw a punch, and landed a square right hook on the Arab nose, then a knee to the groin. Antonio grabbed her from behind, laughing. "Oh, you *are* a little spitfire." He lifted her and held her until his man found a plastic tie and bound her hands. "That will do for now. Hurry up. It's almost dark, and we need to meet our plane."

Jessie's attempt to wrestle free resulted in a biting slap across the face, and she acquiesced. "Hand her down to the boat. Don't bruise her, you idiot." She was passed down to the boat driver and then tied to one of the backseats. The driver's assistant sat next to her with an AR-15 across his lap. The bumpers and tie-downs were released from the yacht, and the boat roared away.

Antonio glared at Jessie for her upstart actions. No one ever contradicted him, but then he changed his attitude, realizing she was just a young, stupid American. He sat down next to her and pushed her windblown hair from her face. "I know you are frightened, my little kitten. Let me tell you what is happening."

"Untie my hands, and maybe I'll listen." The panic she felt was subordinate to the stinging blow across her face.

Antonio nodded to his man. "Elliott Spencer, an old friend from the States, contacted me and said there was to be a Texas Hold'em poker party on his yacht anchored off Catalina. It was a million dollars to buy in, and when I saw a list of players, I had to join in for the fun. Huge bragging rights for the winner. I didn't find out until during the game that it was a ruse for smuggling women. I stayed for the game and planned on leaving, but then I saw you."

Jessie was staring out across the water but turned at his last remark. "And?"

"And I couldn't stand the thought of you being sold into sex slavery, a street prostitute, so I decided to save you and run for it. I don't think Elliott will cause any problems, and I can take care of him if he does. But for now, little flower, feel fortunate that you are off the yacht and in one piece."

Jessie didn't know whether to trust the man. "What about the other girls? We can't ignore them. Where's Meg? She wasn't even on deck when we left."

"Elliott has a thing for this Meg person. I think the whole idea was to kidnap her again."

Instant recall struck Jessie. "Elliott. Oh my God. He's the serial killer she's been running from. He's the reason my twin sister is dead. Meg was the catalyst for all of this, and I hate her. Maybe I shouldn't worry about her demise." She lapsed into a daydream of revenge.

Antonio was pleased with her response. Jessie seemed to believe his far-fetched story. Oh, what a nice turn of events. If she believes I was an innocent bystander, then convincing her to go to Spain without a struggle should be easy. Antonio decided to let her statement pass without a reply. Let her dwell on Meg's guilt. My new little playmate has a dark side. Interesting.

He gave Jessie a consoling squeeze and stepped to the boat driver and whispered, "Did you dump the FBI man overboard? How stupid did they think we were? Well, maybe the other boats didn't recognize a setup, but it was certainly apparent to me. The tracking boat. Can we outrun them?"

"Yes, sir. If you look behind us, you'll see their boat. No way will they catch us."

"And our seaplane is waiting where?"

"Around the west end of the island, at Parson's Landing. About eight miles."

"How long will it take? Are there any Coast Guard ships showing on your monitor?"

"You should be airborne in twelve to fifteen minutes. No ships showing, sir."

"Good. Carry on." He returned to his seat beside Jessie and untied her hands. "Don't be alarmed, but do you see that boat way back in our wake?"

Jessie turned, squinted against the sun, and focused on the chase boat. "Um, I see it. Why?"

"I'm afraid Elliott is trying to get you back. That's his chase boat."

"Can we outrun him?" She grabbed Antonio's arms. "Will he have guns?"

He wrapped his arms around her. "Don't worry, precious. I've called ahead, and there's a seaplane waiting for us around the point of the island. Another ten minutes, and we'll be in the air. No catching us then."

The boat surged forward, and they both fell backward into the seats. Jessie felt a flood of relief wash over her. *My, he is some kind of hero. Storybook shit. But how much of that story is a lie? I'll go along with it for a while. In the meantime, maybe Elliott will settle my score with Meg.*

The distance between the seaplane and the boat grew shorter.

60

Rachael and Amanda watched the satellite monitor and witnessed the first boat take off from the yacht. "Okay, that's boat number one leaving and boat two arriving. Eight more to go."

Rachael's gaze was intense. "That first boat is going south. That's not according to our plans. Are you sure there's an FBI agent on board? Check operations."

Amanda texted the agent in charge and waited for his response, watching the boat's image move farther south. "What? Shit." Turning to Rachael, she yelled, "Let's go. All of the getaway boats checked in except the one that's going south. I've got a helicopter waiting at the Gulch. We need to get in the air. Something's gone wrong."

"Is Meg in that boat?"

"No. Her GPS shows she's still on the yacht. Hurry."

They commandeered a Jeep and raced to the Gulch, calling ahead to have the chopper ready. "Take off to the back side, somewhere around Little Harbor. We need to find that boat. There's an innocent on board."

***

When Elliott entered the room, Derek grabbed Meg and slapped her. "You fuckin' whore."

Staggering backward from the blow, Meg rubbed her face. The slap had been unexpected and painful.

"My, my. What do we have a here? A coup d'état? What're you doing here, Derek? Come to say good-bye? Meg, sweetness, you look wonderful. I'm so happy to have you again. You don't seem surprised to see me."

Meg felt no fear, only repulsion at the appearance of Elliott. Repulsion and then rage. "It was bad enough to run into Derek. Figured you wouldn't be far behind, you bastard."

He started for her. "There, there, darling."

"You'll think *darling* when we're through with you." She rubbed her face again as the outline of a red handprint appeared. She stood her ground.

"Let me look at you, precious. Beautiful as ever. I've missed you for a whole year, but our future will make up for that." He grabbed his crotch and pranced around the room. "Master of the universe, am I." His egotism propelled him.

"Do you know how disgusting you are, Elliott? Even with the plastic surgery, you're still a repulsive toad. Your inflated self-image is ridiculous. I hated every minute I spent with you. Nothing's changed. Idiot."

"Tsk-tsk, darling. My stash of drugs will surely help you change your mind. But now, you're probably expecting help from your family. Unfortunately for you, as usual, your simple sisters have been outsmarted by me. Now Derek, step back. Meg and I have a little trip to take." He pulled a Glock from his waistband.

The gun...an equalizer. She looked to Derek. Think. Think. Derek has to plant the relay on the sub, but how?

Derek left Meg's side and started toward Elliott. The gun moved in his direction. "A trip? Sure, Elliott. I know about your minisub. Wandered down there yesterday and found it. Real smart." He stopped and yanked Meg by the arm. "What do you want me to do with her?" He wasn't sure about his status with Elliott. How much had he figured out?

Elliott grabbed Meg away from him and turned her around. "You know what a handful she can be, Derek. Escort the wench down below." He shoved her against Derek's chest. "Don't disappoint me."

Meg struggled against Derek's grip. He pulled a zip tie from his pocket, pushed her arms behind her, and feigned putting on restraints. "There, I've cuffed her." She grabbed the loose end and held it in her opposing hand.

"Oh, I knew you wouldn't turn against me when trouble came knocking. You lead." Elliott's instincts were running pure; he knew Derek wasn't to be trusted but wanted to play out the hand.

The three left the stateroom, snaked around the exterior of the boat, and then climbed down the two flights to the crew's quarters. "The door's unlocked. Push down on the handle."

There, inside the floating dock, was the minisub, fueled and ready to go. The driver popped the fiberglass top open, and Derek shoved Meg forward. He feigned a fall and caught himself on the side of the sub, attaching the tracking device. Recovering his balance, he grabbed Meg. "Is there room in there for me?"

The driver took hold of Meg, helped her off the dock, and positioned her in the backseat of the minisub. Then he looked at Elliott.

"Did you install the waterproof OEM jammer? Is it working?"

"Yes, sir. As you ordered. It will block any signal coming from the sub."

"Get in the driver's seat then and start the machine, stupid."

When Meg realized that neither the CIA GPS system nor the FBI spray would be effective, she looked at Derek for help. Nothing. She slumped into the tiny cockpit and didn't resist as she was taped to the chair. Trying to fight Elliott would be wasted energy right now, so she settled in the tiny interior, looking again at Derek for some direction. Nothing.

"Oh, dear. Guess I should have ordered a four seater. Next time I'll remember, okay?" Elliott raised the gun toward Derek.

"What are you doing?" Derek knew his options were limited.

"You fool. I know you and your sister are up to no good. How far has this conspiracy gone?"

"I don't know what you're talking about." Derek quickly glanced at Meg and mouthed, "Sorry" to her. He turned back at Elliott, knowing his minutes were numbered.

"No time to talk about it now, but as I shoot you, it comforts me to know that you have become quite a warrior. Trying to save Meg and standing up for your sister. Who would have thought that such a wimpy gay man would grow a set?" He raised the gun.

Derek lunged forward, catching Elliott off guard. "Not this time, brother. I can't let you do it." He wrestled Elliott's gun hand upward and grabbed for his throat. The gun fired a hole through the upper deck. Elliott sent a staggering blow to Derek's chest with the butt of his gun. Derek fell, and Elliott took aim.

Meg tried to untie the duct tape, but the sub driver pushed her hard against the seat. She screamed, "Don't shoot him."

Two more shots. Derek fell. Shoulder and pelvis bleeding.

"No, no!" Meg struggled to escape from the sub.

"Live or die, brother. No one cares." He kicked Derek in the ribs.

Derek curled up in pain.

Elliott kicked him again, and he splashed into the water between the minisub and the dock. "Well enough."

Elliott grabbed an upright and swung into the sub. He moved to Meg and grabbed her breast. "Now for you."

61

Antonio's boat outran the Coast Guard by six minutes, giving the group enough time to transfer to the seaplane and take off. Once inside, Jessie looked around, confusion still coloring her judgment. "Tell me again. Where are we going? So there's no movie? I hate to sound stupid, but I guess I don't get it."

This beautiful American girl intrigued Antonio. His stable of young women in Spain had included many nationalities but not American, so this was a real treat. "First, we fly by seaplane to San Diego, and then we drive across the border. My jet is waiting in Mexico to take us to my villa in Spain. It's a long trip, but you'll find it comfortable."

"Oh, but no movie filmed in Spain? What's going to happen to Rosie and the rest of the girls on the yacht? What will I do in Spain if there's no movie?" She glanced around the small seaplane, feeling instantly claustrophobic.

"I'll make arrangements for your friends to fly to Spain, and you can all have a vacation on me. How does that sound? Just rest now, dear one." The effects of the earlier champagne and drama finally took their toll on Jessie, and she relaxed against him. He pulled her close, and she didn't resist. "Yes, that's right. Next stop Mexico and then to my beloved España."

"Before we go any further," Jessie whispered. "I have a confession. I told you a little white lie. My real name is Jordan." Saying her name out loud empowered her, and she shot a smug smile over her shoulder at her past.

62

The small boats were now pulling alongside the yacht, and one by one the girls were deposited on board, the investors happy, the girls submissive. On board each small craft, one FBI agent, fully armed, took charge when they were out of range of the yacht. The command post observed as the eighth boat neared. It slowed down, and four divers slid overboard with their breathing apparatus and German-made M16s. They began the swim to the yacht.

Grace pointed at the screen. "Which one is Luke? Tell me, which one is Luke?"

"Can't tell, Mom, but he's been trained to do this. Don't worry."

"Trained years ago. He's not a kid anymore."

As the eighth boat took off and the ninth tied up, the Navy SEALs threw a grappling hook over the railing on the stern of the boat and climbed on board. The mercenaries were preparing the final girl's exit and were oblivious to their boarding.

Boat nine had two armed FBI agents on board, one of whom stepped aboard to assist as the girl was being transported. Rosie, the last to exit, was shaking her head, trying to overcome the drugs she had been given. "Wait. I don't want to go without my friends. Where's Meg?"

She wrestled with the mercenary, took a swing at him, and then stomped on his foot. "Leave me alone, damn it." She broke loose and ran toward the stern of the boat. A SEAL grabbed her, clamping a hand over her mouth.

"Hold still."

Fear paralyzed Rosie, and she stiffened in his arms.

A clothesline move dropped the unarmed mercenary following Rosie in his tracks. He slumped to the ground, instantly unconscious.

Rosie broke loose and started to run, but an agent stopped her again, covering her mouth. "We're FBI. You're in danger. You need to jump overboard and swim to the jet boat. They'll pick you up."

"Screw you. I'm not jumping anywhere." She pushed away, but then her eyes widened, reflecting fear. "Watch—"

The agent turned in time to shoot the armed mercenary rounding the bulkhead.

Rosie needed no more encouragement. She lifted her gown, crawled over the railing, and jumped. The cold water took her breath away. Damn evening gown. She struggled to unwrap her legs from the yards of fabric. Boat? What boat? I don't see a damn boat. Shit. She splashed around, trying to tread water with the pounds of wet material clinging to her. Exhaustion was coming quickly. She rolled over on her back and tried to maintain a float. A Zodiac appeared to her left. No motor running. Stealth like.

It took two men to pull her on board. "Give her a blanket," an agent said. Into the mic he relayed Rosie's rescue. "We've got one woman. Says her name is Rosie." Her name was checked off the list.

"Two onboard mercenaries down, two to go. Then we find Meg," the onboard agent whispered.

The FBI agents and SEALs spread out and approached the bow of the boat as Luke joined them in the search. Elliott's other two guards, hearing the gunshots, started for the stern, weapons readied.

When Luke signaled to his men that two more guerrillas were approaching, the squad took cover and dropped the mercenaries as they passed. They started a room-to-room search.

Luke headed directly to Elliott's room. "The suite's empty. Signs of a struggle." He checked the closet and bathroom. "Going below," he announced into the mic. Gun in hand, he slammed open the door to the lower deck, took a quick look, and saw a body in the water. "We've got a man down." He struggled to pull Derek's unconscious body onto the deck. "Get me some help here. Get a medic. He's been shot." He started CPR. "Breathe. Come on, breathe."

"Move back. Let me take over. I'm a medic." A SEAL dropped to his knees and started chest compressions.

"Is he awake?" Amanda shouted through the mic. "Any sign of Meg?"

Derek puked up some water and mumbled.

Luke turned Derek's head away from the medic. "Where is she? Where's Meg?"

"He got her." He started to pass out but fought it. "Sub. Planted the transmitter. Got a jammer." Then the world turned inward, and Derek floated into a sea of his own blood.

"Did you get that?" Luke breathed heavily into the mic.

"Yeah. On our way." Amanda and Rachael, only a mile from the yacht now, closed in on board the FBI helicopter. All eyes were on the tracking device. Nothing registered. "How deep can that sub go? We aren't picking anything up yet. Must be the jammer."

Luke grabbed the spec sheet on the table. "It can dive to forty-five thousand meters. It's an Alvin-class DSV. Can handle three people."

"Mandy, which way would he head? Not out to sea unless there's a boat waiting." Rachael focused her binoculars south of the yacht.

Amanda turned on her laptop and checked the specs on the sub. "The mainland is twenty-six miles. The sub has that range. She thought out loud. "What? Will he try to outrun us? Or double back? Pick up faster transportation from a small cove? Which?"

"Not back toward Two Harbors. He probably knows Derek told us about that hideout, but send some agents there anyway. Probably headed southeast. Let's start tracking here and move toward China Point."

They flew close to the water and slowed their speed. Without the assistance of the GPS, they had to anticipate his direction. They knew the approximate time of departure and the maximum speed of the sub, and they assumed it would hide close to shore until crossing to the mainland.

***

Inside the sub Elliott was humming and feeling quite secure. "Soon we'll round the end of the island by Seal Rock, and then it's smooth sailing. We'll be pulling up to a floating dock and transfer to a more comfortable arrangement,… a ski boat that will take us to Mexico. Same place I had planned for you in July." Visions of a naked Meg filled his brain. He turned and ran his hand up her leg. His arrogance pushed him beyond contemplating being caught.

Meg felt death would be preferable to the horrendous, barbaric sexual encounter he had planned. Climbing out of the mental and physical abyss of his torture had been painstakingly slow and raw, and even the thought of that excruciating journey made her sick. Not this time Elliott. If my sisters don't get here in time, I'll…Well, I'll…She slipped the zip tie off her hand.

"No comment? That's unusual for you, darling."

She needed to take control, fight him. What would do it? What would set him off? "I'm sorry you shot Derek. We were so close to getting away from you." Push his buttons. Yes, push his buttons.

"We…Oh, I see. He really was helping you? And you were going to go with him? Should have known that his gay side would lead him to some kind of conscience."

"Well, at least he really had you fooled." She was sitting behind him and saw him jerk straight in the seat. A reaction. Oh, yes.

Elliott twitched. The thought of anyone fooling him, let alone Derek, was absurd but enticing. "About what?"

Good, he's taking the bait. "About being gay. He's the most gratifying lover I've ever been with. Doesn't need to be sadistic like you. He has real emotion and such a manly body."

Elliott whipped around in his seat and grabbed both of her knees, pinching hard.

"I loved every second we spent together. The touch of his manly body was all I needed to get hot. And we would make love for hours at a time. It was mind blowing." *Chew on that, asshole.*

Elliott leaned forward, grabbed Meg by the neck, and jerked her forward. The duct tape tore her evening gown. "What are you talking about? He's gay."

"Afraid not, Elliott, not by a long shot. He told you that so you wouldn't spy on us." Enough said. *The betrayal will kill him…and,…he probably won't want me anymore.* It was a gamble, and she knew it.

"Driver. How far away from the yacht are we?" The trip was taking too long. "Hurry up. How far?"

"Sixteen miles off the coast of California. Ten miles from the super yacht."

"Take us to the surface. Now." The driver immediately changed direction of the sub and maneuvered it to the surface. Once Elliott could see the sky through the plastic dome, he yelled to unlatch the hatch and kill the engine.

"You bitch. I can't stand the thought of getting Derek's leftovers. You fuckin' whore." He cut the tape from around her waist and yanked her by the hair to a standing position. There was barely room, but Elliott lifted Meg, slamming her against the plastic dome. His knife came forward.

Meg lashed forward with a staggering head butt. He fell back into the driver, recovered, and lurched toward Meg again. Meg caught his hand holding the knife and punched him in the ribs. The driver got out of the way as Elliott fell back. Meg ducked and climbed into the front seat. With a huge kick, she disconnected the jammer.

Elliott screamed like a madman and sliced into the air again. Turning, he grabbed Meg by the shredded gown, pulled her back, and sliced her shoulder. Blood trickled down through the sequins. "I'll kill you, you bitch. You whoring, fucking bitch."

Meg wrenched free and dove overboard. She grabbed a deep breath as she slammed into the sixty-five-degree sea. She fought for survival.

"Where's my gun? Where's my gun?" Elliott frantically searched the minisub.

Meg dolphin-kicked to the surface and gasped for air. Treading water, she unzipped the evening gown, struggled to pull the clingy dress down her body, and finally kicked out of it. She could see the mainland. Sixteen miles…I can do this. Water was her friend, and she knew she could survive. She rolled over on her back and watched Elliott scramble in the sub. Instinctively she rolled again and started swimming for her life. *Come on, Rachael. Find me.*

She didn't hear the shot but felt the bullet ping the water next to her. A full gulp of air, and she dove.

"Take that, you whore. No one defies me—no one." He emptied the gun and started to reload.

**

The helicopter pilot yelled to Amanda and Rachael, "Look, two o'clock—there's a shiny reflection in the water."

The women raised their binoculars and searched the horizon. "I see it—oh no, now it's gone," cried Rachael. "Head that way."

The navigator shouted. "Yes. We're picking up a signal on the GPS now. Finally. It's the sub."

**

Elliott focused but could no longer see Meg on the surface, so he fell back into the seat. "Dive." He slammed the dome cover. He knew traveling on top of the water took less time but insisted they submerge again. "Coast Guard could have ships in the area. Any radar activity? How close are we to rendezvousing with the powerboat?"

The driver glanced at the navigation system and made his calculations. "We're six miles from our destination, and there are no major ships in the area. Just fishing boats and sailboats. But, sir, the jammer's disabled."

"Damn. Any bait barges close?"

The driver scanned the screen again. "Yes, one off the port side, maybe half a mile away."

"Head for it. Radio my boat to meet me there. Wait until the last minute to surface. Will docking be easy...fast?"

"Yes. Should be an easy transition."

"Good." Elliott was still shaken over Derek's betrayal, and the thought of ever touching Meg again almost made him retch. I hope she's dead. The sharks will finish her off if I missed. Bitch. Fucking bitch.

**

The minisub slowed to a crawl and surfaced, gently squeezing alongside the bait barge as the ski boat idled, tied up to the opposite side. Elliott's driver opened the hatch and threw the tie-downs over the pilings.

The barge captain pried himself out of his slimy beach chair and limped over to Elliott. Disgusting fish parts and slime covered the planks, and the smell was nauseating. "Howdy. You dudes can't be looking for bait in that stupid sub, so there'll be a charge for tying up your boat or whatever you call that funky thing."

The sub driver looked at Elliott for direction as the owner untied the ropes and put his foot on the sub to shove it off his barge.

"Throw the idiot overboard. We don't have time to fool with him." As Elliott stepped onto the slippery dock, he noticed two of his men were shading their eyes and looking up. "Hey, assholes, get to work. Transfer my stuff to your boat. Hurry the fuck up." He turned his gaze upward and continued, "What's going on?"

"Expecting company? There's a chopper heading our way, high speed."

"What?" Elliott focused and spotted the helicopter bearing down. He recognized the FBI insignia. "Start the boat. We have to get out of here." He slipped on the dock, found his balance, and sprinted the short distance to the ski boat. "Hurry."

"Sorry, I need to run the blower for a minute. Otherwise we'll blow up," the driver said as he turned on the blower.

Amanda recognized Elliott immediately as he scrambled into the boat. "That's him. Where's Meg?"

"What do you want me to do?" asked the pilot.

Amanda pulled out her rifle and loaded it. "Get us closer. I can take Elliott out with one shot. Close in and hoover." Rachael reached for her rifle.

Amanda was on the radio. "Any boats in the area or Coast Guard choppers, we have Elliott in sight. No Meg. Get Search and Rescue on the water, in the air, off Pinnacle Rock, headed to the mainland."

The pilot transmitted their location.

"Get the troops here for backup." Amanda pulled the door open and was met with a rush of air. She raised her rifle and joined Rachael, setting up for the shot.

The FBI helicopter maneuvered closer, and several of the men working on the dock cowered and then jumped into the water. Rachael heard the safety click off on Amanda's rifle. "I'm taking the shot."

Elliott stopped, staggered, and fell over the edge of the dock when the shot found its mark; half of his body was draped into the water. The boat driver turned off the engine and raised his hands in submission.

Turning on the outside PA system, Amanda said, "FBI. You, in the white T-shirt, tie the boat to the dock. The rest of you, facedown on the planks." She looked at Rachael.

She could see through the plastic dome that Meg wasn't on board. "One of us needs to get to Elliott and make sure he's dead, and the other should go find Meg."

"Lower me by the cable, Mandy. He's made my life hell longer than he has yours. My treat."

Amanda helped her hook up her Kevlar vest, and with Glock in hand, Rachael rappelled down to the barge. As she unhooked the cable, her focus moved to the helicopter, signaling for them to leave. Elliott moved slightly. When she turned back, she saw the blood trail had moved to the edge. He's still alive. He had slumped to the right, against the stern of the boat, and remained motionless. She clutched her Glock and leaned over to check his neck for a pulse.

The minute he felt her fingers on his neck, Elliott reared back, pulled a gun from his waistband, and slammed it into her flesh. Safety off. It landed next to Rachael's forehead, and a loud bang erupted.

Amanda's shot clipped his shoulder, and he fell off the edge of the barge. Rachael grabbed his hair and pulled him above the waterline. Elliott's eyes were open, a glaze passed over them, and he seemed to stop breathing. She looked around for help and spotted the barge master. "Get over here and help me pull this guy out of the water."

"No pulse?" Amanda asked.

"Can't find one," she reported over the mic, and then she stepped into the sub's small cockpit. "There's blood by the plastic hatch. More blood by the freeboard. Meg must have clocked him."

Rachael stepped onto the barge, ran back over to check on Elliott, and watched as more blood spilled out of his wounds. Spurting blood meant blood pressure—he wasn't dead. "You don't look so dangerous anymore, you son of a bitch. What happened to Meg?" Silence. Elliott had passed out, or at least he was pretending to be passed out. She kicked him for good measure and pushed the button for her mic. "Amanda, Meg's gone for sure." She shaded her eyes and scanned the rough ocean. "Elliott's taken care of. Get out of here and look for Meg."

Amanda grabbed the PA and yelled, "Got it!"

Rachael looked up at the helicopter. "Good luck, sis. Bring our girl home."

***

Meg was already tiring, her arms dragging through the water, her legs refusing to propel her forward. I know my job, she kept repeating over and over. *Stay alive until Amanda finds me. Stay alive—, my job.* Minimal swells rocked her as she turned over and floated on her back. She heard the helicopter before searching the sky and finding it. Oh, thank you, God. Renewed energy allowed her to tread water and wave her arms to the heavens.

Within minutes, Amanda had spotted Meg splashing, a tiny speck in the massive Pacific, and the FBI helicopter bore down on its single survivor.

"Hover here. Let's figure out what to do." She strapped on the safety harness, opened the side door, and shouted through the PA. "Hey, sis, need a lift?" Meg's fragile face looked up from the center of the circular maelstrom of ocean water, and Amanda froze. "You strong enough to climb into the harness?" When Meg shook her head, Amanda yelled to the navigator, "Send down the basket." The pilot maintained a 150-foot elevation as the basket was deployed, staying high enough to ensure there was no motor wash to impact Meg's attempt to crawl in. Helpless to assist, Amanda watched Meg fight the swells while trying to muscle her weight into the carrier. "Shit, drop down to twenty feet. I'm going in." She yanked off the harness, her Kevlar vest, and gun, and pulled on a life vest as the pilot decreased the distance between the helicopter and the surface of the water.

"Altitude," he yelled continuously; the navigator replied each time, indicating the distance. "Okay to jump."

Amanda hurled herself into the ocean and landed twenty feet from Meg. With sure strokes, she erased the distance and grabbed her, turning her around backward and holding her tight. "You're okay now, Meg. Don't fight me."

Meg relaxed.

Amanda gave short instructions. "Hold on with your left arm, swing your right leg over into the basket." The undulating waves cooperated and gently assisted Meg into the basket. "You're naked."

"I know. Necessary." Meg was too tired to explain.

After signaling for the navigator to raise the basket, Amanda floated until a bare rescue hook was sent down for her. Once inside the helicopter, Amanda located a FBI jacket and helped Meg to dress.

Then the tears came. "Oh, Mandy, thank you. I knew you would find me, but I didn't know if I could wait. I'm tired, so tired."

Amanda cradled her baby sister and rocked back and forth, whispering, "It's okay. You're safe. Let's go find the family. They're worried sick. I love you."

The helicopter headed directly for Descanso Beach, and the sisters sat in silence, recuperating until Meg finally asked, "Did you get the bastard?" With energy and strength rebounding, that's all Meg could think about.

"Did indeed and this time for good. The asshole's dead." Amanda twitched. *Rachael really didn't say that.*

Meg began to cry happy tears. "Oh, thank God. Wait, Mandy. I want to see him. Like now. I don't believe evil can die that easily."

The pilot banked the helicopter without being asked and headed for the bait barge. Meg saw the spilled blood and the prone body as they approached. "My God. That's a beautiful sight." She looked at Amanda and laughed. "Shit, I'm so depraved that it's scary." They waved at Rachael. "Maybe now I can go on living without fear. Thank you. Oh, Mandy, thank you. I love you so much."

Amanda squeezed her and said, "Ditto."

63

"Let me out of this damned nightgown." Stella struggled against her restraints and threw herself against the locked door. It was the second day in lockup, and her mood swings were getting more violent. A registered nurse entered the room, and with the help of an attendant, she was given another sedative. "No, no more shots. It will hurt my baby. Call Josh. He'll come and get me."

Sharon watched through the small window as Stella finally relaxed and the attendant helped her into bed. He took the restraining jacket off and substituted it with Velcro wrist cuffs attached to the bed rail.

"Have the blood tests come back yet?" Sharon feared the answer but realized everyone's future depended on the findings.

"I believe so, but you'll need to talk to the doctor. She's in right now. Come on, I'll take you there." The nurse gestured to follow her down the hall.

Doctor Schmidt stood as Sharon entered her office. "Come in. Sit. My goodness, Stella is quite a handful." She nodded as she opened the chart on her desktop. "The blood work is in. Stella's actually is in excellent heath, but I know that's not your immediate concern."

"No." Sharon leaned forward, bit down on her upper lip, and closed her eyes. "Well?"

"She's pregnant."

64

The FBI reunited all the girls who had been kidnapped, returned their personal property, and explained the situation to them. Most girls were happy just to be alive, with the exception of Rosie, who didn't settle down until Meg showed up. "Finally. Shit, I thought that maniac had you again." She had stayed at Descanso Beach long after the other contestants had left, waiting for her friend, never mind the wet glamour gown and messy makeup.

"My sisters saved me, thank God." She adored Rosie. "Look, I have to meet with some of the muckety-mucks to clear up some stuff. I'll see you later. Dinner?"

"Dinner's good. Let's make the FBI pay. How about that?"

"Good luck with that." Meg waved at Rosie as she took off in her cart. After a quick stop in the public restroom to change out of the pilot's jacket and shorts and into fatigues, courtesy of the FBI, she dashed to the police department for their final meeting.

"Has anyone reached Payden yet?" That was the opening question after the FBI and Catalina Police finished their confidential work. The Penningtons and Luke were invited to furnish some missing details.

"The Spaniard has slipped through our fingers. Had a private jet waiting, and he took off with Jessie. Destination—Spain."

Meg felt sick. She was responsible. It doesn't mean that this Spaniard is a deviant like Elliott. God, she has to be okay. This is my fault. First her sister; now her. "You know, let me do it. I know Payden better than the rest of you."

"Not your job, Meg. The FBI can handle this." Amanda didn't feel Meg was up to the task or responsible for it.

Grace put her two cents in. "Amanda, it's your sister's decision. Let her run with it." Luke placed his hand on Grace's arm, signaling it was time to butt out. Quite unlike her normal behavior, she acquiesced.

"I'm going," insisted Meg. "No more discussion. Like now. Time's wasting. Text me when you figure out what steps you're taking so I can tell him." She headed out the door, grabbed the first available cart, and drove up the road to the stables.

Payden was driving the John Deere, dragging the arena, oblivious to the last few hours of trauma. Lights had been installed, and they were turned on, illuminating the freshly tilled DG in the ring.

"How's it going, Meg?" When she got closer, he stopped the tractor, looked around for Jessie, and froze. "Oh my God. What happened to you?"

Meg stood there in wrinkled fatigues, her hair in shambles and no shoes. "Is this the costume and makeup for the audition?" He checked his watch. "You're either really late or awfully early. Where's Jessie?" He climbed down off the John Deere as Meg walked over to him.

"I don't know how to tell you this, so come on." She looked around the arena. "Let's go unsaddle Jessie's horse and talk for a minute." They walked into the barn and then into an open stall.

"Hey, little lady, you got me worried. What's going on? You look mighty serious." He uncinched the saddle, pulled it off with the blanket, and slung it over the stand.

She gave him all the details, watching his face for reactions. Worried, mad, tense, fearful? What? As Meg finished retelling the story, the emotion of reliving the trauma finally hit her, and she broke down.

Payden tightened as she related each detail of the kidnapping. When Meg couldn't find any more words, he nodded. "I know you did the best you could. I'm glad you're safe." He was overly polite and formal. "Excuse me, but I have to leave now." He turned and started for the house.

His reaction and the abrupt end to the conversation surprised Meg. "What are you doing? Let's go and meet the FBI and find out what they're planning to do."

Payden pulled out his cell phone as he walked, taking total command. Meg followed, listening in on the conversation.

"Do a full background check on Antonio Nadal. Call my helicopter pilot. Get Abel. Meet me at the heliport on Pebbly Beach in half an hour. We'll be heading to LAX. Have him alert LAX of our arrival. Have the corporate jet gassed and ready, waiting for me. We'll be going to Spain."

"Where?"

"Madrid. File a flight plan. Check LAX, John Wayne, Ontario, and Mexico for private and commercial flights that have taken off for Spain in the last twenty-four hours. I'll need two security personnel and one personal attendant waiting at the plane. Plan on taking off from LAX in two hours. Got that?" He closed the phone and continued on into the house.

Meg was still trying to catch up with him. "Hey, wait for me," Meg yelled at him as she stumbled up the first stair. "I thought you were a retired insurance salesperson. Do they loan you corporate jets for that?"

"Long story, but the jet is mine. Gotta go." He brushed past her. "I'll need to borrow your cart. I'll leave it at the Pebbly Beach."

"I'm going too," Meg declared. "I'm the reason for Jessie's problems, and I need to take care of it." Stubborn Meg had reappeared, and she wasn't going to be ignored.

He didn't stop for her. "Not a good idea. You'll just be in the way."

"Too bad. I'm going." She jumped into the cart as he was taking off.

"I don't have time to argue." He looked at the messy girl beside him and saw the determination on her face. "All right. We'll go to your house first. Grab your passport. You have one, don't you?" He didn't wait for an answer. "Grab a change of clothes. You have ten minutes. Don't keep me waiting." He slammed the gear into forward and punched it as Meg grabbed the upright for support.

Meg phoned the family on the way to her house, and while they all objected to her going, they knew it wouldn't matter. Meg does what Meg does.

The hop from Catalina to LAX was uneventful, and Meg was seriously impressed with Payden's private jet when they boarded it. His preparations had paid off, and the scheduled touchdown in Spain would be an hour before Antonio's plane would land. The CIA was in charge of contacting the Spanish officials, Interpol, and the American consulate to coordinate the release of Jessie. So all would go as planned, it seemed.

After three hours of flying over the Atlantic and enjoying a light meal, Payden and Meg began to relax. Another ten hours to go. She had pumped him enough to find out that he was a billionaire, having sold his computer company to Apple two years prior. He hadn't told anyone because he enjoyed his simple life in Norco.

"So, Meg, where do you see yourself five years from now?"

"Hmm. Good question." She glanced at the clouds floating by the jet's windows, feeling a welcome euphoria. Payden...searching for an answer from me. Interested? "The only thing I know for sure is that it will be somewhere around water."

"I like water."

65

Three months passed. While Elliott's wounds were serious he had recovered and was incarcerated at San Quentin, awaiting his trial date. Bullhead authorities were working with Santa Cruz PD to combine the six female abductions and murders, along with the murder of Carlos and Sasha. Money laundering, black-market body parts, transfer of illegal aliens, and now human trafficking were the other charges filed against him.

Marisa crossed the Mexican border before the FBI could catch up with her, and Derek was in custody, willing to turn state's evidence against Elliott and furnish names for his Mexican contacts and supply information on his other nefarious acts. Because of Elliott's endless criminal tentacles spread over the world, Derek was placed in protective custody until after the trial.

Stella remained at the hospital as her baby grew. "Did Josh call today?" The attendants were instructed to give her a positive answer and then find an excuse for the call not going through. They could control her without medication, if she believed them.

Josh and Rachael couldn't come to a decision about the child or their relationship.

"I can't abandon my kid, but I don't even know if it's mine."

Rachael shook her head. "You'll have to get tested. Is your department going to bring charges against Greg?"

"Ah, shit, Rach. Greg's a good guy. His moral compass got fouled up. Family does that to you sometimes."

"Your opinion." Rachael still carried a lot of distrust for Greg, family or not. "Are you sure you don't want to have Stella and Greg charged with kidnapping and all that other stuff? If Stella went to prison, at least you'd know she'd be off drugs, and then your baby might be okay."

"Her mom and Greg are willing to take her in. They'll keep her healthy. I really don't want my kid to be born in prison. Can you get that?"

"Sure." She walked over to him and put her arms around his neck. She said, "I love you" before planting a huge Pennington kiss on his ready mouth.

***

The family joined together in Yorba Linda for Christmas again. It was the first year for Luke to experience the wild Pennington women's holiday, and he was a minute short of amazed. Payden had been invited to join the group, along with Jack Jakes, Amanda's guest.

"Luke, don't cut such large pieces of ham." Grace was again assuming the mother superior role in the kitchen.

"Ham, be damned. I'll do as I please, or you can take over."

Meg let out a howl. "Wow, did he tell you, Mom? How come he can say what we've been thinking for years and get away with it?"

"Bedroom privileges, I hear." Rachael put in her two cents as she entered the kitchen.

"Enough, you two." Grace enjoyed the tease.

"So, Payden, what's the word on Jessie?" Meg was curious.

"About the same. Says she's happy." He took a sip of merlot. "I think something's wrong. Jessie acts more like Jordan than like her old self. Can't figure it out. There's no way that Jessie would have gone along with this billionaire playboy. Not her style."

Luke put down the carving knife and looked at him. "That's my turf. Want me to do some checking?"

Payden grabbed a bite of ham. "I plan on going back in January." He took another piece. "I'll check with you tomorrow. Let's enjoy today."

"Right." Luke went back to his task.

Amanda helped Rachael set the table. "Any news about Stella?"

"No good news. Josh and I are keeping track of her. Not sure how any of this is going to end."

When Grace announced that dinner was ready, the clan gathered around the dining room table. Luke stood. "Before we start, I'd like to say a few words."

Grace interjected, "Luke, we usually don't say a prayer, but…" She paused to looked around the table. "Well, okay. Go for it."

"Not exactly a prayer. Maybe an answer to a prayer? More like a gift to the entire family." He reached into his shirt pocket.

"Wow. Is that a written proposal to Mom?" Meg teased. "Watch out, Mom. Looks like senility is setting in early. Has to read the words?"

"Shut your mouth, you little scruff." Grace threw her napkin at Meg. "Go ahead, Luke. Don't mind the brat."

"I received an e-mail this morning from the warden at San Quentin."

Rachael tightened her grip on her water glass, and Amanda shot a look of concern at Meg.

Meg jerked upright. "Don't tell me Elliott escaped."

"Let him finish, Meg." Grace reached for her hand.

Luke waited until the family fell silent. "It reads, 'Elliott Spencer was transferred here yesterday. There was an incident during the night. He burned to death in his cell. Details will follow.'" He sat down. The shocked silence lasted only a minute as the family absorbed the information.

"Positive ID?" Amanda pushed.

"I'll take care of that," Luke answered.

Meg slowly stood and raised her wine glass. "To Dad. Thank you for the best Christmas present I've ever had."

"I'm just the messenger."

"Right."

The End

ACKNOWLEDGMENTS

Thanks, family, for allowing me to use your first names in the book; hopefully Derek will forgive me for portraying him as such a despicable character, but I did give him a solid dose of redeeming value before the end of the story. Jenny Ruvalcaba, my artsy grandaughter, designed the book cover, and Annie Jacques, my grandaughter with the beautiful long legs, posed for the picture. Thanks, kids. I'm one lucky lady to have such wonderful daughters—Suzie, Cindie, Karen, and Becquie—who put up with my ranting and raving when my characters decide to do their own thing and mess up the plot. How dare they!

Special thanks go to Rosie Taylor, Catalina Conservancy, and Greg Salcido, Los Angeles County Sheriff's Department, who volunteered to be my beta readers and added so much to the authenticity of the story. I owe you big-time. To Sharon Larson, my publicist and BFF, thanks for covering my six and for reminding me to persevere instead of doing whatever pops into my nomadic mind.

Others need to be mentioned and applauded for answering all those questions regarding guns, poisons, autopsies, drugs, and other means of mayhem. Those would include Dr. Steve Kishineff, Zonnie Krause, Jeff Jacques, Lesley Trejo, and Jerry Duke.

And finally, thanks to all of you who have read my books. To those who would have preferred a big red ribbon tied around *The 7th Victim*, I hope you find some closure with *Deadly Aftermath*.

Life is good. Enjoy.

Made in the USA
San Bernardino, CA
20 February 2015